About the author

Stevie Davies comes from
was a lecturer in English Literature at Manchester University from 1971–84, leaving to become a full-time writer. She has published six volumes of literary criticism, including two studies of the revolutionary Milton, two books on Emily Brontë, one on Virginia Woolf and a feminist reappraisal of Renaissance poetry.

Her first novel, the acclaimed *Boy Blue* (The Women's Press, 1987), won the Fawcett Society Book Prize in 1989. *Primavera* is her second novel, and her third novel, *Arms and the Girl*, was published by The Women's Press in 1992.

About *Primavera*

'original and poignant . . . Stevie Davies' first novel, *Boy Blue*, won the Fawcett Society prize. *Primavera* proves that it was not just a flash in the pan'
The Scotsman

'Stevie Davies' *Primavera* is vernal and blooming . . . as charming and evanescent as a masque'
The Observer

'Davies' writing is uniquely beautiful. *Primavera* is a prize-worthy novel'
City Life

1996

Also by Stevie Davies from The Women's Press:

Boy Blue (1989)
Arms and the Girl (1992)

STEVIE DAVIES

primavera

First published by The Women's Press Limited, 1990
A member of the Namara Group
34 Great Sutton Street, London EC1V 0DX

This paperback edition, 1992

British Library Cataloguing in Publication Data
A catalogue record for this book is available from the British Library.

ISBN 0-7043-4299-5

Phototypeset by Input Typesetting Ltd, London

Printed and Bound in Great Britain by
BPCC Hazells Ltd
Member of BPCC Ltd

To Bill
with my love

Contents

Prelude: Art

It was in the Uffizi Gallery in Florence that Jack Middleton, in the sixty-eighth year of his age and with three further years of his life-span still to run, passed through a door which led to transformation. There had been no clue that morning, awakening in the hotel room to the sound of parakeets – no, they were chambermaids furiously squabbling in the corridor outside his room – as to the existence of a threshold in that tainted summer of a stifling city, over which one might pass and be forever changed. On the contrary, normality declared itself in a sciatic back and creaking joints as he swung his legs over the edge of the bed and sat there feeling lamentably old. His paunch rested out over his lap; he kneaded his eyeballs with the heels of his hands. Maureen, who had been up in the night violently sick from some mackerel she had eaten in a restaurant – *dive*, Jack said, angry at the dollars Maureen's food-poisoning cost him – remained comatose but groaning softly in her sleep near the edge of the bed. If Maureen, who had shooed Jack out of the nuptial bed at home over a decade and a half ago, sleeps any nearer to the edge of the obligatory double bed they share in Florence, she will undoubtedly pitch out. So Jack has several times pointedly observed to her on this trip. Tight-lipped Maureen, who at the age of sixty-two can look back to a punishing total of nearly four and a half decades of Jack's coercive company, thought in the privacy of her own heart, *Shut up, Big Mouth*, and kept her distance.

Jack wants a woman. He wants and needs and craves and clamours for a woman. He dreams of female flesh stripped bare for his inspection. He tongues hard nipples and claws his fingers into soft stomachs. The scantily clad sight-seers drifting down the narrow pavements of Florence between light and shadow offer a feast of flesh to his hard and hungry eye at which he is forever destined to be an unsatisfied voyeur. Maureen sees his eyes that travel and his rapacity that is always checked; Maureen knows, and averts her heart from Jack. She has a lifetime of grudges scored up against her husband: coarse, angry, opinionated Jack who wears his bitter need like a badge of office. Maureen comes of a long ancestral line of Pennsylvanian aristocrats on her mother's side; her father, like Jack's mother, was English. She is a lapsed Quaker and resembles one of the pioneers in her serene and upright bearing, grey hair drawn back into a sheath, classic features that have been beautiful and still turn heads to muse upon who she might be: *this great lady*. Maureen is indeed every inch a lady, proud though not over-bearing like her mother Bess whom Jack so detested, anglophile and cultivating English customs and speech, traditional in her tastes for gracious living, hospitality, cookery, gardening. She knows right from wrong, and knows that Jack is pretty near always wrong. Maureen has loved her husband as her husband has loved her: with an entire devotion, as the father of her five children, now full-grown and departed the nest, latterly as the old sinner with an extraordinary if intermittent capacity for justice, humour, the milk of human kindness. The roots are still there, a deep lace of familial belonging, but the plant of love in its old age shows crazy, bizarre and tortured, a thorn in the wilderness.

Jack gets up and staggers to the window, pulling the threadbare curtains to view daylight over Florence. The room is seedy, plaster flaking from dingy walls, the furniture basic. Jack, with his savings, stocks and the income he still derives from part-time tuition in cello and composition, could have afforded a far better room than this *poky hole*, and one part of him feels he dishonours Maureen by condemning her to such squalid lodgings; the other part is just plain mean, and intends to remain so. As he is fond of telling his glazed-eyed offspring, Jack went through the Depression of the thirties, and knows the value of money. He always clears his plate, even if the mackerel is pretty near inedible and liable to contain certifiable traces of botulism. His own stomach is like his mind this morning, sour: a well of bile. He hopes the bug in the mackerel which infected Maureen in the night, thus spoiling his night's sleep, isn't going to put him out of action.

That really would be damned bad luck. Women bear illness so much better than men: they are born martyrs and don't need nursing. Maureen doesn't ask for anything when she's sick. She just lies there and endures. But when Jack, that titanic figure of a man – built on such a heroic scale that he reminded himself in youth of Michelangelo's 'David' – gets sick, everyone knows about it, he makes sure of that. The patriarch is a piteous attention-seeker then. He moans feebly for Mother, bad Mother, who went and died, unforgiveably, inconceivably, when Jack was seven.

Jack wants Mother. He is still searching around for her, even after nearly sixty-two years. When he married Maureen on the lawns of 'Shadows', the great white-timbered house her family had owned for two centuries on the rolling, pine- and oak-forested, maternal hills on the Pennsylvanian-Delaware border, Jack thought and continued for twenty years to believe, that he had found Mother. Then he was a penniless musician and teacher. Maureen's mother helped them to buy and restore the tumbledown farmhouse on the hill opposite 'Shadows', in twenty acres of forest and pasture, with a stream and small lake. They named it 'Red Earth', and there Maureen bore him five children, Josie, Frank, Tilly, Angela and Tom. Jack and Maureen's children echoed through the tall timber, competing with the birdsong in their dappled world; they shattered the age-old quiet of the pool with their riot, and glanced like light along the windows of 'Red Earth' in their racing play. Then they were all gone. Then, too, Mother was gone. Jack looked round for Mother: Maureen turned her back on him. *Why? Why did you do this to me? I was so happy with you.* 'Ah,' Maureen might have said, but didn't, 'but was I perfectly happy with you, Jack?' Maybe it was possible to have had enough of an ambitious and powerful husband, with a turn for barbed witticism, furiously appetitive in bed but short on gentle, sensitive words, tender kisses and the art of cuddling and caressing essential to the comfort of all human creatures – including Jack, who knew he was missing something but couldn't tell what it was and hence put it down to some mystifying defect in his wife. Maybe it was time for Jack to be weaned from Maureen's breasts he sucked so sore.

Maureen wanted a woman. Just as passionately as Jack, and with scarcely less famished eyes and aching heart, she yearned toward a woman's love. With age and practice, she learned to feign deaf and actually not to hear Jack's rasping voice, with its peremptory habits of speech. She avoided contact with that ramrod body that lay on hers so hard and heavy, trying to express its love in a vehement sensuality forlorn both of grace and sense, as if one should bellow in the quietened ears of the dead, *I love you, damn you! Why don't you reply?* She wanted gentle, searching fingers to receive in her own; to lay her head on some listening breast and exchange wisdoms; to sit in a window-seat with some pleasant contralto companion with whom she might share books, memories, recipes for jam, the sewing of a gay ribbon round a hat. Maureen turned, in the absence of such a friend, more and more to her ageing mother. Jack drank. Maureen watched him drink. She observed him from halfway across the world in her tall tower at 'Shadows' soaking up liquor like a decaying sponge; she watched his music ebb away till the pool was almost dry. Jack could have divorced her. He could have discarded her and started again, with any one of twenty fetching young cellists who gravitated to the allure of the maestro. But he had two problems. His father, a strict Baptist, still spoke within as the voice of conscience. But this has always been the lesser of the problems. The second is worse, and tautologous: Maureen is Maureen. She was there, is there, will and must be there. Beyond her desertion, his fidelity. Beyond his tyrannous and lifelong custom of being Jack, there remains that root of love clawing down into her heart: gnarled, twisted, impotent, life-guaranteeing. They both witness and attest to its existence. Which is no earthly use either to Jack or to Maureen, and has no bearing on the fact that Jack wants a woman; and also Maureen (Bess being fifteen years dead) wants a woman.

Jack thinks, having been down to the hotel restaurant and breakfasted in poignant solitude on rolls and fragrant coffee, that it is time Maureen recovered in order to accompany him on the strenuous agenda of sightseeing he has planned. Over breakfast he worked out their itinerary, with the help of a map, a guidebook and the waitress, an attractive French student with whom he conversed in that extraordinary and super-confident pidgin American-French with which Jack has already confounded several European cities. The waitress, convulsed as she was by the exuberant way the capacious

American thinks fit to *parler* her native *français*, yet rather took to Jack, in the way many do. There is something truly genial and warming in the way his pale blue eyes acknowledge his own absurdities; a real human interest in you that goes beyond the allure of those nicely globed breasts of the waitress at which his eyes can't help cadging a stealthy and delighted look. This warmth and fellow-feeling, so hard to resist, is another thing Maureen has long held against her husband. *Charm*, she calls it, *old fraud*, she calls him: elegiacally.

'J'éspère que vous vous amusez aujourd'hui,' the waitress says pleasantly as her gentleman gathers his maps and leaves the table.

'Mercy bean,' says Jack, smiling broadly. *'Et vooz oh-see, mademoiselle.'*

He is still recalling with relish the fetching young thing and how the young do seem to take to him (*oh God, oh God! If only* . . .) when he turns the key in the lock and enters the bedroom, which welcomes him with a stale and sickly odour and the whey face of Maureen propped up on the pillows and looking exceedingly groggy.

'I've brought you a glass of iced water,' says Jack magnanimously, handing it over and perching on the edge of the bed, but not too near, for after all it's still possible he hasn't caught the bug and there's no point in inviting the beast into his own cast-iron gut. 'How are you feeling now, Molly? Better?'

'I think I am coming round a bit,' says Maureen, gathering all her forces to respond to his peremptory rallying call.

'Well, good. *That's good.* Do you think you'll be up to a trip to the Uffizi? I've devised two programmes, one strenuous if you're fighting fit, the other more restful. See, here's my map, what do you think? We can take it as easy as you like.'

Maureen stares blankly at the map around which her husband's ball-point pen has charged and darted. The world is composed solely of moving dots to her queasy eye; she feels unable to move a muscle, and even to raise the precious ice-water to her parched lips seems Herculean labour. *I wish I were home at 'Red Earth' with the dogs and the neighbours, I wish I were not sick and lonely and at your mercy in a foreign land.*

'I can't move this morning, Jack, I'm sorry. I'll try this afternoon. You go off and enjoy yourself.'

'I can't go on my own.'

'Of course you can. You don't need me.'

'The hell I don't.'

'Don't look like that, Jack. I feel so weak.'

'Like what? I'm not looking like anything. I'm just thinking of you, wondering if you need me to prod you a bit – get you going.'

'You look like a sentencing judge. Please don't. I didn't choose to be unwell, it's not my fault. Please.'

'You needn't plead with me, dear. Of *course* it's not your fault,' admits Jack begrudgingly. Though in a way, of course, it is her fault. If she hadn't insisted on the mackerel, just because she remembered having it as a child; if she had joined him in the scampi, which really was delicious . . . 'So you think you may be up this afternoon?'

'I'll try, Jack.'

'Good, dear. It would be a terrible waste to come all the way to Florence and just lie in a sickbed for a week.'

At Jack's monitory tone, Maureen turns over on her side and covers her face with her hand. He has never in the course of forty-two years seen her shed tears, and she does not plan for him to see her now. 'Sometimes you are not a very nice man,' says her muffled voice. It is a very mild way of saying *You self-centred bastard I despise you*, but naturally Jack takes it hard. Jack Middleton not a very nice man? – the idea. He removes himself abruptly from the bed, which springs up to support Maureen again, and is cataloguing the persons who do not merely think but *know* Jack Middleton to be a very, very nice man. Generations of students know it; whole orchestras know it; the hotel manager here and the very waitress are discriminating enough to perceive it. *But if Mother says no* . . . He nearly kneels to beg poor Maureen's pardon, but instead, in a milder voice, says, 'Well, dear, I'm sorry you feel so bad. I'll wander round this morning and return at lunch-time to see how you are. If that's all right?'

In the bathroom he lathers up, and cannot forbear to sing, notwithstanding the deplorable Italian failure to provide plugs to recharge the battery of his electric shaver. Favourite melodies from *South Pacific* and *Oklahoma* come to mind, and the golden, expectant light filtering in through the narrow window from the city prompts him to exercise that grating, hideous and uncertain instrument, his voice, unique amongst professional musicians as exhibiting distinct symptoms of tone-deafness:

'Nothing walks like a dame,
Nothing talks like a dame,
There ain't nothing like a – '

He has to pause to scrape the stubble off his chin; blood flows; he staunches it with flecks of tissue paper. The high point today will be the the viewing of Botticelli's *Primavera* at the Uffizi, a picture he has waited half a century to see. As he pats on aftershave he imagines the moment at which Jack Middleton will stand in person before that great panel of tapestried paint, a solitary spectator in the great, silent halls of Renaissance art, sharing for the first time that lyrical dream of Venus and spring awakening. What a moment that will be! A moment to flourish at dinner-parties, a moment for all time.

'O-o-o-Oklahoma!' Jack trumpets, on the strength of this, emerging from the bathroom in his undershirt and shorts. There is no response from the stricken lady on the bed, not even the *Shut up* any sane person must be meditating to Jack's pernicious ebullience. Anxiety and pity on Maureen's account (zipping up his trousers, holding in his stomach to tighten his belt a notch) give way to irritation that nothing can be done to precipitate her on the road to recovery and the sharing of the adventure. Jack meditates an experimental 'Ballyhai!' but, thinking better of it, descends to the minor key, enquires in a gentle tone as to whether Maureen needs anything, strokes her head with gauche and clumsy hand, and leaves for the Uffizi, pulling the door to behind him softly. He will bring her flowers; he will be more tender of her feelings. He knows he ought.

Jack navigates to the Uffizi without aid of map, taking as his lodestar the tall grey tower of the Palazzo Vecchio. He has an unerring sense of direction; strides along as buoyantly as a young guy of forty. He enters the portico and, yes, here's the inner vestibule, here Vasari's monumental staircase, here the elevator, into which Jack steps, to sail to the second floor. Appetite is whetted; zest for life and art and love and new discovery shines from his eye, so that the sandwiched mortals in the lift take light from his radiance and smile back to him. He's always been a hungry person, and a hopeful: could never rid himself of the prescient intuition that round the next corner, through that door there, someone or something marvellous was waiting to declare herself, himself. *Now* . . .

No, not quite. Not at all. This is neither the time, it seems, nor the place. For the entire world has not only come to view the *Primavera* but is determined to contend with Jack for place in the Botticelli Rooms, using every known technique of unsavoury jostling or elbowing. Jack looks on from the threshold in disdain as Norway in the form of five blond and barefaced youths presses back a miscellany of nationalities, and the population of India drifts and sifts helplessly out of range of the picture, colourfully costumed, picturesquely doomed, tossed aside by a contingent which Jack is ashamed to recognise as a party of American tourists. The Americans angle forward, brash rangy boys and girls of spectacular height in Bermuda shorts, the older generation attired as if for a round of golf, and there are cries of:

'Get a load of that!'

'What an eyeful!'

'Is that the Birth of Venus?'

'No no it's the Primavera.'

' "What Botticelli wanted to depict, in allegorical form, was life and death, beauty and eternity, dream and reality!" ' The girl shrieks this text at the top of her voice above the Babel din of many languages. 'That's what the guidebook says.'

'You don't say.'

'It sure is a cute picture.'

'Can you see, Cindy?'

'Not real well. Let's try and get to the front.'

Meanwhile the Germans are losing this war hands-down. The Teutons are a party of courteous and immaculate academics who, having been elbowed out of range of the work of art itself, are still desperately conversing about its meaning, its *Platonische Philosophie*, how it is *sehr interessant, wie man nur es sehen könnte*, how there are two Venuses and this is the heavenly one, no it isn't it's the earthly and Flora is spring, *jawohl*, but as we can't actually see the picture properly we shall adjourn elsewhere for *Kaffee und Kuchen*. Jack, surveying the human swamp, thinks gloomily that he will do the same. Over the heads of the crowd the lyrical painted personages can be seen to waft in their life-sized silent dance, with expressions of inscrutable amusement. Art and life, thinks

Jack, have painfully little in common. And Americans – well: as he turns back through the door he has not quite entered, Jack is treated to the information that a rouged and lacquered lady more painted than any known Botticelli would just *love* to take home that sweet darling *Primavera* and hang it on her wall; wouldn't it look just something else in the entrance hall, honey? What Honey thinks of his spouse's yen Jack manages to evade hearing: he threads the shoaling bodies speedily, thinking, *I'm more than half English and, thank God, it shows.* He finds his way to Room 28, and Titian's *Venus of Urbino* and, through the throng, glimpses a world of golden flesh so softly melting to the imagined touch that as he is leaving the Uffizi he realises that his back teeth are grinding, his fists clenched so that his nails dig into his palm, as if under stress of some agonising long-term pain.

Yes, Maureen is feeling very much fitter. Yes, she will do her best to accompany her husband on his afternoon expedition. Jack cheers up immediately.

'Now are you sure, dear? I don't want you to feel bullied.'

Perish the thought: Jack bully Maureen? Her pallid, anxious face breaks for an instant into a wry grin which Jack finds it possible to ignore. He confides his intention to return to the Uffizi and have another go at the *Primavera.*

'I thought you said it was terribly crowded in there? I don't think I can manage anything gruelling, Jack. I'll simply collapse.'

'Nonsense,' says the student of the Medici, who is also, it appears, a devotee of their imperious bad manners. 'Get you out of yourself. I really don't think it will be as bad this afternoon.'

Through the baking sunshine Maureen's body floats and flies, but not as lightly as her mind which balloons along above her head as if attached by the slenderest of membranes. Her gauzy, lemon-coloured blouse is awash with perspiration. Nothing greatly matters to high-flying Maureen, tugged like a kite across the Piazza della Signoria, great bells chiming and echoing within her very skull; her husband's hand is firm below her left elbow, nudging her shoulder-joint somewhat upward whilst propelling her person totteringly forward, according to his customary procedure. Maureen goes along with it all. Her mind has floated so free that it has fled

Italy altogether; has found its way home across olive groves, vineyards, cities, seas, ports and airports to where the three dear old dogs bark a choric welcome and that nice new lady who has moved into 'Shadows' is waiting for her. A gang of urchins surges round her, brings down the kite; they are dark-haired, ragged, cynically smiling.

'*Avanti*,' orders Jack. 'Go on, scat. *Avanti*!' Having little further Italian, he fires off some Latin: '*Non habemus pecuniam. Valete*!' a blank cartridge with which he does nothing but startle himself. 'Keep a hold on your handbag, Molly. Pick-pockets. Go on, scram. Vamoose. *Arrivederci, ragazzi*.'

The loitering boys sheer off derisively to seek better pickings. A dove descends at Maureen's feet as she stands there in her swimming haze.

'Oh how lovely! Look, Jack, a beautiful dove. Just at my feet.'

Jack is patting each of his pockets in turn, checking up on cash and cards. He hasn't a great deal of energy to spare for ornithology just at the moment, and besides he is beginning to feel a little queer, he couldn't specify in what way.

'The dove, of course, appropriately enough, is Venus' bird,' he remarks informatively.

'Of *course*,' raps back Maureen. *Know-all*, she thinks, *old windbag*. And she drops down on one knee (oh the relief from standing) and holds out one hand to the gentle bird. She looks at its bright pensive eye; the pensive bright eye looks back into Maureen's. It seemed wonderful, the way it came fluttering down slantwise to enter the vacuity of her vision and settle there at her feet.

'Beautiful creature,' says Maureen to the dove. 'I've nothing to feed you, I'm afraid. *Columba . . . Columba*.' Her schoolgirl Latin slides up to the surface of her mind, quite unexpectedly. 'That's what you are. *Columba*.' It is an astonishingly halcyon moment, rapturous almost, in a quiet way, for Maureen, naming the bird.

Jack looks down through the fainting heat of the piazza at his crouching wife, who represents herself as a splash of tart lemon colour, as if the surface of the eye could register taste, rather tangy, like a pear-drop. This heat is really getting to him. But at least she's cheering up. She has always been so good with living creatures, plants, animals, human young: less centred with adults (he means himself, and those fellow ruffians his academic friends). He levers her up; the bird hops off, is airborne with a soft roar of wings. He takes the opportunity to remark, 'I'll bet you're glad now you decided to take my advice and make the effort to come out.'

But Jack is already faltering. His time for indulging the savage rudeness of the old dispensation is almost run through, and if he has any more barbs or goads up his sleeve he will have to discharge them now, before he enters the portico.

'Oh, this is much better! Hardly anyone here at all.'

A single line of spectators is standing before the *Primavera* in attitudes of musing respect, their postures scarcely less graceful than the wistful figures flowing together over Botticelli's panel. Jack leads Maureen over the threshold to join them. They stand a little distance behind the other viewers and take their fill of the beauty that is offered. Jack feels extremely odd as he stands there trying to enjoy the moment toward which he has tended with such passionate curiosity so many years: hopes he isn't going down with Maureen's accursed bug; wonders if he ought to take a seat until the sensations pass over.

'Do you notice,' says a very gentle English voice just ahead of them, breaking the reverential hush, 'that all the feminine faces seem to be reflections of one face? Do you think that's intended?' The voice belongs to a fair-haired English girl in a soft white blouse and a floral skirt, tall and full-figured.

'Mmn,' says her friend, as a query rather than a reply; and the person tucks a hand in the fair girl's arm. They continue to stare reflectively.

Somehow Jack can't concentrate on the picture; it swirls in a meaninglessly pretty fashion before his listless eyes. He has come all the way from Pennsylvania to pay it the compliment of his homage, but all he can think of is the small figure of the crop-headed youth before him, one hand twined with casual intimacy in the sister's (it had to be a sister's) arm, the other hand in the pocket of white cotton trousers. The youth is of indeterminate age; his hair is dark brown and rather well cut if you like that ragged fashion they all patronise nowadays. Jack can't see his face. He finds he is covetous of seeing his face. He finds he's roused, unbelievably, just by the back view. That portion of Jack's anatomy which finally gave up the ghost over a decade ago, to his intense shame and distress, stirs and hardens, as he runs his eyes over the boy's slim flanks and stares fixedly at the fair skin of his nape, between the hair and the loose collar. *Good God. What's all this?* He would like to kiss that delicate skin, and turn the youth between his hands – gently, so gently – to kiss his throat, and – no, this is all wrong, for the youth says, in what seems to be a girl's voice, to the fair-haired companion, 'I got out a book about Botticelli last week, Rosie – it said that every single flower and plant had a meaning, quite specific – the cornflower and the marigold for instance (can you see them there?) meant – well, I can't remember what exactly, but something. The Book of Nature.'

'It's so beautiful – more than I could have imagined.'

'It is, it is.'

Jack who has always, for reasons he imperfectly understands, been inquisitive about sexual variation and deviation, now nudges Maureen and hears himself enquire in one of his most resonant whispers, 'Molly, is that a boy or a girl, do you think?'

'A boy, I'd say.'

'No, I'm a girl,' says the turning youth, and beams without embarrassment in such a way that one can see quite plainly it's a girl: *no doubt at all*, thinks Jack, reeling. Her face is just like someone's he knew long ago. He's just dredging for the name when the similitude fades and fails him.

'Do please pardon me,' says Jack. 'It was unforgivably rude of me to blurt like that.'

'Oh that's all right, I don't mind a bit. It's been happening all the time since I had this haircut. Anyway I'd rather have been born a boy than a girl. It's an easier life altogether.'

'Would you really?' asks Maureen, taken aback. 'I wouldn't. Not in a million years.'

'Oh yes, definitely. Freedom. Value. Authority. Swaggering round being a lord of the earth. Absolutely the preferable state.'

'It isn't quite like that when you have to be it,' says Jack. 'Take my word.' He is still agitated by the meeting; his mind is a churned pool, all tremor and dazzle. Her call to him is loud and poignant, though she is so undersized and slight (a head smaller than Maureen) and not in any respect akin to the buxom Cleopatras he chases nightly through his dreams and wildly fantasises under the warm shower at 'Red Earth'.

'If you'd ever had a baby,' says Maureen, 'you could never wish for a man's estate over a woman's. Never.'

'Oh but I have,' replies the stranger; and her face darkens, her words lose energy and focus. 'He's called Oliver. He's five.'

'But what a lovely name: Oliver. Is he with you in Florence?' Maureen wants to know. She would like to meet a child in this wilderness of artworks, palazzos and piazzas and encyclopaedic, strutting Jack with his rage for culture and his guidebook.

'No . . . no. He's with his father. They live in Harrogate.'

'Is that – Harrogate, England?'

'Harrogate, England,' agree the Englishwomen with broad smiles. 'We live in Bradford, England.' More smiles. 'But Rosie's going away to Lesotho to dig irrigation ditches in an unpronounceable dry place. She won this farewell jaunt for us in a Persil competition.'

'Hello, Rosie,' says Maureen. She takes to the large, soft-eyed girl: like a maternal landscape, comforting and receptive.

'Hello,' says Rosie, taking her hand. 'It's lovely to meet you.' And she goes on prattling of chance meetings in unlikely places, of French meteorologists under the Pyramids, of expatriate Sudanese in the Himalayas.

'And your name?' asks Jack, ignoring the other one, the nobody. He can think of names that would evoke her: Cherubino would do well, or Viola, or Donatello's David.

'I'm Jenny,' says Jenny.

And that is the end of him, he is fished for and caught, and twists on the end of her line. Jack feels, as he helplessly trails her with his beggar's eyes, as vulnerable as those supine female nudes his eyes rape on the walls of the gallery, as disadvantaged as a woman unclothed and presented to the penetration of the general view. It's an awful feeling, squirmingly awful, this loss of the immunity of his gender. *Don't go,* he wants to say to her. *Stay, I'll die if I don't keep you. For Jesus' sake.*

Somewhere on the other side of the door is stranded the man he was, the unregenerate, superannuated old jackass, and there will never again be permission on this earth or in the next world to resume that threadbare self, which now has purely antiquarian interest. He departs from himself as if he'd inadvertently left an autonomous reflection on a mirror. The old Jack wanders off into the crowd and strays towards Santa Croce in search of a wife to bully perhaps, and an audience to impress with majestic remarks. The new Jack, humiliated by the onset of a terrible tenderness in the eyes in his breast in his bowels and in his sex, looks round for a place to sit down. He is leaning on Jenny, who looks up at the old man with concern.

'Are you feeling all right?'

'No, not well. Not good at all. I must find somewhere to sit. Molly, I'm not well.'

He's coming down with the bug, thinks Maureen. *Now we shall see languishings, now we shall hear 'Oh Molly Oh Molly Oh help me I think I'm dying', and a whole box of tricks brought out for Mother's benefit.*

'You do look seedy, Jack. Best get you back to your bed.'

Jack, who shows reluctance to let go of Jenny's shoulder, compels her and Rosie to come along too.

Clamorous Jack lies still and suffers in silence, to Maureen's slight alarm: he *must* be ill if he's showing this uncharacteristic stoicism. Why is he not moaning and groaning, kicking at the sheets and pointedly enquiring of her as to why he was ever born? She herself is quickly back to normal, better than normal, for now she has these two dear young people with whom to see Florence. While Jack lies there and sweats, Maureen gads. But it is at her own pace. The three women chat their way round Florence, they amble and perch, their thirsty eyes drink light: light on creamy and golden stone, on green, red and white marble, on vast pink dome and pale statues the folds of whose stony garments run like milk. They sip coffee, they listen to one another. Nobody drags on Maureen's hand, punishing her with the moody pressures of a jogtrot itinerary. If she wants to be quiet, they let her be. They listen to her stories of children and grandchildren with every appearance of interest, and because of all this she is able to soak in the beauty of Florence through every pore as a merciful human place, to which she will always stand in loving relationship.

How would the black beetle feel if compelled to evacuate its carapace and live soft-side out? The eye of day would scorch it through, the rain would wash its jelly body out like an inky blot. So Jack cowers, minus his shell of worldliness and cynicism. She comes to sit with him, Maureen being gone with Rosie on a minibus to Vallombrosa. How can she be interested in an antediluvian wreck like himself, who'd want to hang around with a fat old horrible man wearing carpet slippers and a prehistoric tartan dressing-gown in a stifling hotel room when they could be visiting the monastery at Vallombrosa? How can a girl who's missing a once-in-a-lifetime jaunt bear to sit still in the company of decaying senescence, and look at him with such an electric glitter in her eyes? Jack could swear she was excited by him: but no; but no: she'd have to be quite freakish, aberrant, to return his feeling. And the English are so polite, he knows that. They queue, and agree to everything that is put to them.

'I wish you'd gone with the others, Jenny.'

'Do you?'

'No. Of course I don't. But I feel guilty. You're missing out.'

'Am I?'

'Stop it, Poll Parrot. You tell me.'

'Of course I'm not missing out. I'm stuffed with monasteries and mausoleums. I wanted to stay with you more than anything.'

She is pulling the curtains wide, pushing at the sash window which wouldn't budge for him this morning, but now shoots up with a crash to admit lemony light and air full of voices.

'How can you say that?' *Stuffed with monasteries*. That's rank heresy in Jack's book, not to mention bad language for a woman. But there is a crazy perfection in everything he hears her say. He's heard her swear uncouthly, and she walks with an unladylike swagger. Okay, so swearing and swaggering must be acceptable behaviour. In future, clean-tongued Jack shall swear from a reformed mouth.

'How can I not say it?' She turns from the window, her hands being open to him, her elbows defensively caught in to her sides. 'I love you so much.'

He watches with disbelief as her eyes brim with tears. Can she really have said it, plain and straightforward, over there in the glow from the eased window, like some gentle puritan smitten with grace: that old-fashioned spirit in her that reminds him of his own people, Maureen's rather, ancestors way back. The portraits of her Quaker forbears, those powerful quietists, look you straight in the eyes from the walls of 'Red Earth': *Did you honestly imagine we were dead and gone?*

'And I love Maureen too. I love you both. I can't explain it. I can't help it. It just happened.'

That's a let-down, *I love Maureen.* That puts a check on Jack's racing imagination.

But 'We love you too,' he capitulates, taking the slenderness of her hand and grasping it in both of his as if to leave an imprint. 'It has been special meeting you, Jenny. Like a recognition. I don't feel as though I'll ever be the same again. If there is ever anything I can do for you, you just tell me and I'll do it like a shot. You never knew your mother and father. Let me be your mother and father.'

Head in his lap, she twists the fraying tassel of his dressing-gown cord. The words in the wilderness drop down like manna, each one an atonement, a soft rain of mercy, but – no – it wasn't a parent she came here to seek.

'Bradford, England,' meditates Jack out loud. 'Bradford, England. I think Bradford, England must be the home of the gods.'

Jenny bursts out laughing. 'Oh, it is,' she says. 'It definitely is. You should see it. Far more gorgeous than Florence – all cloud-capped towers and castles in the air.'

'I can believe it,' replies Jack in all seriousness. 'May I come and visit you over there one day, Jenny, in Bradford?'

'Oh, I don't know about that.' Jenny's face is veiled whenever she speaks of home; and of her child Oliver and her estranged husband Alexander she won't speak at all. 'It's a northern town, industrial, very poor. It smells of coal-smoke. It's cold. You wouldn't like it.'

Jack is prepared to like Bradford, England, if it turns out to be located on the inside of a coalmine. He worships the ground that Jenny treads on: though she seems to his sensuous eye more like a wispy plan for a woman than the accomplished fact. She wears tight jeans and coloured T-shirts, her footwear leaves something to be desired. Her brown hair, cropped close, is rough but shiny. She wears no make-up, scent or jewellery, the essentials of female seduction to Jack's way of thinking. Her small, oval face is unremarkable, lips rather full, only the eyes astonishingly powerful: a dark sort of blue, almost navy, like those of newborn infants which last a month and normalise to brown or pale blue. Jenny's haven't normalised. They disturb him. When she's gone, late that afternoon, Jack's heart knocks and bangs like an old tin can dragged over cobblestones, just at the remembrance of those eyes.

He sits with the shabby green cardigan she has forgotten to take away with her crushed between his hands and rubs his cheek against it. He sniffs it. It smells of Jenny, faint faintest reminiscence of a familiar body which threads its arms into those sleeves, armpits, shoulders, delicate little breast across which the buttons (one missing) do up; that body, the one-and-only body to which he aches to offer his tenderness, and may not, for he's an old man and she's so young (though older than she looks, surely, to have been to art college and have a child of that age?) Jack, accusing himself *doting old fool* and *senile infatuation* but not *dirty old man*, no never again, as long as he lives, only gives over his adoration of the cardigan to fold it up with motherly care and insert it under his pillow, with no intention of returning it to its owner.

What's this under his pillow? thinks Maureen, straightening out the rucked-up bedclothes. Jack doesn't seem to be sleeping well since his illness, he threshes, and when he's done threshing, he gets up and prowls. Last night she heard him awaken weeping, he was crying like a child. It scared her. It embarrassed her by invading the tabooed area of the not-said, the forty-two-year silent contract of defensive estrangement. The enemy was at the wall, his poor hands tearing at the barbed wire: the enemy who was your likeness and your mate. Jack was crying without restraint, lying on his back with his eyes wide open, tears coursing down, she glimpsed the glitter on his eyes from the moonlight as she turned reluctantly on her own pillow.

'What is it, Jack?'

There is a pause. 'Nothing. Just a dream.'

A grown man to cry for a dream! Jack is obviously entering second childhood. He was sitting up now and blowing his nose with considerable furore, as if ashamed of his display. Maureen has frequently had occasion to wish over the decades that Jack could find it in him to blow his nose with less ostentation both in public and in the sanctuary of the private world. She wished it again now; longed for the peace of her single bed back home at 'Red Earth' where Jack's uncouth snoring doesn't penetrate, and his dreams don't rock her. The walls of 'Red Earth' are twelve inches thick and provide her with soundproof immunity to her husband and his more seismic manifestations.

'Are you all right now?'

'Yes. Yes. Go back to sleep, honey. Sorry I woke you,' He leant over her and kissed her cheek. Maureen lay in a state of rigor mortis until she was assured that was all he was going to do. She relaxed.

'What was your dream?'

'Oh . . . just some nonsense. It's all scrambled now.' His voice was husky; he was clearly holding out on her. *He doesn't want me to know. Probably dirty.*

'What are you doing with that cardigan under your pillow?' she asked surprisingly, rising to one elbow. Jack's shadowy bulk was lying down again, turned away from her, his arms hugging the pillow like a spar in the sea of unruly sheets his agitation had whipped up.

'What cardigan?' he mumbled.

'The threadbare old green cardigan I found under your pillow this morning. The cardigan with the button missing. Knitted in four-ply lambswool, Size 10, with a St Michael's label inside the collar and – let me see – fraying slightly at one cuff, I think it was the left – five buttons, dark green, somewhat triangular in shape – *that* cardigan, Jack dear.'

'Oh *that* cardigan,' rejoined Jack acidly. 'Good God, woman, you couldn't have browsed through it more thoroughly if it had been a book.'

'Well?'

'Well, what?'

'What's it doing under your pillow?'

'Really, Molly. I don't investigate the state of affairs under your pillow. I fail to see why you should concern yourself with mine. Good night.'

'Whose is it?'

'Good *night*, Molly.'

'It's Jenny's, isn't it?'

'Yes.'

'Dear oh dear.'

'What do you mean, "dear oh dear"?'

'Just that.'

' "Dear oh dear" yourself,' riposted Jack with helpless petulance. 'Can I sleep now?' *I know how to shut her up*, thought Jack maliciously. He turned over towards her and reached out a hand, which he placed lovingly on Maureen's shoulder. The lazily wafting tendrils of the sea anemone shrank back into the knot of self at his exploratory touch. The hand was withdrawn. Maureen was silent. She let him sleep. She lay and reflected, in a state of stressful complexity. She likes Jenny though Jenny is immature for her age which must be around thirty. She has no feeling of jealousy at all; but there is a sense of danger, not least to the young woman whose nerves lie so near the surface of her skin, whose brittle insecurity like that of a delicate graven glass seems to have called Jack's great clumsy fingers to settle round it. There is danger in Jack's tears: when did Jack ever cry? Men don't cry, in Jack's book, and she has always believed this maxim to be a proper one. Who is going to hold up the world when Atlas turns aside to weep? Danger for Maureen. Deep in their shared past, at their reticent, tender, tentative beginnings when they had restored 'Red Earth' (vines grew up through the floorboards of the now gracious living room, ivy ate at the gables) Maureen received Jack for better or worse, bore his children, inspired his music: and the bad old plant is fixed in her poignantly and for all time.

Don't leave me, Jack. Don't leave me.

She stole one faltering hand over to her husband and laid it on his shoulder. Jack did not stir from the abyss into which he had plunged. He will never know to his dying day that Maureen's pride crept into the lee of his sheltering body one night in Florence, and begged *Don't leave me, Jack.* He will not know that in his sleep his right hand unconsciously felt for her left hand, gave it a friendly squeeze and lapsed away again. Nor that he then began to snore, with rhythms severely maladjusted: sometimes in triplicate, at others in single ebullitions, punctuated by momentous silences which, being interpreted, proclaimed, *What's coming next? Bet you never heard one like this!* Florentine youths sang and kicked cans down the echoing alley beneath their window, Jack snored, and 'Shut up!' hissed Maureen, shaking his shoulder. 'Go and sleep in the bath if you've got to make that racket. How do you think little Jenny likes ancient snorers?' Jack shut up immediately and was not heard from again all night.

The girls have flown. Florence goes out like a light. Jack loiters for the duration in her footsteps and adores his cardigan. He stands in front of the *Primavera* and thinks up elaborate schemes whereby he must attend a conference of modern composers which just happens to be located in Bradford, England. He has consulted a map and learnt that Bradford is in an area called Yorkshire, proximate to Leeds where he knows there is a piano competition, Manchester which has a famous music school and Sheffield which has a choir. He finds he may have to make essential journeys to all three cities in the coming year.

Maureen is happy now to be going home to Pennsylvania. She can never at the best of times bear to be away from 'Red Earth' and 'Shadows' for long without fretting, and is fond of saying that she is a 'home bird' in contrast to Jack, that vagrant cuckoo. She has telephoned the new owner of 'Shadows' whom she liked so much and told her they were coming home tomorrow and how much she looked forward to entertaining her. Nicki's voice sounded genuinely delighted: 'My dear Maureen, I can't wait to see you', eager like a child, but mature and comfortable. At Vallombrosa, looking out towards the forest of dense pine and beech, Maureen had been reminded with a pang of her homeland, and with that pang the memory of Nicki's face and hair and indeed her whole person had so vividly flooded Maureen's mind's eye that she had almost cried out to Rosie, her companion, *Oh look at her, do look!* The remembered face turned queryingly out of shadow; sunlight low as if in late afternoon called out the copper shine in that curly tempest of auburn hair; Maureen was aware of the athletic, deep-breasted beauty of her body as well, so sensually aware that she startled herself. *What does it mean?* she pondered, and then reproved herself, *It must be all these nude statues of ladies everywhere. I'm getting as bad as Jack.*

Going home – you're joking. Jenny's plane taxies in to Manchester Airport, it's pelting with rain. Florence and the *Primavera* and the wonderful old American she took to so inexplicably are already discounted as participating in the falsifying light of holiday. Jenny shoves Jack deep into her pocket amongst the siftings of dust and linen fibres and fragments of bills long paid. Some girls come home to the phlegmatic north of England, their minds flown with the glamour of Etruscan youths on beaches like breathing statues, or the bronzed boy-children of Lemnos. Jenny comes trailing home with her own kind of epiphany, an old man in an objectionable raincoat. She crumples it now with scornful fingers like some phony postcard. And somehow blames him for his failure to endure as other than art.

Part One

1
Life

Jack's life might well have one further year left in it to unfold but it could hardly stretch to two: so might have testified a consultant at locating the bloodclot nosing its way along Jack's artery toward his brain, gathering substance as it pursued its journey. But as spring advances, the second year on from Florence, there is absolutely no sensation of decay in Jack: only a regenerate feeling of deep, core joy, a youthfulness he is sure he never experienced during the anxious and turbulent period of youth itself. He is far too happy to bother with medical check-ups, and besides where's the time for ophthalmologist, urologist, cardiologist and all those other plutocratic ologists to whom Jack used to direct portions of his bank balance; and thought it money well spent. When one has dedicated one's life to bouncing to and fro between Philadelphia and Heathrow like an ardent ping-pong ball, there is neither time nor inclination to fuss about one's state of health. He would have said he never felt better in his life. He has Jenny. There is nothing further to wish for, except more of her, more often. He tells this morning by morning in the womblike darkness of his den, to his family of animals: the great Newfoundland pup Thoby, the schnauzer Paul, and the grizzled little dachshund Nancy, assembled at his feet in furry congregation. 'Jenny is mine and I am hers,' he instructs them. 'Yes,' he says, 'yes, Thoby. How about that?' He is bursting to confide in people, and if he were to visit any consultant would undoubtedly rave to him of Jenny, and Bradford, England, and how she's beautiful, and how he'd changed: mellowed, maybe, but savagely sleepless.

Jack has lost the faculty of sleep. He awakens at two or three a.m., bright-eyed and alert. And in those hours of pampering solitude, in which he is free to do all he wants to do, in the order he wants to do it, emperor of darkness till light glimmers along the bars of the blinds and Maureen is heard to stir, sometimes the magical old gift revisits him. Musical notations drop like soft, needed, merciful rainfall into the well of his long-barren mind. He keeps sheets of score-paper on the bureau under the great spherical oil-lamp, on which to catch these drops. The joy of composition when one had resigned oneself to impotence: the gratitude, the grace of it. And hence he must repeat with every morning this aubade: *Bless Jenny*, for her extension of quickening power. She coaxed life from its sources, and the music that was found, though little in quantity and simple in form, had a tilt, a slantwise irregularity, which made it, to his ear, new and haunting.

Far-away-eyed Maureen, who does visit her consultant for a complete check-up, is told that she is in tip-top condition for a lady of sixty-four, and that there is no reason to doubt that she will live to the age of ninety-two. 'Oh don't say that!' gasps Maureen into the consultant's benign, expensive face, in genuine alarm. 'I shouldn't like that one little bit.' Imagine being a crazy, incontinent old woman everybody hates; put away in an old folk's home with the other crones whose mouths are toothless and who dribble, weep and leer; or, worse, descending like a curse on your seventy-year-old daughter. No: no. *Though I cared for Mother when she was in that condition. I thought it my duty; and I wanted to do it.* But Maureen is proud in a different way from autocratic Bess whom she so longed to please; and couldn't. The smiling physician amends his prognosis at her request; shears twelve years off her life-span and offers a coffin at eighty. 'Make that seventy-five,' Maureen haggles. 'And a painless coronary in the night.' Done. Maureen goes home very satisfied and writes her cheque.

'He told me I'd go on till ninety-two,' she tells Jack and their neighbour Nicki from 'Shadows' over supper. 'But I beat him down to seventy-five.'

'You'll never seem old,' says Nicki to Maureen. 'Not you. It's just not in you. Ripe, yes, old no. I've met people who seem somehow to include all ages. You're one of those.'

Maureen has Nicki. For her as for Jack, the world's fulcrum has shifted, to include another being as part of herself. She contemplates the frequent excursions of her delirious, risible husband across the Atlantic with equanimity, managing to hold her laughter as the pretexts become more and more outlandish, at least until he is out of the room. The Atlantic to his giant eye has shrunk to a puddle. Like the snake that opens his jaw to an angle of nearly 180 degrees to squeeze in the world-size egg, Jack's imaginative appetite has a megalomaniac quality in regard to the laws of probability.

'I've decided to attend an international cello symposium.'

'Oh yes, dear. Where might that be?'

'Er . . .' Jack coughs. 'In Manchester, England.'

'That's nice. When would you be going?'

'The day after tomorrow.'

'So soon! Do you have a ticket?'

'Yes.' He shifts from foot to foot, furtive-eyed, like their son Tom when twenty years back he smashed the greenhouse window with a golf club.

'I hope you bought it at the cheap rate?'

'Oh yes, dear, of course.' That means he's been holding on to it at least three weeks.

'You didn't mention it.'

'Oh, no, well, I thought I might cancel.'

'It's a pity you *didn't* tell me, honey,' says Maureen shaking her head. 'I could have made a batch of cookies for you to take across to Jenny. And her little boy. Give me advance notice next time, Jack, for goodness sake.'

'I will. I'm sorry,' mutters Jack, head lowered. He wonders why he crassly didn't: Maureen doesn't seem to mind one way or the other where he is; what he's about. In a way that very tolerance, or indifference, disturbs him. Doesn't she care about him any more at all? It's as if his wife lives with her head perpetually averted, her eyes looking out over the pine-clad valley towards the facing house of 'Shadows'.

He caught her early yesterday morning at her bedroom window, just standing, staring. She was wearing a dress he hadn't seen before, of cerulean blue, long-sleeved, high-necked, of some soft material his fingers would have liked to stroke. Her long hair was loose, all down her back, thick undulations of hair, nearly to her waist; crinkling from being habitually bound up. Her hands rested on the sill at either side, and she leaned more on the left than the right, her body rather gracefully angled, so that the folds of the blue dress fled away from her right hip. From where Jack stood in the doorway, her figure poised there had a beautifully generous quality: loss overcame him, keen and sharp. She didn't stir when he deliberately creaked his shoe on a floorboard he knew to be loose. He cleared his throat. Nothing.

'Maureen.'

No reply. She was swaying slightly, as if to music she alone heard, or made, drowning him out. As Jack walked to join her, the glittering view from the open window approached his eye. Half the top storey of 'Shadows' was showing, its white wood glinting in the sunlight, the remainder of the house concealed in the darkness of the forest.

'Maureen.'

Her eyes that turned to him were drugged as those of a somnambulist, or as if she had turned up the volume of the inner music to a deafening pitch.

Her eyes retreated to 'Shadows'. There across the green bowl of the valley the answering house, the answering bedroom window, and, as Jack now discerned, the answering woman. Nicki was standing in Bess' old bedroom at 'Shadows', mirroring Maureen in hers: a small, only just discernible figure in red with folded arms, just standing there looking out.

'*Maureen*,' said Jack, in some agitation.

'I hear you, honey. I'm just coming. I suppose you want your breakfast.' She made it sound like a sombre accusation.

'Am I disturbing you?'

'Not in the least bit.' She turned with ease from the window; did not wave.

Why am I not disturbing you? You should be disturbed, thought the attention-seeker. *Am I not your husband? Wives obey your . . . and all St Paul's laudable etceteras*. Jack, who was meditating a fit of moodiness, recollected that Jenny has set him right on this as on an abundance of other issues.

'Let *me* get you the breakfast for a change,' he offered meekly. 'It won't be up to your high standards, of course, but – let me. I so want to do things for you.'

'Certainly not,' said Maureen, scandalised. She has not had the benefit of Jenny's feminist revelations; and sticks to her conviction that men should be kept well out of kitchens. She was herself again; stalked out and began to cause things to sizzle in fry-pans.

I'm safe, I have Nicki. Nicki stands between her and Jack's dictatorial shadow as no one has stood in her life before. Nicki grew up chivalrous and chirpily gallant, like a boy. When Jack's tongue gets waspish and uncivil (rarely nowadays since Eros tamed him down, but he's still at heart the same bad old animal he ever was) Nicki calls him off before he's had a chance to get going. Maureen has never before heard Jack directly taken on and worsted. Jack hasn't either. At first she nearly clapped her hand over Nicki's mouth and said, *Oh no Nicki dear, we don't talk to him like that.* She herself has always ruled him by indirection, insinuation. But when Jack barked, they all stood still and suffered. Nicki goes straight in and collars the hound whenever its manic side makes an appearance. Jack looks mildly astonished but not displeased to submit. It has all been reciprocal habit really: the habit of bullying, the habit of fear.

Maureen's sense of safe home-coming increases daily, combined with an odd counter-emotion of moving into uncharted and risky waters. What *is* this with Nicki? Is it friendship? Baking trays of gingerbread men with currant eyes and buttons for Nicki's school fair together; measuring Nicki for a green silk blouse she wants to run up for her, *Oh do stand still you wriggler*; singing duets at the piano and trying hopelessly to contend with Nicki's rich contralto: this is the friendship of shared life with a woman for which Maureen yearned. But how may she describe this further, unsafe dimension which is not friendship of this motherly yet equal and rational sort, but which awakens Maureen in the dead of night and panics her with bright longings in the secret places of her body, numb so many years? She is ashamed and afraid. She hugs a pillow in her arms and rubs at the light between her thighs with inexperienced fingers, with a view to putting it out; but instead it glows there as she lies thinking of the beauty of Nicki, with a more and more powerful insistency. She has never had an orgasm; privately felt that all such rumours of physical joy for women outside the child-bearing sphere were indelicacies fathered by the male world. Maureen's deepest pleasure, harmony both of spirit and flesh, was in nursing her babies. Now thinking of Nicki she puts up both hands to cup her breasts, decades dry and barren, and tears squeeze through closed eyelids to think of how it is all over: giving the child to suck. Oh the poignancy of that anachronistic need, to yield to bud mouth and searching hands, the flood of sensuous comfort as the milk is called forth from her glands, the fainting of her womb as it contracts in answer to the call. Bluish-white milk, beautiful surplus, overflows the steadily sucking mouth; blue veins lace the breast; aquamarine eyes intently stare up into hers and the working mouth pauses to grin. And somehow her love for Nicki is figured forth in this overpowering ache to sustain and to be cherished in return. But how impossible. It is impossible. And not only that: but grotesque, obscene. What is she but an elderly female fantasist abdicating that dignity which is her birthright, her inheritance, and for which Mrs Maureen Middleton is known in the community, as her mother and grandmother before her: refusing to submit decently to reality.

Grow up. Be your age, reprimands the dead Bess from under the grey rectitude of her gravestone. *You always let me down.*

Maureen, hearing that chilly voice which put a blight on pleasure in her childhood, stayed away from Nicki for a week. She felt it would be fairer to Nicki to let go honourably. After all how could that glorious creature genuinely care for this old bag of bones, this dreaming dying clay? She can't possibly. It isn't natural. Obviously, as Maureen sees in a blaze of comprehension, she has been forcing herself on Nicki, exploiting a relationship from which Nicki is too kind to extricate herself. She lets go, with steely self-discipline. When Nicki knocks, Maureen isn't in; when she telephones, Maureen punishes herself by answering with cool, remote politeness and points out that she has to keep an appointment, would Nicki please excuse her, she's in a hurry? She refuses the flattering delusion that Nicki's voice is growing with each day more hysterically anxious; discounts the evidence of tears and entreaty in the voice. She sternly reminds herself of the facts of her shrivelled womb, her wrinkled husk of a face, her fifteen year survival of the menopause.

One morning Nicki doesn't phone. A terrible relief. Terrible. But thank God, she's weaning her. She must see it like that. Loss as success. She can't stay in the house with the phone's silence. Climbs into the car and drives off down the long, winding lane, rather fast. In the lane, Nicki's car appears round a bend. Nicki swerves suddenly and blocks off the whole road. Gets out and runs to Maureen who strives to slam her car into reverse but the lever's jammed. Nicki beats on the window. Maureen fights the gear-stick. Nicki runs round behind Maureen and lies down flat on the road; hollers, 'Talk to me, damn you, or run me over!'

Maureen, in a real rage, winds down her window and yells, 'Get out of my way. Go on – get *away*.'

Nicki won't budge. She lies there and Maureen can hear her crying, or laughing. All the rage goes out of her, she gets shakily out of her car.

'Come on, sweetheart. Get up.' She offers a hand.

'Will you talk to me?'

'Of course I will.'

'What have I done, Marmie?'

'You haven't done anything.'

'I must have. You wouldn't just – cast me off – for nothing. I must have said something to offend you. Tell me what it was. I take it back, unconditionally. Please – *please*.'

'You don't have to plead. You've done nothing. Get up, come on now.'

'Not until you forgive me.' Puffy-eyed Nicki is leaning up on one elbow but showing no disposition to arise. She looks bleary and unkempt. 'I've gone to pieces. I'm in shreds. It's totally your fault,' she accuses Maureen. A driver stuck behind Nicki's car is hooting in irritation.

'Nicki, will you get up and move your car?'

'No.'

'Then I'll have to come down and join you.' Maureen squats beside the recumbent Nicki. Their neighbour Mr Scott backs up from behind Nicki's car, cursing through his open window.

'Why have you done this to me?'

'For your sake, Nicki. I'm an old woman. I've no business to be monopolising you.'

'You mean you don't love me.' At last, the words are there in the open between them.

'Oh yes I love you. That's the whole point. Too much. Not in the right way.'

'Don't say so. Oh Marmie don't say so,' Nicki sobs, and Maureen cannot restrain herself from putting out her arms to her. 'Just let me go on loving you. I won't be a nuisance, I won't make demands on you. You don't know what you mean to me, you just don't know or you couldn't . . .'

'Nicki, I'm an old woman – '

'Will you quit saying that? Will you just stop it? I'm not a child, to be dished out this babyfood.'

'If you're not a baby, why are you lying in the middle of the road having a tantrum?'

'I don't mind where I have my tantrum, quite honestly, as long as you pay attention to it. I'll willingly have it in your living room. But you have to agree never *never* to shut me out again. If you really want to get rid of me, I will undertake to go. But I have to understand, I have to be consulted.'

Later as the afternoon sun is dragged into the cauldron of the western hills behind 'Red Earth', long shadows stretch in like arms through Maureen's bedroom window; but Maureen, out of harm's way, is lying with Nicki on Bess' bed, embracing her, whispering words of love never ventured in her life before to anyone other than her children as they slept. They have been drinking sherry, plenty of it, and it would be rather hard for either to say how they came to be lying together on Maureen's patchwork quilt, the embarrassing threshold having been traversed wellnigh unawares.

Nothing here partakes either of compulsion or of novelty; nothing is less than equal or other than easy and familiar. In this embrace Maureen feels more herself than she has ever felt. Her fingertips listen to the soft beat of Nicki's life, at her wrist and breast, they travel as lightly as thought over the surface of her closed eyelids, the thin skin of her temples, the fullness of her mouth. She looks at that lapsed-out face close to hers and Nicki's eyes open and that's a world, unbearably gentle and vulnerable, taking her in. With slow, hesitant mouth, Maureen kisses the downy softness of Nicki's cheek, brushes her own against it, then kisses the edge of her mouth, then full on the lips; and Nicki's arms are powerful round her but not like Jack's to manacle and buckle her to him, no, not like that, like the mother to her child to shelter, adore and include, one arm crooked round her head and fondling her hair, the other at her back. To receive back what one has given and been, all these decades of outpoured tenderness to hard and thirsty mouths that take, take, take, and male hands that could bunch into fists, and their stressful, thrusting bodies. Eve remains at home unfallen in Maureen's garden; and Adam is shown the door.

Jack Middleton is suspended at longitude 60, latitude 30,

30,000 feet above the Atlantic Ocean, that trifling pond. He has ordered a cognac from the tartan stewardess but it comes in such a mean and stingy little bottle that he at once orders it a companion. He sips and surveys the vast blue void below, across which a few rags of cloud drift. Nothing is impossible. He is on his way to Jenny in the springtime of his life. Jack is young and vigorous again, and the world lies all before him.

The bane of Alexander Reinhold's life, Jennifer Reinhold, his estranged wife, is observed by him, to be loitering at the end of his garden, in the form of a cloven head which at times dips down and at others bobs up and cranes over the privet hedge. Pity Alex cut back that hedge at the weekend to a level over which that midget can peer. *Memo to self: grow hedge another metre*. Now she's disappeared. Maybe she'll give up and go away.

What did Alex ever see in her? He has often interrogated himself on this with some severity, but he really can't remember the source of the attraction at all. Jenny has none of the qualities a man desires – requires – in a woman, to make it worth his while to house, feed and clothe her. Not that Jenny had ever caused much expenditure in these terms. She had the appetite of a mouse and went around in a shirt and jeans. When Alex tried to educate her dress sense, Jenny said she was comfortable as she was, didn't want to go to a Law Society dinner anyway and why didn't he take his mother? Thin stick of a woman. Hardly a woman at all. Take a tape measure to her and you'd get the vital statistics of an adolescent boy. No breasts to speak of. Little bony hips. He'd made the best of her: called her delicate, slender, the articulations of her joints like the precision engineering of a bird's wing. Fondly, *my Jenny wren*. But the worst of Jenny was, she had no idea how to please a man. No conception of what a man likes, and how he has to be played up to. Baleful, stinging Jenny with her unfocused, sharp retorts. Standing on her dignity as a woman, all five foot two of her. And when he struck her that time, not flinching. Not weeping when he needed her to cry. If she had melted to him, yielded, and crept to his bed in the depths of the night, he could have forgiven her it all. She deserved everything that came to her. Alex gave her fair warning on a variety of occasions. He said,

'If you go on neglecting your child and your husband, I will have you out of here, without one penny piece in maintenance.' Why was she so surprised when he brought the heel of his shoe down upon her as we smash insects? She cried then all right.

'What's the problem? I told you this would happen.'

'Yes, but I never thought you meant it. To take a child from its mother – '

'Motherhood was not so sacred when you had the chance to do it. You were a scandalous mother.'

'No. No. I was just human. I wanted to be free.'

'Well, now you are. Free as air. So fly away.'

Pity the court made Alex pay her some maintenance. Still, he got rid of Jenny, that was the main thing; and Oliver was released from her pernicious influence. Greenham Common, CND, Greenpeace: all Jenny's pie-in-the-sky delusions.

Of course she was a doddle when it came to the divorce, a pushover; had no idea of how to defend herself by attacking him. Her lawyer was a graduate of Bombay University, whose English though voluble was nonsensical. Alex, himself a divorce lawyer of considerable stature, graduate of Johannesburg and Oxford, used his best friend as barrister. The xeroxed letters from Rosie, all gush and girlish sentiment, did the trick in smearing Jenny as a lesbian (though as far as Alex knows she is not), not to mention the statement by the head teacher and neighbour attesting to Jenny's crazy mismanagement of the boy.

But wouldn't you imagine, thinks Alex, still at the kitchen window, in intense irritation, brawny arms folded over his apron, *that having spent all that money and gone through utter trauma to get clear of her, you could expect the silly bitch to leave you alone?* Jenny is at the gate, her hand hovering over the latch, indecisive as she ever was. *I'll get a guard dog*, thinks Alex, *that's a brain-wave. That'll see her off.* Jenny has a phobia about animals. Thinks everything with teeth is about to bite her. *Of course the woman is profoundly unstable. Had no parents herself and consequently doesn't know how to be one. Like female gorillas brought up in zoos who sit on their offspring rather than suckle them.* The potted books of psychology lawyers read all say this. Maybe she should be put away, for her own good. During their marital disputes Alex more than once pointed out that this was a practical option, and related the case (which he invented on the spur of the moment) of Rhees v. Rhees in 1980 in which this was done to the wife, who was diagnosed as psychotic. Or there might be drug therapy available on an out-patient basis? White as a sheet Jenny tottered back a pace, and 'I'm not mad, Alex,' she pleaded, 'I'm perfectly normal.' Oh how it echoed, the hollow space of uncertainty beneath her words. He might well try this one again.

The door is opened to Jenny by a large buxom girl in a blood-red dress and black leather boots. Jenny, who has seen Alexander glaring at her from the kitchen window, is relieved that she has to deal with the new au pair rather than her blond and brutal ex-spouse.

'I'd like to speak to Oliver, please.'

'Oliver he is not here, sorry.'

'Where is he?' asks Jenny quickly, nursing the alarm she carries around with her, in the pit of her stomach, in her womb, in the breasts that failed Olly from the very first by producing too little milk, engorging and erupting into sore, infected places, until in the end they shrivelled back into less than the nothing they always, humiliatingly, were. And Alex sat up with Oliver to do the night-feeds, crooning to his child in his striped pyjamas by the gasfire, a black pane mirroring the back of his head, listening in to the World Service: as Alex has fed the son she failed and failed, ever since. *What am I doing here? He's more of a mother than I'll ever be, with all his faults.* The burning shame of her inadequacies: she doesn't need Alex to point it out; never has. And if she had a second chance, would she do any better this time round? Forgetting to pick him up from playgroup, drawing the breakfast pots as still life rather than washing them up, letting him take a bottle to bed so that he'd be quiet and she could read, hating it, hating it all, the nappies, the night-waking, the noise, the colds and mess and boredom. Loving him but saying in her heart of hearts, *this bores me*; at root an unaccountable terror of Olly from the moment of his birth, total recoil from his huge violet-eyed need and dependency. The impiety of that, it so ashames her now bereaved of him that it registers as a cringing soreness in her chest, and sometimes in the middle of the night she finds herself shielding her breast, bowing her head over the wound of guilt, huddled in her bed. The infirmity, it seems to Jenny, was born in her, and though she knows she cripples herself yet further by this fatalistic reasoning, she feels that too was fathered upon her by whomever sired her, on whom, in whatever oblivious and forgotten bed.

'Excuse me, but who are you?' asks the au pair.

'Oliver's mother,' says Jenny tonelessly. At the very moment she announces her identity, Alex appears, slightly in the wake of his voice, which is saying, 'It's all right, Renate, run along. I'll deal with this person.'

'Alex, I need to see Olly.'

'Jennifer, go away. You have no business here.'

'I do have business. This is my house you've stolen. That is my child.'

'Go – away – and – stay – away, or I will take you back to court and get your access order rescinded. I am not joking. I've just about *had* it with you. I haven't ever got tough with you, Jennifer, yet. All I've done is snap my fingers at you. Unless you get off my property and stay off it, and stop hanging round outside my son's school gates disturbing him, unless you abide by the agreement *to the letter*, you are finished. Do you follow?'

Alex seeks to conclude his harangue by slamming the door but Jenny's foot is in the way.

'Do you want me to use force?'

'You won't do that Alex, you know you won't. Imagine what the neighbours would say. You can't afford to make a bad impression. And what about the au pair? She's taking all this in, you know.'

Jenny can see that the living-room door is ajar, a breathless presence may be intuited there. She herself is trembling uncontrollably; has never in her life asserted herself against Alex in the way she is doing now. Her face burns, her mouth is dry. *Keep going, keep going*. She woke this morning with the image of Oliver so piercingly real, a face like his father's, bitter, Aryan, contemptuous, that she heard herself cry out to him for mercy as she woke.

'Would you mind coming out here, Renate?' asks Alexander. The girl immediately issues forth, insouciance itself.

'This woman is Oliver's mother.'

'That I know, Mr Reinhold.'

'She is never to be admitted to this house. She is never to approach Oliver when you take or bring him home from school. She is an unstable character. Got that?'

'Certainly, Mr Reinhold.'

'We shall be buying a guard dog, Renate, to protect the property against trespassers.'

'Oh Mr Reinhold I do *not* like dogs especially those great ugly bullhounds. Would I be in charge of this dog?'

'For goodness sake.'

'I would not mind a (how do you say?) *Pudel* – or a nice spaniel. But these bullhounds, they give me unwholesome experiences.'

'Yes, well, we can talk about this, Renate.'

Alexander, deflated, runs a hand through his blond hair and grins at the au pair through gritted teeth. One has to be polite to au pairs to a degree unnecessary with wives; otherwise they decamp in the middle of the night and leave you in lumber, holding the baby.

'Do not worry about the dog,' he adds as an emollient. What outrages him about modern European women is the way they have abdicated their basic responsibilities. Menfolk are no longer free for serious work. Oliver is the apple of his eye, his son and heir, but he shouldn't have to be wiping his bottom and cleaning his teeth, that's women's work. Back home in Jo'burg he wouldn't be seen dead in an apron. Now he wears his stigma with pride. Back home, of course, Alex was considered to be undesirably liberal on questions of race and gender. This chaos is what comes of tolerance to inferiors: they told him that but he didn't like to believe it.

'Will you undertake to leave Oliver strictly alone, Jennifer?' he goes on. 'If you can't make such an undertaking, I have no option but to start proceedings at once.'

'Are *you* such a wonderful father?' Jenny suddenly bursts out. '*Are* you? How can you judge me, how dare you?' She hears her voice falter and gasp. Craven, querulous Jenny knows she's beaten. *Did you honestly think you could take him on? Him and his ancestors and his legal system, his tribal certainties, his fathers and his fathers' fathers?*

'I am a good father, certainly.'

'Oh yes, Mrs Reinhold,' chimes in Renate. 'Mr Reinhold is a true example of fatherhood. *Jawohl.* Better than any fathers we have at the current time in Germany.'

Renate beams at Alex; Alex stands an inch taller. This is more like it. This is what he likes to hear. Nubile, luscious Renate would really know how to please a man. He looks down pityingly at Jenny from the top step. Her hair needs washing. Her wardrobe is the rail of the Oxfam shop. It's odd how she suddenly and inexplicably caves in. One gentle tap in the right place and you split her like an egg. Now she's weeping, and pleading.

'Please don't take Olly away from me altogether. I *couldn't* live with that. I couldn't.'

'Then you'll have to promise,' he says mildly, not unkindly.

'Yes, yes, I promise. I'm sorry, Alex. Sorry I bothered you. I shouldn't have.' Spineless and lachrymose, she hates herself for this incapacity to keep what's hers; to hang on to her pride and rights. *There's something missing in me. I wish things away before they're taken.*

'You should see a doctor,' advises the voice of sanity.

'Yes, yes, I will.'

'You need some sort of counselling.'

Jenny doesn't reply. She turns away irresolutely. There is still the crying need to see Olly and touch him, or to see his clothes or toys or anything that comes from and leads back to the peace of him. It doesn't go away, the need, however abject she becomes. He is bricked up behind a wall in her mind, and she hears him crying there, on and on, day and night.

'Is Olly well?' she asks quietly.

'He's well.'

'Did his cold clear up?'

'It did.'

'Do you keep on with the Actifed?'

'Of course. Don't worry.'

'What did he have for breakfast?'

'Cornflakes.'

'The gerbil also had a cornflake,' interpolates the au pair, smilingly adding her contribution to this feast of goodwill and compromise.

'Who?'

'The gerbil, Bertie,' Alex explains testily. 'Olly was feeding him cornflakes.'

Jenny has trouble wading down the garden path through that hampering element, the air. She carries away with her an unexpected loot of precious details. Oliver wearing his blue pyjamas and red dressing-gown opens his mouth for the spoonful of Actifed which will dry up the catarrh in his tubes and protect him from ear infection. Now (as she hasps the gate and turns for the bus-stop) Oliver is eating cornflakes at the old beech table in the kitchen. He spoons them in with the milk and sugar, his white-blond head shorn of the curls she used to encourage, his pale eyes fixed upon his gerbil in its cage. Jenny can see the eye of the gerbil, black and softly vigilant and its paws that scamper on its treadmill with tiny squeaks. Now Oliver's hand coaxes Bertie to accept a cornflake: Bertie nervously obliges. Jenny sees it all in a close-up lens, slow-motion, the boy's eye, the caged creature's in its sawdust world. Pain spasms in her breast, to see all this so clearly and to have forfeited it – his hand with the spoon in it, the milk in the spoon, the milk in his mouth, his soft throat swallowing.

Tomorrow she will see Jack again: Jack her comforter, her advocate. He will plead for her, atone for her, denounce the Judge himself at the bar of Heaven. But who is that vainglorious foreigner to imagine that she can love him as she loves her child, her kin? He comes from another rainbow world, which is called Cloudcuckooland; he has stepped off a picture into a soiled and implicated life in which he has no business. *Oh Jack*, she rages at him in the silence of her heart, *Jack come here quick quick for pity's sake and take the blame.*

Jack is more kind to Jenny than she knows how to bear.

'Jack, don't *be* like this,' she complains, turning away from his gentle hands and gentler words. 'Just don't. Be carping and cantankerous, be querulous and despotic. Be yourself. For God's sake.'

'I can't be, honeychild, I just don't seem to have the knack any more.' When Jenny turns away from you, it isn't like Maureen turning, in aversion. There isn't any trace of rejection in it; rather an invitation. The ripple of soft little knobs which are the vertebrae of her spine delight his eye. His fingers dwell on them with breath-soft motion, Jenny shivers. 'I love your back, Jenny, so slender and delicate.'

'Stop it, Jack. Be cussed and beastly.'

'Why do you want me to?' He lays his cheek against the nape of her neck.

'Because I've got to lose you. You're going home.'

'You *are* my home.'

'No . . . no. I know I'm not.'

'Oh, I wouldn't deceive you, Jenny, about this.' He raises himself on one elbow, speaks gravely as he feels called to do. 'It's too serious. Having you is like – it will sound absurd, I know – having my mother back. Though why you should entrust yourself to a broken-down old relic like me is beyond me to fathom. I can't imagine I'll keep you but while I do have you, Jenny blessed dear, by God I'm going to make damn sure I love you honour you cherish you serve you and, yes, even obey you.'

Jenny laughs; turns back to him and hoops him in her arms. 'So you're even going to put in the obedience clause?'

'Sure I am. No problem at all.'

'You're besotted.'

'Besotted is the word. I feel damn good about that. Damn good.'

'One day you'll wake up. You'll see me for what I am.'

'What might that be?'

'What Alex saw – what Oliver must see – Rosie hasn't yet – what I see whenever I look in the mirror. Someone off-centre – all baffled ego and inadequacy – marginal.'

'Your skin is thin and you're terrifyingly vulnerable. I see that.' Jack winces at the name 'Alexander' and does not trust himself to repeat it. The aged lovers of young women have gone off with coronaries in mid-sentence under less stress of emotion than the rage and envy that overwhelm Jack at the very thought of that – base Indian – 'He threw away a pearl, richer than all his tribe.'

They lie and listen to the swish of the net curtain which the early morning breeze sucks in and out of the window. Another rented flat in the vicinity of Victoria Station, seedy and anonymous, with a faintly sour odour from its being a thoroughfare for nomadic transients of all nationalities: Arabs, Canadians and a Mr Horace Jowelela from Nairobi who declared himself 'Richly satisfied' in the Visitors' Book but felt called upon to regret the derelict monstrosity across the street. The entire block is due for demolition. It rots and crumbles in every way that a once elegant work of architecture can find means to rot and crumble. Boards along the base advertise doom to trespassers, the apocalypse of falling masonry or death-trap floorboards. Scaffolding declares a sketchy interest in preventing violent collapse; but at every available niche and crevice and all along the remainder of the roof the building replies with a vagrant and cheerful insistence on metamorphosis. It sprouts a wilderness of grasses and fireweed; bushes and young trees waver and rock in a light wind at its summit. The eyesore greets Jack now arising to fetch Jenny's tea, with malevolently anarchic welcome. Its gutted windows are black holes, its façade a patchwork of charcoal smears, like the wreckage of a child's drawing.

'How about that?' says Jack for the tenth time. 'What a wreck! Wouldn't it be something else to see it demolished? I like seeing these old places when they dynamite them. One great implosion. Now you see it, now you don't. All gone in a moment.'

When he's gone, Jack can be heard humming *Gaudeamus igitur* in the kitchen, to the chinking of cups. The ruin over the road continues to scrutinise Jenny, lying in a daze of lassitude, through the multitudinous cavities of its eye-sockets. It whispers words like 'Oedipus complex', like 'sugar daddy', it mouths with a jeer words like 'home'.

'There was no tray, so I improvised.' Jenny's morning tea arrives in a small brown plastic teapot, accompanied by a carton of milk and two biscuits on a circular breadboard, eight inches in diameter, which is planted on her quilt.

'Thank you, Jack, I'll always take my tea on a breadboard in future.'

'Better try the tea. Is it all right?'

'It's great. Really good.' Jenny sips and smiles bravely.

'Are you *sure*? Shall I get rid of that and start over? Is it disgusting?'

'Certainly not. It's your best ever.'

'What shall I get for your breakfast? Bacon and egg? Danish pastry? I love to serve you. Back home I'm not allowed in the kitchen. Otherwise I could develop my skills for you.'

Back home. Back home with your legal wife, your legitimate children, the manifold grandchildren, the dogs, the neighbours, the grandfather clock and church twice on Sunday. Jack at once detects that the room is darkening from the dilation of Jenny's pupil.

'Come on now, darling, you are my – '

The telephone rings. It is a modern affair whose tone imitates a police siren.

'Ignore it,' says Jack.

'Disconnect it,' orders Jenny.

He pads out and pulls the plug on the phone. With a slight stirring of anxiety, he disclaims the reality of any allegiance beyond this fortress.

Maureen worries. She is too happy. She wanders the corridors and thirty-one rooms of 'Shadows' like the jaunty child she was never permitted to be nearly sixty years ago by the severe mother whose love by every childish art she fruitlessly sought to win. She remembers how Bess sat, in majestic old age, and cast reproachful looks upon her unerring daughter from the high-backed chair like a throne; but how the gorgonising look was replaced by a vulnerable radiance like that of a lover (lips parted, eyes wide) when Robert appeared in the room. Robert the banker who didn't need a bequest but was sole beneficiary of their mother's will; slovenly Robert who didn't give a damn about that unnecessary old woman, and always consulted his watch five minutes after arrival: which Bess, observing with ever-renewing pain, forgave. For what must be judged iniquitous in a daughter was only natural in a boy. A boy must be given his head. A boy must be allowed to pound up and down the gracious staircase on which a girl must not set the sole of her tiptoeing foot; a boy might smash a costly vase, torture his pet rabbit and eat with his mouth open, sprawled out across the table. Lord of creation, none of his most crass behaviour might be held against him; on the contrary, each rough and thoughtless act, by strange calculus, was further testimony to Robert's high estate. So Maureen's English father, reserved and timid, was given to understand. Bess insisted that the children grow up with his English accent and diction, but pointed out that her mate was useful for elocution but little else. He might perhaps have been only too thankful to have been banned the nuptial bed and its exhausting imperatives soon after the birth of the heir who was to become Bess' chosen consort. 'Are you a man?' enquired Bess of her spouse, at a dinner-party, 'or only an inferior sort of weasel?' Off went the self-confessed inferior weasel to his golf-club and his cronies. Maureen, with no recourse to a golf-club, grew up closer to the sewing machine and the kitchen range than to any living being. Now she has the run of a liberated Bastille, glowing with happiness, and it doesn't seem quite right. She tells this to Nicki and is scolded.

'The queen is dead. Long live the queen.'

'How do you mean?'

'Your mother was a vindictive tyrant.'

'No, Nicki, no. She acted according to her lights. She was sincere.'

'Hitler was sincere.'

'It wasn't *like* that. I idolised her. I wanted her love. She couldn't give it.'

'Well my sweetheart, "Shadows" is mine now. And therefore yours. Idolise me instead.'

'I do, I do.'

'I can give you my love. Without reservation. Bess is dead and gone.'

'You can't imagine how Jack hated her, Nicki.' They are sitting on the window-seat in the living room, their fingers lightly laced.

'I bet I can.'

'At first he hated her for my sake, because he resented the fact that I was made so little of.'

'Good for him. Good old Jack. I'd have cheered him on.' Nicki is chivalrous. She stood between her father and mother as a child of seven and took the blows on her behalf. She threw herself in a running tackle at the paternal trousers and bit into his calf. She banged him on the head with a garden spade shrieking, 'Leave – my – mother – alone!' Nobody thanked her. But she pressed ahead, and took her punishments like a girl; a girl of Sparta. Her love has very little alloy of possessiveness. It sees what is beautiful and generous in Marmie and seeks its greatest fulfilment; all that threatens or impairs Marmie is a slight to Nicki.

'Then when I turned to Bess in her last illness, and she seemed to relent a little toward me – well, not quite that, but at least to need me and depend on me – Jack started to say I'd abandoned him for her, and hate her for that.'

'And did you?'

'Yes,' says Maureen quite simply, after a pause. 'Yes, in a way. He's very hard to live with. Autocratic, appropriative. *Very* hard.' She shakes her head. 'And yet – ' Her eyes scan the gap between 'Shadows' and 'Red Earth' anxiously, as if she were expecting someone already very late.

'And yet what?'

'Since he's gentled down with this little Jenny of his – I miss him. Does it hurt you my speaking like this?'

'No, no, no. I want to hear. Jack's no rival to me. Jack's a different species. You'll never understand, I want what you want for yourself. God what joy to be able to feel and say that, what *joy*.'

'And what joy you are to me.' Maureen stretches out her arms and takes Nicki's shoulders lightly, wonderingly.

'And will go on being. Through thick and thin. Till death don't us part. Go on about Jack.'

'Just that he's *there* – or should be there. Like a standing stone, it's always been there, doing no one the slightest good but just being. And if it weren't there . . . it's unthinkable. Something immemorial lost. I don't mean that I begrudge him Jenny, though I worry for her, she's such a wisp. And it's not that I fear to lose him physically. If he died tomorrow, Nicki, that would just be in the natural course of things – a relief from oppression in a way, but the marriage left intact. It's this soft falling away of Jack that terrifies me – he's always been such a pressure on me I could have screamed – but sometimes lately, in the evenings, I've looked him in the eyes and thought, *He's not here*. And now I look out of this window and I think, *He's fled away, into some other world*. We were married out there on your lawn at "Shadows". My mother stood out there – look – just there – in a lavender dress, between the cypress and that pine, and my father gave me away just there under the great larches.'

Nicki peers out. The lawn inclines gently to the magnificent larches which are budding out now their powdery-green new needles: deciduous conifers midway between the everlasting and timely worlds. There is a thin mist drifting on the lawn: it's only six o'clock in the morning and Nicki has risen early to keep company with Maureen who only catnapped last night. To Nicki's musing eye, they are all still there, in light slippers on the cold grass, the ghostly wedding guests. They waft to and fro in gauzy dresses trailing pale skirts of mist; they swirl about greeting one another, for the sacramental part of the wedding is over, the eternal vows have all been made, and the minister is free to mingle with the evanescent congregation. Birdsong congratulates the nebulous bride, who billows whitely at the centre of the swell. The leaves and rustling creatures murmurously applaud.

'Oh if I could have been there, Marmie, to see you in your splendour! If I only could!'

'I was very proud then, Nicki – proud of my figure, my dress, my hair all down my back, my lineage, proud of Jack.'

'I've seen the pictures. You were right to be proud.' Nicki has stood and stared at the walls of 'Red Earth' crowded with black and white prints of Maureen aged twenty, on her wedding day, wishing there were a door or threshold over which, Alice-like, love might step, to greet the outlived self, and say, with wonder, *So this is you*, and introduce oneself, *I am Nicki. I am waiting to love you decades hence*. So she has often eyed the photographs of the bridal maiden on Maureen's walls: the solemn expression on painted lips and unsmiling eyes, an odd mingling of royalty and childishness in the upright carriage.

'Ah but if you'd been around then, you wouldn't have been waiting for me in the here-and-now, would you?'

'Sage doctrine, Marmie. And you wouldn't have looked twice at me then. You'd have said to yourself, "Who's that great lumbering horse-faced thing?" '

'All I wanted was my babies, and my finery, and my husband. I had no idea one could love a woman, Nicki, think of that. No one ever told me.'

Nicki has loved girls before, even during her marriage with Cameron there was someone. She never imagined loving an older woman; that was unexpected, disquieting. Always before, Nicki played the man. It excited her to control and possess. All her life she has taken men on fair and square, in their own terms, asserting her rights, teaching her children and schoolchildren to insist on theirs. Her mother was a weakling; Nicki was not going to be kicked around. When Cameron turned nasty, he found the door bolted on him and a legal suit which has left him with only two pairs of trousers one of which has holes, as he still bitterly complains, and Nicki with the wherewithal to purchase and renovate a thirty-one roomed mansion in Pennsylvania. Nicki, her father's only son, had as her paternal inheritance the ability to hit back at Father, to screw girls like a man does, to raise her teenage offspring, Shelley and Pete, in a feminist household in which she is both breadwinner and authority figure. Then came Maureen. Then it all fell down. Then she became a vulnerable child again and took rest, and was fed, and now lays her head with an unspeakable feeling of trust and consolation against Maureen's ample breast. There is nothing she will not do for her: nothing. Even cede her to another.

'Could you sleep in my arms, Marmie darling, if we went back to bed? You look wiped out.'

'I think I could.'

'Come on then. I'll lie very quiet and still, I'll watch over you.'

'You sleep too.'

Nicki lies in an ache of tenderness comprehending moment by moment the soft give of Maureen's breast against her own. Maureen's breathing deepens but still she murmurs words of love from some recess within the chamber of sleep. *There must be something radically wrong with me*, thinks Nicki, and tears pour down her face. *I never felt like this before in my whole life, never to my children, never to my husband, neither to my mother when she died. I was glad. I was free. Fettered now. No fight left in me.* It's like being granted another chance late in the day. *I'm nearly forty, think of that*. Wherever she looks, 'Shadows' is full of wraiths. Its passageways throng with Maureens: an infant, a child, a young woman, a visiting wife, a middle-aged daughter caring for a bedridden mother. The great bedroom with the four-poster is the one in which Maureen was born and in which Maureen's mother died. There the parameters of her beloved lady's life lie down together in the one bed: Maureen's unwelcome, enforced arrival from source; that reluctant source's enforced departure. Nicki does not like that room and keeps it locked. It retains its stale atmosphere however often you open the window to ventilate it. Though Nicki has never been superstitious, and knew perfectly well that the severed hands she saw crawling up her curtains at the age of seven were tricks of the light, she has unpleasant, hagridden feelings in that room. A skeletal, neurotic figure straightens up and turns, frowning; some gnarled and twisted emotion, compounded of amity and guilt, seems stored like contaminated waste between floorboards and ceiling. Nicki and Maureen share a bed in what was Maureen's nursery. Shelley and Pete, when they are home from school, have the pick of all the other rooms; but they are fledged and growing ready to leave.

Maureen wakens; squeezes Nicki and then stretches.

'How are you feeling?' asks Nicki.

'Much better. I had a funny dream of Jack.'

'What was your dream?'

'Oh – nothing very profound. He was mooning around, getting on my nerves. I said, "Can't you make yourself useful?" Next thing I knew he was planting a row of pansies in a trough; humming a tune to himself.'

'A nice dream?'

'Yes, I suppose so. Yes. The pansies were nice. Jack was – just Jack. I'm going to get your breakfast, my darling girl. You've been so good bringing me sleep. Nobody else has ever been able to do that for me.'

Maureen skips downstairs in her bare feet, singing. In her white nightgown, with her hair flowing out free all down her back, she feels like a child again; all the buoyant energies of her childhood are loose in her, and when she trips on the third step from the bottom and falls rather heavily on her right shoulder and leg, the shock and pain hardly register for a full minute, through the giddy lightness of her spirit.

Jack tosses his lifetime's allegiances aside with the messy insouciance with which he abandons his clothes for the night. He will be anything Jenny wants him to be. She doesn't like macho attitudes, incontinent remarks? Okay, she won't get them. She prefers him to act and think in ways he has been taught to call 'womanly'? Sure, no problem. She is jealous of his five children, ten grandchildren, and one lawful wedded wife? That's okay, Jenny, they don't exist. We'll feign they don't; scissor the bond; build a wall against the vision of variant loves and duties by taking your face as my entire horizon.

Jack stares and stares at Jenny. He wishes he could by process of such greedy looking become her, and wonders where he could find jeans like those she wears, with a view (despite one or two refractory anatomical impediments) to impersonating her. He notes Jenny's soaring happiness, and how she seems to have forgotten her boy altogether, making a home with him high in this demolition-workers' paradise. He hears her singing from the shower at the top of her voice; receives her merciless teasing as a glorious privilege (though he never let his children get away with that kind of behaviour); and marvels over the beauty of her most ordinary action. *Infatuated, doting old fool*, admonishes an inner voice, that of a worldly, experienced old guy who has seen it all before, the puerile rhapsodies of senescence. Jack takes little note. He has abdicated as male; is remade as his mother's child. Jenny, regnant, presides within his eye.

As the days pass, some faint anxieties worm their way into the hinterland of his mind. Waking, his eye alights on the travel clock Maureen gave him just before he left home for the airport, tucking it sheepishly into his pocket, her first present to him for years, decades: he hardly knew what to say in thanks. Jenny, by fiddling with its technological wonders, has managed to break the alarm. Now he wonders how his wife is getting along; feels the pressure to call her. But Jenny wakens then, beguiles him to cuddle close, by crooking one warm arm around his neck, and wants to tell him her dream, which is complex, garish and sensual, and whose fascinating trove of meanings she lures him to discuss, until it is time for her to command the breadboard and its cargo of tea; and the moment has passed. Jack observes that, whenever he surreptitiously replaces the plug of the telephone in its socket, Jenny has made sure to remove it by the time he looks again. It becomes a silent tug of wills between them, this establishment and disestablishment of communications with the world beyond the high nest. But Jack is not trying very hard.

'Fight for your boy, Cherubino.'

'He's a good father.'

'What's that supposed to mean?'

'Well, I personally hate him but he's a good father.'

'I doubt it. Anyway you're a good mother.'

'No. No, Jack, I was – lousy.' Jenny colours up, can't meet his eyes.

'Nonsense. And even if it were true, a young child belongs to its mother. You are *Jenny*. That's what counts to Jenny's child.'

Jack is unsure whether he means Oliver or himself. He flies to her cherishing tenderness as once from other vicissitudes he withdrew to the world beneath his mother's apron, and found in that darkly curtained privacy a refuge. One arm wrapped round the pillars of the temple, her legs, the other furiously sucking his thumb as if milk might someday derive from that as yet unpromising organ, Jack received upon his quietening eye a suffused reddish glow of daylight mediated through the apron's warp and weft. He remembers being yanked out of there by a horny hand attached to an arm furred with black hairs, and an uncouth voice which contemptuously named him *mother's boy, effeminate brat.* Still Jack creeps back over six decades later, his primal intuitions intact. 'Let me help you get Oliver back,' he begs Jenny, as if on his own behalf.

'What do I have to give him?'

'What do you . . . ? You have *yourself.*'

'There's no appeal.'

'Under American law, that bastard would never have got custody.'

'This isn't America.'

'Oh Jenny, you gave up too easily. You didn't fight for yourself properly.'

'Oh Jack.'

'And your lawyer was useless. Let's start things going again.'

'I can't.'

'Don't you want him back or something?'

'Jack, how *dare* you?' Stung, Jenny blushes fiery red. She winces away from his embrace; can't remember having hated anyone as she hates him at this moment. 'Take that back, you bastard.'

'That's better.'

'What's better?'

'You're fighting. You need to get mad at that kidnapping bastard just like you get mad at me. Do it, Cherubino; do it. Let fly. I'll tell you something. When our children were small I used to put my hand out like this and get them to punch it. *Wham bang*: small fists slamming in to punchbag Daddy. Then I'd say, "You're not trying: try harder: didn't hurt a bit." Boy, did that make them wild. "Did a gnat bite me? Was it a flea?" That's what you need.'

'What a pity I didn't have the benefit of your educational genius, Jack.'

'Come on, try.' Jack raises his right hand. It is gnarled and hard, still powerful. 'Use a bit of anger against me. What do you most hate about me?'

'Your children. I hate your children.' Jenny's punch dwindles to a tap.

'You're jealous, that's why.'

'And your wife. – And your happy home. – And your three obnoxious dogs. – And your several thousand grandchildren. – And I hate the fact that you've plugged the bloody phone back in when I want it out.'

'Come on, harder, you're just tickling, I can't feel a thing.'

With unexpected force, Jenny brings her fist slamming into Jack's hand.

'Christ! What was that for? That must have been a big one.'

'I hate the fact that you're going to leave me. And I hate you for trying to strengthen me so that I can live without you.' Jenny kisses the atoning hand and washes it with her tears.

The telephone rings.

'Oh hi Jack dear, it's Nicki Fairburn – hi, how are you? I've been trying to get through to you.'

'Well, *hi*, Nicki – I've been having a little trouble with the phone but some guys came in to fix it. Nothing wrong is there? . . . Oh no, really? . . . Oh *no*. I am so sorry. But when did this happen? . . . She fell down how many stairs? . . . Well, look, honey, I'll change my flight and be back with her as soon as possible, yes, it's sure to be okay at this time of year. Thanks so much for calling.'

'What is it?'

'It's Molly. She's fallen and cracked a bone in her arm and twisted her shoulder and leg. She kept trying to call me but couldn't get through because – you know why.'

'Oh Jack, I'm so sorry.' Jenny is white; she flinches at the implied and justified blame. She phones British Caledonian and changes Jack's ticket for tomorrow. When she looks round, Jack has already shifted several objects from the coffee-table into his old leather shoulder-bag; and has poured himself a tumbler of sherry.

'You do understand I have to go to her.'

'I do, of course.'

And I'll go to bed at noon.

Jack awakens with a start from a nap on the plane. His legs are stiff, his feet hot and swollen. He has in his mind the white face of Jenny as she stood at the airport barrier, her eyes too wide, a violently blue stare. Jack is conscious, with some anxiety, of an amorphous pain in his right arm and a kind of a squeezing in the breast. By the time the stewardess has served him with a cognac, the symptoms have subsided and he has convinced himself that he is not suffering some kind of seizure.

The plane takes a roll and judders; the pilot mentions turbulence and the seat-belt lights go on. Jack's Canadian companion is discussing at great length a doughnut he ate fifteen years ago in Philadelphia, apparently his sole surviving memory of Jack's hometown. The film begins; the blinds go down. All time is problematic, all questions of place indeterminate. Jack slides sideways unawares into sleep.

Someone is calling him. *Jack, Jack, come home.* Jack will run home in response to the call. Quick, quick. He speeds past a grove of larches, past the pool with the goldfish the gulls eat. *Jackie darling come on home.* He rounds the gable end of the house, nearly runs smack into the neighbour Mr Pogue who shares the access path. Hurry hurry: *I'm on my way*! and, barging past a butterfly, sprints towards the scource of the voice.

2
Home

'I so much wish you could have been there with us in Florence, Nicki, two summers ago when we got to see the *Primavera*.'

Jack is home. His wife and neighbour await his arrival at the supper-table in the kitchen; can hear his shoes squeak on the parquet as he pads about, snap of case-locks, the barkings and rushings about of the Newfoundland puppy, Thoby, inchoate with joy and relief at the return of the wanderer.

'I hardly knew you then. How impossible that seems.' Nicki shakes her head wonderingly. 'When I look back, I hardly know myself as the person I was then – isn't it odd? – I was so wild and so ungentle, it embarrasses me now to think of it, paying the world back for – whatever it was. I'm a new Nicki now – thank God, thank *you*.' *I suppose it will end*, thinks Nicki, *I'll see through it all, I always do – but I can't feel it coming*. It troubles her often, how to say thank you adequately.

We're all changed since then, muses Maureen. *Utter incomprehensible transformation – scary, crazy. Still going on.* Like being dragged through the mesh of some long process of chemical change, every cell of her being seems deranged. She tastes different to herself, running her tongue round the inside of her mouth; and the mirror's vivacity is a daily testament.

'That picture, you know, we met Jack's little Jenny under it at the Uffizi – I'd had food poisoning, was in a parlous state – it haunts me – he's brought me back a book about it from Foyle's Bookshop. Do you want to see?'

'May I?'

Maureen lays Mirella D'Ancona's botanical interpretation of the *Primavera* on Nicki's knee.

'It must have weighed a ton to carry.'

She opens it reverently at the reproduction of the whole

picture after its restoration, and smooths with her fingertips the satin surface of the paper. Zephyrus, the swarthy god of the west wind of springtime, puffs renovation into Flora from whose mouth flowers pour; Venus the reconciler presides centrally, robed in red, and her low-flying son Eros aims his blind malicious arrow into the swaying dance of the diaphanous Graces. Mercury, hand on provocative hip, caduceus raised to the trees, blends all the opposites in his androgynous person and marries heaven and earth. The figures that swirl before Nicki's eyes inhabit the marginal area of blessedness, where to be old is no disqualification from the ravishments of springtime, and growth through the delinquencies of love is always extravagantly possible.

'How do you like your present?' asks Jack from the doorway. 'Does it bring back good memories, Molly?'

'*Very* good memories.' She beams at Jack, relieved to have lured back the bad old creature from the other world of his desires.

'So what's been happening here? All these flowers. Your poor old arm?'

Jack is more than a little puzzled by his reception, bewildered by worse than jet lag, the soreness of losing Jenny and the baffled wish to take his wife in his arms and, laying his head in the crook of her neck and shoulder, sway her comforting body to and fro as in the ancient world of their bygone youth. Always when he sees her there is the echo of their first call to one another, and then, immediately, swift as the echo of an echo, sadness and anger at her remoteness now. His home, Jack found as he carried his suitcase into the bedroom he no longer shares with Maureen, is festooned from end to end with flowers. Vases of red roses and white camellias preside over every bed in the house. In the dark wood-panelled den, the grand piano lit on one side by a field of light in the form of a huge glass pane, is lit on the other by crimson and white peonies like the globes of exotic lamps. Maureen is celebrating his return with a festival of flowers. It bodes well but also stirs unease. Maureen has never done anything like this before. 'Oh, hi there,' she normally says upon his return, as if she can't quite place him but is sure the name will occur to her, and carries on kneading dough, polishing silver. But it's not just the flowers. He thought he'd find her in a plaster cast with all those breakages, but when he first put his head round the door was unnerved to find her pottering as usual, the limp a trifle more pronounced and her left arm in a sling.

'Hey Mrs Middleton. How are you doing? I thought it would be a wheelchair job at the very least.'

'I hope you're not too disappointed,' said Maureen, the asperity of her words dissolved in the shame-facedness of her grin. 'I rather think I've brought you all the way back from Europe for nothing. Just a twisted ankle and a badly bruised arm. In the first shock of the fall, it seemed worse.'

So Jack came roaming through a world of flowers, unsettled, sanguine, on the prowl for clues as to what this welcome might portend. And as he enquires 'All these flowers? Your poor old arm?' raising his spoon to his lips, tasting the fragrant onion soup, it darts through his mind to wonder if Maureen is going to offer to come back and share his bed. For comfort and warmth, for sharing, not for sex, although . . . He flashes Maureen, in this sudden illumination, a glance that would have dazzled Jenny, for he sees it all, the slidings asleep in shared embrace, the comforted awakenings, it is all intensely real to him in imagination. He'll make amends, atone for the years of neglect, his crabby temper, his egoism. Jenny's taught him tenderness –

Jenny the white-nightgowned figure who wanders the banks on the other side of the river of Time like a ghost. He will have to see the face of Jenny's wraith, he knows, pressed up against the cold pane in the early hours of the morning, staring tearlessly in past the silent form of his sleeping wife beneath the quilt. *But Jenny you will not deny me comfort?* he pleads with the cruel sufferer. *Yes yes I will: if I may not provide it.*

'Goodness, what a beautiful welcome of flowers you've given me, honey.' And he beams with a tender radiance. 'I'm so touched, I can't tell you.'

'Oh, they're not for you,' Maureen says quickly; then claps her hand to her mouth. 'I don't mean it *that* way. Pardon me.'

'If they're not for me, who are they for?'

'Honey, I've invited Lewis and Serena, and also Jacques – if he can come. I want a celebration get-together. I want all our old friends to meet my Nicki. We've been cooking for days for them – didn't you smell the baking as you came through the house?' She feels quite sorry for Jack, he looks so crestfallen, but can't help shooting Nicki an amused look.

'Strictly speaking, she baked, I sampled. A great arrangement,' says Nicki. 'More croutons, Jack?'

'Thanks,' says Jack, slumped into himself. He's been abolished. Again. But never mind. Yes, he smelt the baking: not for Jack. Yes, he saw a glory of flowers loading every surface: not for you either, Jack. Yes, he saw his wife of forty-four years arch and bright and joyously recreated: but not because you're home, Jack, oh dear no, it's for the red-haired mannish next-door neighbour who sits at your table offering you your own croutons that your wife dances. Khaki shorts and green T-shirt: he glances sidelong at Nicki's athletic legs and thighs under the table, and looking up quickly catches the conspiratorial smile that passes between the two women. He comprehends nothing, less than nothing.

'I'm glad you're back,' says Maureen gently. 'But sorry to have brought you on false pretences.'

'Oh,' says Jack tonelessly, folding his napkin, threading it into the ring. 'Never mind.'

'It was my fault,' says Nicki. 'I felt she wanted you, you know.'

Jack takes a deep breath; crushes down the resented flowers in his mind, ignores the void in his heart where Jenny had been torn away, and hears himself affirm, 'Nothing matters as long as Molly is well and whole. I'm glad you called me, Nicki. Of course.'

Sharp intake of breath, she turns her face away, not to cry out *Jack, Jack* across the twisted years of mutual forsaking, growing apart though knotted together indistinguishably at the one root; to hear the voice of his allegiance shakes her unbearably. She gathers the dishes together with her one free hand, in a rattling commotion of silver on china, agitated by her vulnerability to this gentler Jack Jenny sends home to her. She can't afford the humiliation of this. Embarrassment, pride, a kind of virginal fright stiffen her in resistance. She slips the bruised arm from the sling to balance the plates.

'Here, let me do that.' Jack arises.

'Certainly not. Since when did I allow you the run of my kitchen?' Cold voice; cold eyes, demarcating territory according to the agreed formula, and the yearning cry of *Jack, Jack* is now just an echo of its former self. 'Off you go.'

'Suit yourself.' Jack shrugs; ambles out, hands in pockets. He wishes she'd die. What is she but an impediment? Useless old woman. He'd visit her grave for a decent month or two and look stagily bereft. Sympathetic widows would bring him hot roast dinners in foil containers, lashings of sympathy, well-stewed. He'd scoop up Jenny and bring her home to 'Red Earth' in bridal white. That will teach Mother to abandon Jack. That will show her.

Later that delicate, high-spring evening he looks out through the back window towards the edge of the pine-glade which surrounds the house on three sides, and there are the two women twined in one another's arms, with the dogs, Thoby, Paul the schnaüzer and the decrepit dachshund Nancy. Then Maureen begins positively to gambol with the creatures, shrieking with laughter, throwing the ball for Thoby. That black fur-rug lollops for the ball and pounces; delivers it to Maureen who again prances, teasing Thoby with feigned throws. He stares open-mouthed. Her sling is abandoned; even her limp, the consequence of his drunkenly crashing the car that time fifteen years ago, is in abeyance, let alone the latest injury. She looks half her age. Unlicensed: who gave you leave? They play beyond the pale, and they will go on playing when he is gone. The great dark pillars of the pines tower behind them, a grid criss-crossed with slant rays of light which break into the pool of green shadow. Now the two women sway together, hugging each other in the rocking light, Nicki a head the taller, from shadow into light, from light into shadow, the auburn head and the grey.

Jack, confounded, makes his way out into the dappled green world in which he suddenly finds himself an untutored foreigner. The air of his garden is evocative, resinous; the slippered sole of his foot remembers nostalgically, as if it left an age ago rather than just over a week, the softness of the carpet of wood-fibres and pine-needles into which the returning traveller sinks, raising aromatic fragrances.

The ball is thrown again. Thoby, wholly occupied with greeting Jack with rapturous licks to his face and hands, ignores the ball. The ancient Nancy creeps after it and noses it in a snuffling, hopeless manner where it lies in a tangle of briar and nettle. Nancy looks over beseechingly but no one takes notice.

'Hi, Jack.' No further notice taken of Jack either. He bends his head, jet-lagged as he is, old and sapless and used-up under the monumental bodies of the pines, under the women's scorn, and he thinks, *Just as you have gone, so will Jenny go.* She will go off with some potent young guy, he knows that, has always known it, it's just a matter of time. He sees it now, and the image is an excruciating death. Modestly she takes off her clothes, slides down between cool sheets, and here comes the potent young guy towards the bed in which Jenny waits, magnificently equipped, toweringly erect. Excoriated, he wants to cover his own flaccid sex. Wants to call her and beg her not to proceed but, no, he must let Jenny go back to her own generation, free her from her dependency on the illusion that there is a future in his. The warm, aromatic air issues its balmy fragrances to Jack; it flows in paradisally around his pain. But his pain gets up and walks slowly back into the house, thinking *I deserve this.* His heart is raw as red meat, walking down the long, straight shadow of a pine whose path takes him to the back door and (in the low evening sun) stretches up the wall of the white house, cleaving it sheer in two.

Maureen's bedroom door stands open, he glances in. Something's different in there, what is it? At first he can't make out, then it hits him; their bed is gone, the great king-size bed in which they had slept together since their wedding night has made its exit. It's a shock – not that he had entertained real hope of being recalled to his rightful place in the comfortable dip on the right hand side, but that this was the bed in which he first loved his wife, in which all five children were conceived, where when he was ill she nursed him and when she was – rarely – ill he sat and badgered her to get well, anxious, agitated, *Are you feeling better Mother?* at five-minute intervals; on this bed she suckled their babies and toddling athletes trampolined, they changed the sheets together every Saturday morning and he napped for an hour after every Thanksgiving and Christmas dinner. The bed has a poignant meaning for him. But not, obviously, for her. How eager she had been to turf him out: *You snore, no one could sleep through that, it's like an earthquake,* which Jenny corroborates but he denies. In place of their marriage-bed stands the slimmer three-quarter size bed from her mother's house at 'Shadows' – Bess' second-best bed they had kept dismantled in the junk room, Jack balefully earmarking it for matchwood summer by summer when he rummaged and pottered in there. Bess was his rival for Maureen, Bess won. Is still displaying her trophies cunningly in his sight. It almost fascinates him, the degree of Maureen's allegiance to a mere mother. How could a mother usurp a husband? Jack goes in and fingers the patchwork quilt tentatively, runs his hand along the bedstead. *Congratulations.*

'I'll fix you some tea,' says Maureen. She has sobered right down. Nicki has departed. 'What are you doing in there?'

'Oh, nothing. Just wandered in. You've changed the bed.'

'Yes. I never liked the other.'

I never liked the other. Did she really say that?'

'But we had that bed ever since . . .'

'Yes, I know, Jack, but its days were done. Nicki and her boy dismantled it for me and took it over to 'Shadows'. You didn't mind her having it, did you?'

The ghost of Bess skips in between the sheets of Jack's marriage-bed and lies there cadaverously grinning. Jack accepts the takeover with dull eyes. 'No, dear, I don't mind. Although it might have been nice to be asked.'

'It never occurred to me. And besides, you weren't here. How *is* your little Jenny, by the way? I do feel for her in her distress. Is there any chance of her getting the boy back?' There is absolutely no hint of malignity in her enquiry. And yet the fact that she has made it effectively closes the bed issue.

'No, I don't think so, Molly. She has said goodbye to her son.'

'Unbearable. For a mother to lose her child, that is – unspeakable, there are no words . . . Come on, Jack, your tea.'

'Thanks, dear.' His voice, refusing its habitual refuge of the conscious querulousness of self-pity, is gravelly and tired. He sits obediently.

'I'm sorry, Jack.'

'I'm sorry too,' says Jack.

What each regrets is neither stated nor understood. It cannot be a subject for enquiry. Maureen is life itself. One cannot say 'I love her' or 'I hate her', neither complain of her inhospitality nor make an issue of her clemency. After forty-four years she is simply the matrix of all that is; remains, however, begrudgingly, and however one is allured by dreams of emotionally less impoverished worlds, the source and terminus of all reality: home.

3
Loss

Growing up at the children's home in Sheffield, Jenny could never attribute much reality to Jenny. Now sitting at the window of her two-bedroomed attic flat in Bradford, England, that home of the gods which she has been too ashamed to let Jack visit, she has exactly the same sense of her own insubstantiality. Pictures were real, always, on the walls, in the glossy art-book the warden gave her one Christmas which had the Botticelli *Primavera* to captivate her childish eye, and especially those pictures her own excited fingers chalked and crayoned. Tongue between her lips, breathing slow and heavy, Jenny put forth on the page a teeming world she could bear to live in, beautiful and strange. But she herself was a matchstick figure, supplied with a surplus batch of unmediated emotions, which sat and rocked itself in its own arms in the corner and watched the play of light and shade on that more cumbrous flesh and blood which denoted the solidity of her fellows. She was airy and light amongst their materiality, nothing held her down to earth. She veered between moody and retentive, gushing tears for no known reason, attaching herself to unlikely persons like the porter with a beseeching passion and then detaching. Then as now, looking out from the tainted unsatisfactoriness of her cheaply furnished indoor world towards the wedge of moorland thrusting in between the human habitations, she had the status of an intimation, a possibility, a shadow merely; tries now as then to throw the shadow on to the other world of the page to seek clarification of its nature.

'*No, no, no,* Jennifer,' expostulated the pursed mouth of the Mrs Bloxham whose task it had been to standardise the nut-brown uniformed Jenny to take her place in life: 'Wrong hand, dear.' Jenny gripped the pencil hard in her left hand, forcing the teacher to prise off her fingers and poke it into the clenched right hand. 'Come on, Jenny, you can if you try.' The right hand was lame and dumb. It forged her name like an old lady's querulous signature. It was a counterfeit hand, impotent to transmit the pictorial codes that teemed in Jenny's brain above or beyond the range of language. Mrs Bloxham turned away to harangue another miscreant about a paper dart. Jenny promptly returned the pencil to her good left hand. Now the right half of her mind poured out its calm and fluent, self-delighting messages. Jenny wrote her name again, but backwards – YNNEJ – reversing the letters; and began to draw, with obvious joy and absolute panache. The shadow was again thrown across her page. 'Oh *really* Jennifer. *For heaven's sake.*' The pencil was yanked away and the knuckles of her left hand rapped smartly with a ruler. 'Naughty, naughty, girl. You've written it backwards again. Haven't you?' No. Rap. '*Haven't you?*' No. Rap again. Thrusting both hands under the desk, Jenny grasped the recalcitrant left fist in the collusive right. 'You see, Jenny, you're mirror-writing.' Patiently, for the hundredth time. 'Now try to frame your letters the correct way round.' Jenny looked blandly into Mrs Bloxham's bespectacled eyes that were now on a level with her own, and wet her pants. The wet ran pleasantly down between her legs and puddled between them on the floorboards.

Slowly, slowly, Jenny consented to turn her letters; consented to be ambidextrous. Like some elderly stroke-victim she reversed her vision, structuring the world from left to right, faking real. But the matchstick figure became the home's claim to success. Jenny's gift, even in its mangled and compromised form, selected her from among her more substantial sisters who went for shop-girls, typists, mothers and the dole queue. It secured her a place at art college and, out of the blue, Alex, a lovely home and adorable baby. Why would a golden godlike male desire such an eccentric, scrawny little bag of bones as herself? She often asked herself, in the first excess of rapture, but could obtain no answer. It was another shadow merely, behind which some obscure glory lay. She painted his picture in oils and hung it on the living-room wall above the fireplace in their Harrogate house; he'd show it round with pride: *my wife did this of me, my wife has a real talent.* She did him as Apollo in a brilliant sunburst.

Apollo soon noticed that she didn't hold together properly, there wasn't much to her as she stared vacantly from his unwashed windows, doodled on paper serviettes while the baby screamed blue murder from his crib, denouncing her to the very heavens. The reality of Oliver was overwhelmingly intense, her fear of him absolute. She didn't blame Alex for casting her off, her shadow bent its head to receive its sentence and passed out of her own front door in silent compliance.

Her Bradford flat is leased to her by the Khans who live below, and she works as a part-time helper in a local primary school. They are lovely, gentle people, especially the womenfolk, and she is teaching English to the wife and grandmother, Shahan and Parvati; but that number of children is bound to make a noise. In the street the little dark children are sprinklings of bright clothes, and voices like birdsong. Jenny knows them all by name and is striving to overcome her unaccountable fear of them. Sometimes one will go to the chip-shop for her and bring back cod and chips. To them she is Jen-Jen, the nervy foreign lady who does not speak their language, the only white person in the street – who has a boy of her own, a pale-faced, white-haired child, but only has such a boy on alternate weekends. They see her and White-Hair coming in with the shopping or setting out in Jen-Jen's beaten up old Escort to walk on the moors. Whereas Jen-Jen has a friendly smile, White-Hair has none. He has informed Jenny that the Indian children's skins are dark because they are dirty.

'Who taught you this?' aghast.

'Nobody had to tell me. I used my eyes and nose. The curry smells round here turn my stomach anyway.'

She knows it came from Alex, whose blond beauty, like shining metal currency, stamped with an imperial face, now suggests not Apollo but 'Kruger Rand', her nickname for him. Hearing on the news that the West is disinvesting in South Africa, she looks forward to the fall of his namesake. Since Jack's arrival in her life some seeds of healthy anger have begun to stir deep in Jenny.

Jack is soft; wherever you touched Alex he was hard. His pectorals were well developed through weight-lifting, and indeed he is the owner of a pair of dumb-bells with which he amused Olly as a toddler by swinging and juggling. Jenny remembers stroking the contours of those magnificent breasts with tender, wistful fingers when they were first married, and feeling moved to lay her head upon his chest: but Alex tensed, rigidly embarrassed. 'Men don't feel anything there,' he explained. 'Only down here,' removing her hand. She had violated Alex's sense of himself as male; she might as well have enquired of that Aryan god as to the pedigree of his racial origins. Hard breasts; hard thighs; small hard behind; hard butting thrusting prick. Jenny tries not to remember how he drove into her with that organ, raising himself upon his hands as if engaged in an arduous course of press-ups. The worst of it was, Alex could go on and on for an hour or more of the most relentless gymnastic exertion. At first there was an excitement in her sense of his power. Later it dawned on her that she wasn't actually feeling anything; really, nothing of her own. She must be frigid, something missing in her womanhood, as Alex sometimes delicately mentioned. Jenny tried moaning and groaning earlier in the exercise, which sometimes brought remission of sentence. Latterly, she just lay still with her arms folded, staring up at him. 'Castrating lesbian,' muttered the wilting hero as he dismounted. They must be sniggering at him in the locker-rooms, he was convinced, when he learnt of his cuckolding by an ancient scarecrow. *Obviously size belied performance*, agreed the imagined comrades-in-arms. *Poor old Alex.*

Jack, though covered in a gnarled old skin, was rounded and yielded to the touch.

'I'm like an avocado pear. Soft under a bit of rind.' She was drowsing on his breast.

'How true.' There was a short pause.

'Jenny?'

'Yes?'

'How can you love an avocado pear?'

How could she not? Her devotion astounded Jack, for her mist of delusion was transparent before his eyes: he knew he was no oil-painting, never since Mother's death had he liked to look in the mirror. And now with age, finding his ultimate form as a whale, as a mammoth, as an oak, an avocado, he could hardly think of himself as a man at all. Especially with this business of impotence.

'We do the best with what we have,' he said, meaning the best for Jenny. But there were operations you could have, he told her wistfully – pull a string and up it pops like a jumping jack. If she liked, he'd try it. Would she care to pull his string?

'And be jumped at by jack? No thanks,' she said.

'Oh, so you prefer a gelding?' Bitter, humiliated Jack could not look her in the eyes.

'I like you. As you are. So, so kind.' Tears were in her eyes, for Jack's hands and whole person were gentle and generous. Disempowered as male, Jack's power was full as human; he yielded in every possible sense.

She came to him with a gaping hole of need which Alex had punched wider open. She brought Jack her wounded sex, it wasn't much of a gift, but with tender, listening, inventive fingers he began to heal, to revive. The gratitude was unbearable. It commanded expression but there was no language for it. Gratitude choked on words, melted into tears, bestowed several thousand kisses upon hands and forehead, loaded Jack with demonstrative affection his experience had never compassed. Gratitude hugged and cradled his body as he bent over the frying pan, it ran for his newspaper, it forgave the excesses of his more diabolical utterances. If this took some doing, for he was a naughtier child than Olly had ever been – more possessive, more boisterous, more manipulative – all that she gave came back to source with an immeasurable surplus of warmth. To be with Jack was to inhabit one of the less credible parables of Scripture: to be the child whose father runs to receive him from afar, to be the foreigner at the roadside to whom the Samaritan extends his grace. It has been, for Jenny, the experience of home-coming.

But Jack is made of a material mortally perishable, and subject to periodic vanishings. Here at the window of the squalid attic flat, she is stranded in a reality which he can't mediate for her. Bradford drops away before her down the steep sides of a well. She likes its people, the variety of their cultures, the village feel of the streets, and knows she has a chance to work at belonging here, drawing strength from Jack before he retreats one more pace, beyond the veil of drizzle that now obscures the window and soon will persuade her to close it, to the land from which he will never again testify to his existence. She is going to set herself to becoming a *real* mother now, a source of comfort and confidence to Olly; it's not too late. Olly's little friend Lawrence is coming today on a weekend visit. That's a start. It was amazing that his parents agreed, and what the child will make of her place of abode is beyond her to imagine. Lawrence lives in a converted rectory in a nice area even for Harrogate, a few streets from Alex. If the weather stays mild, perhaps they can picnic on the moors, which could not offend even the most couth child's sensibilities.

She begins to clean the room for the visit but her body is obsessively remembering the touch of Jack, calling out in desolation not to be vacated. *I can't be anyone without you* is its forsaken cry, *and I don't want to be either*. She respires with thoughts of Jack, reminiscences of his presence in fondling touch all over her body. Her skin whispers to her in the privacy of her solitude, until she is deafened by the voice which surrounds her, and which is her: *I want, I want, I want. I need.*

She vacuums the threadbare living-room carpet; arranges flowers in a milk-bottle. Her flesh aches for Jack: humiliating, abject craving, a dependency she never knew before he taught her how to love herself enough to be loved. *Damn you, Jack,* she shouts at him in the silence of her mind. He should have left her in that graveyard of suppressions, it was quiet there, not much in the way of noise filtered down to where her body lay like a carcass, anaesthetised. There was a kind of liberty. She was never so pusillanimous before, so cowed like a spaniel. *Heel, heel.* And she races obediently to lick her master's hands. *Good dog. Down now, down girl.* Goodbye, master. *Stay, stay.* One day she'll wrench him off. She'll stray from his side and set up in her own right: a free creature. Who now reluctantly lies down on the mangy hearth-rug where he has left her, and jerks in her sleep at the wild dreams that beset her, and cocks her head at every imagined footstep outside the door.

Jenny meets Oliver and Lawrence at Bradford Interchange. They have been put on the train straight from school by Lawrence's mother, and are still wearing their uniform, royal blue blazers and caps, with golden mottoes in the Latin tongue expressive of Playing up, Playing up and Playing the game. It appears that the boys have been participating as mourners at a funeral, for they walk lugubriously side by side, their satchels slung over their left shoulders, small cases held in their right hands, and their faces are the pictures of grief.

Oliver does not run to his mother as usual, but prefers to stride in manly but miserable fashion beside his comrade.

'Lawrence has tummy-ache, and the gerbil's dead,' are Oliver's first words to his mother. Jenny seizes him and forcibly kisses his hot little cheeks.

'Sorry about the tummy-ache, Lawrence. What do you think is the matter?'

Lawrence can't say. Thinks it might be school sausages. Thinks he might be about to throw up. He puts down his case and hangs on to his stomach melodramatically, pointing out to Jenny exactly where it hurts. Jenny feels she could have done without this particular manifestation of childhood reality, but reflects that real mothers take this kind of thing in their stride. Can he last until he gets home? He thinks he can, for the throe has suddenly and magically passed and Lawrence gives it to be understood that he is looking forward to his tea, which he hopes might include doughnuts and chocolate éclairs. Does Lawrence ever get nervous tummy-ache? Lawrence does not know; but he can tell her reliably that he and school sausages do not agree.

During the tummy-ache inquisition Oliver has sidled round to the side of his mother which his comrade cannot see. He has inserted his hand into hers, laid his cheek against her arm and is sucking his thumb. Jenny squeezes that delicate hand surreptitiously, and rubs the back of it with her thumb. If she catches him up in her arms and loves him out there in public, the scrupulous Olly will bolt back into himself and no more be seen.

'So sorry about the gerbil, Olly. What happened?'

'We don't know. Yesterday he was fine. Today he was lying on his back in the sawdust. Daddy thinks he died of old age.'

'Shall I get you a new one?'

'I don't want a new one. I want Bertie.'

'There's no answer to that.'

'He's buried under the sycamore. In a shoe-box, wrapped in a poem:

> Here lies Bertie underground,
> He was a gerbil, fat and round.
> Bertie died without a sound.
> Do not stamp upon his mound.

I made that up.'

'It's good. Says it all in just a few words. That's called an epitaph, Olly.'

Olly does not wish to know that; but believes that the buried Bertie will find solace in perusing the manuscript as he lies there, it will while away the tedium of eternity. Daddy has promised a dog.

'We have a dog,' says Lawrence. They are walking across the car-park to the Escort. 'It's a poodle, named Fiona. You should have a poodle, Olly.'

'I don't want a poodle, thanks very much,' says Oliver with the asperity of intransigent loyalty. 'I don't want an Alsation or an Irish wolfhound or a terrier or a red setter. I *want* Bertie back. And that's all there is to it.'

'That's okay, Olly. You have a right to those feelings,' says Jenny. 'They're good feelings.'

'And if I *can't* have Bertie back,' adds Oliver, 'I shall have a stick-insect.'

Jenny starts up the car. The two boys are in the back, Lawrence's tummy-ache apparently subsiding in the excitement of roughing it in a beaten up old Escort that advertises its charms by back-firing when you start it up.

'Why a stick-insect?' Jenny wonders, nosing out into the rush-hour traffic.

'Because you can't love a stick-insect,' Olly says. A safe pet. Nothing irreplaceable when it abdicates its angular life and implants the suckers of its twiggy legs on the Tree of Heaven, fading back into the insentient nature which it can hardly be said to have left. 'And its diet is so simple: it eats privet leaves and lives in a jar. No problem to care for.'

Lawrence looks round the dingy flat with some interest, but as far as Jenny can see, no active distaste.

'Is this where you live? Your real home?' he asks. He is a square-faced, snub-nosed boy, with a southern accent plentiful in diphthongs which betrays signs of having been elocuted into him at an early period of his training. A boy of excellent manners, Lawrence has clearly been instructed not to question Jenny as to why she lives away from Oliver's father: it was a liberal gesture on the part of his parents to entrust Lawrence to her care, given her circumstances. Jenny replies that, Yes, this is her real home – for the time being; until she can get a proper house.

Oliver is on the floor with the toys she keeps for him here, and which he associates particularly with his Bradford home: wooden soldiers, a model bus, key-cars and a magnificent transformer which Jack bought for him last time he was in England. 'We won't let that bastard win him by bribery, Jenny. At the very least I can stock you up with toys he'll like.' Jenny let him do that for her, though generally she has refused all offers of financial help. On every floor in Hamley's they bought toys. Jack threw his money about. They bought dolls and cuddlies, a toy circus and a baby piano, magnetic building sets, optical instruments. All the way back on the underground Jack, his lap loaded with red and white Hamley's bags, muttered, 'This will show the creep' and 'By God, Jenny, wait till that bastard hears about this.' When they got back to the flat, they played with the toys a little, driving the cars between them over the rug, winding the musical box: which filled Jenny with a sense of boundless desolation, or emptied her of happiness rather, as if her barren and unchilded life were being enacted in front of her eyes; and she tearlessly packed the expensive toys away in the bags. 'I think that's enough, Jack.' Often she wondered what Jack felt about her child and the tearing, inarticulate love she bore for him; but Jack never said. Was he jealous? Did he pity her? Was he guilty? For herself, this loss of Oliver daily disgraced her, testifying to a failure which she also, unfairly, placed at the door of Jack. *If you hadn't come along* . . . And she missed Oliver. As if the green-clad Fates came in with their masks and surgical scissors and snipped through the arterial cord which was equally Oliver and Jenny. As they did at his nativity, so they repeated it now, shearing him from her flesh which was his flesh. With each raw morning as she awoke, they cut him loose again. She can't get used to it. Detached from his mother, Oliver is his father's child. It strikes her sometimes how like Oliver Jack was in this, losing his mother at around the same age. But whereas Jack's mother died, Oliver's is there, on the calendar, cyclically lost and found like a briefly recurrent season; like a timetabled ghost.

An albino boy, Jack called Oliver on the phone to Maureen that time when she overheard; when she stood in the doorway of that alien flat and heard from the cat's mouth how she was a *pathetic little waif*, her child a *queer like changeling*, how Jack just felt so damn sorry for her, honey. She finishes serving Oliver and Lawrence their tea, of sticky buns and Coca-Cola, which they will eat watching TV; and she perches on the arm of the plastic settee next to Olly, with her cup of tea, sipping, looking down on the wheat-coloured head one longs but is not permitted to rumple. And she thinks *albino boy indeed*. She will never forgive Jack for that impertinence. Never. But Jack is irrelevant. He is a ridiculous intrusion of unreality into the difficult continuum of the real: the unfolding procession of lights and shades within which she must struggle for bearings and balance. Jack's rotund figure retires to the perimeter of her mind, she banishes him like a Lord of Misrule, like a vain clown who has presumed to intrude his presence into affairs of moment. *How ill white hairs become a fool and jester*. Jack the knave hangs his head in her mind, shuffles his feet, temporarily abashed, meditating his come-back. *Banish plump Jack and banish all the world: I do, I will*. She turns her eye from that pretender with Roman severity. She will live for her child, care for him, work for him, perhaps ultimately get him back. Surely that is right for Olly; hence for Jenny. *Hard luck, Jack. You're going to lose*.

'Have some more cake, Lawrence?'

'Yes please, Mrs Reinhold.'

'Jenny.'

'Yes please . . . Mrs Jenny.' She loads his plate.

'Not feeling unwell any more, Lawrence?'

'Oh . . . not really, thank you. I like this black-and-white television, Olly, it's quaint.'

'I don't,' says Oliver. 'It's boring. At home, I have a colour set in my bedroom – and Daddy's bought a video. It's great. I do *not* like black-and-white.' He is not eating much; looks tired and drawn.

'At home?' asks Jenny quietly. 'But this is your home too, Olly, isn't it?'

'Well – yes, sort of.'

'But it is really, sweetheart, not just sort of. Mummy is here, and your bed, and toys.' *I shouldn't be doing this*, Jenny knows, *I should just let go: not lay this heavy burden on him*. 'Eat up your cake, love. I thought it might be nice if we invited a couple of the children downstairs up to play with you tomorrow. They are sweet children, Lawrence, rather shy, but friendly.'

'No thanks,' says Oliver, glowering. He sits bolt upright, as if to attention, his knobbly knees held tight together, his pale face glacial. 'I don't like this programme,' he adds. 'Let's turn over.' He goes and twiddles with the knobs.

'Why not?' asks Lawrence.

'*Daddy wouldn't like it*,' replies Oliver, without turning round. He plays on the programme buttons like a piano; conjures up and annihilates several silver worlds: ping, ping, ping.

'Why not?'

'Because he wouldn't,' says the back of Oliver's head.

'Why not?' enquires Lawrence indefatigably. He is prepared to sit there why-notting till the cows come home.

'They are all foreigners round here,' says Oliver, turning from the televison set. 'No speakee English.'

'Oliver! You are parroting utter gibberish. You belong in a zoo. You ought to be ashamed.'

'Mummy likes them,' explains Oliver to his friend. 'But we don't.'

'Oh,' says Lawrence, losing interest. 'Mrs Reinhold, could I have a bath please, if it's no trouble?' Jenny has never heard a boy ask for a bath, voluntarily. She hopes they have enough hot water in the tank for his ablutions.

'Are you sure?' she asks feebly. Lawrence is definite; at home they put a premium on hygiene. His mummy hates germs.

The moment Lawrence is out of the room, Oliver's thumb goes into his mouth; he presses up wordlessly to Jenny and wraps one arm around her waist.

'I want you to feel at home with me, Olly, that I *am* your home.'

'I do,' mutters Olly, face buried against the cleft beneath her shoulder. The defensive, inward-turning posture of his whole body articulates the desire *Do not dig me out of here. This is where I want to be buried.* His eyes are screwed shut, his cupped hand is an umbrella to his eye against the light, the thumb he sucks has snared his mother's person by prudently threading itself prior to insertion in his mouth, through the button-hole of her cardigan.

'Good, love, darling, sweetheart, dear old Olly – because you're my home too.'

'But Mummy – ' Oliver mouths around the thumb, which is consolatory in direct proportion to the extent to which Father forbids its use, at Oliver's advanced age.

'What?'

'Why won't you come home and live with us again? You don't have to stay here in this slum, with all these – ' Alex's voice ventriloquises through Oliver's throat. Jenny recognises the lingo: *slums, nignogs, ghetto, darkies, wogs, coons*. The ventriloquist's dummy lying in her arms with his warm, soft flesh that was yielded from her own: how long would it take to turn him fully to wood?

'You know all that,' Jenny says, trying to eradicate the animus from her tone. 'Daddy and I love you just the same, but we are wrong for each other.'

'If you don't come now, Mummy, it will be too late.' The thumb is out; his face confronts hers to discharge the desperate ultimatum.

'What do you mean, Olly?'

'Because of Renate.'

'The au pair?'

'Yes. He's going to marry her. They've gone all lovey-dovey, it's disgusting. I caught her creeping out of his bedroom three mornings running. I've looked in the keyhole.'

'Oh *Olly*. Are you sure they're getting married?'

'Honestly. They told me at breakfast on Thursday.'

Jenny takes a deep breath. It was bound to come, Alex marrying again. 'Do you like her, Olly?' she asks thinly.

Oliver shrugs. 'She's all right.'

'Just all right?'

'She's not as bad as the last one, the foul Gisela. She doesn't pinch me behind Daddy's back and she can cook terrific pancakes *and* toss them.'

'Oh well, at least that's two things she has in her favour. Is she kind to you, Olly? Does she seem to – love you?'

Oliver shrugs again, with a kind of perplexity. What has love to do with au pairs? It is irrelevant. Lawrence can be heard rendering a long and circular bath-song, with accompanying splashes and a hearty refrain of *Quack quack quack*. It is good that Oliver has friends, even if they do get in your bath, use up all your hot water and exhibit there a fearful musicality.

'It would be best if you came back,' says Oliver, definitely and distinctly, as if his mother might be hard of hearing, or simple as to the deduction of consequences. *'Now.'*

The phone rings. It is Jack.

'Hello my dear sweet girl. How are you, my beautiful?'

'Distracted. There is a boy in the bath singing *Quack quack quack*. Someone else's boy. There is a boy on the settee with a slight temperature. My own boy.'

'Poor you. I do miss you.'

'Yes, Jack, but I can't talk about it just now. There *is* such a thing as Reality: and most of it happens to be located in Bradford at the present moment.'

'Okay, Jenny. I understand. Another time.' His voice coddles but does not declare its grievance.

Lawrence is removed from the bath, very scalded and shrimp-pink as to the body but threateningly white about the area of his mouth. His hair is soaked, as with each *quack* it apparently required to be ducked in the tap end of the bath. Jenny towels him down, coats him with talcum powder, dries his hair, buttons his pyjamas and gets him to ring his parents, who, however, are out. Observing that he appears a little green about the gills, she enquires about the state of his tummy. He thinks it is reasonable, but confides that he keeps thinking of slugs which naturally conduces to queasiness. Jenny wonders about the night ahead. She reads them several stories and puts them in their beds to read and relax before sleep.

It is a long and spectacular night. Lawrence ceases to throw up at six in the morning but is closely followed by Oliver, who begins at seven. The boys have groaning competitions over their respective buckets; the flat stinks of disinfectant. Every five minutes or so Lawrence reminds Jenny that he wants his own mummy. Jenny drinks some whisky at nine a.m. and begins to sing. The doctor, arriving towards ten, looks sharply at the bibulous young woman who introduces him to the two whey-faced boys and chronicles their gastric symptoms at inordinate and tipsy length. He advises sips of water and leaves, severely. Jenny eventually gets through to Lawrence's mother who is less than pleased at the news of her offspring's condition, clearly puts it down to Jenny's feeding his delicate system with Indian curry, suspects dysentery but points out in a business-like way that a child in that condition should not be moved, and that it will be more convenient if Jenny will keep him until he recovers. Jenny mentions that it is not tremendously convenient; but Lawrence's mother has rung off and apparently dashed straight out of the front door, for she cannot be recalled. Jenny calls Alex and informs him of their son's indisposition. Alex, like the good father he is, will come instantly.

'No,' says Jenny. '*No.* I want to look after him, I just thought you'd like to know.' Alex will come later in the day; just to make sure; doesn't want to think of his boy ill so far from home.

'I won't let you in, if you speak to me like that!' yells Jenny.

Alex points out that Jenny is a drunken slut, and that if she can't tone things down, her access will be in jeopardy.

'Or your custody, your randy bastard,' Jenny replies.

Alex adds that, if that's how she wants things, it's fine by him. She does the boy infinite moral harm by her influence, and now it appears that she has poisoned him.

'Please, Alex, I've been up all night,' pleads Jenny with abject terror. She sees the divorce court arrayed in fullest panoply; Alex's barrister all in black, so sharp in feature, pleading unanswerably against her legion infirmities. All of which she cravenly acknowledges. The scalpel of the law frees the boy cleanly and for all time with minimal damage to his healthy tissues, from that tumour, his mother. 'Please, Alex. I'm just tired.'

Alex, after a brief pause, accepts that she spoke under stress. He will be over tomorrow, to remove both boys. Putting down the phone, with shaking hands, Jenny takes another dose of medicinal whisky. In the bedroom, Lawrence is sitting up, fiddling with a jigsaw on a tea-tray; Oliver lies still, on his side, with his eyes open. Jenny gets into bed with him and holds his clammy forehead in the palm of her right hand. They doze, with emergency interruptions, through the remainder of the day.

At four, Lawrence starts to whine for Lucozade and biscuits. At six, Oliver begins to recover. At ten, Jenny starts to throw up. Half an hour later, Jack rings. 'Oh get lost,' says Jenny, haring for the bathroom. The receiver bounces softly on its cord into a state of repose, emitting to absent ears the lengthy pause of Jack's shocked silence.

4
Age

The combined ages of the lively company assembled in Jack and Maureen's flower-lit front room is three hundred and thirty-four years precisely. So Jack computes as he pours drinks for his guests on the evening of the day which Jenny has crowned by addressing to him the polite injunction: *Get lost.* At seventy-four, Lewis, a friend of Jack's Harvard days, of half a century's standing, is the oldest of the bunch, and his fourth wife, Serena, at fifty-seven, the baby of the party. Serena is very conscious of this, and starts out as she evidently means to go on: flirtatiously eyeing and appealing to her seniors in a juvenile and winsome manner which Jack finds peculiarly repulsive. Jacques, nearly seventy, has worn well, much better than himself if you judge by looks alone, as Jack tends to do. No sign of paunch showing in the spry, lithe Jacques. Jack gave him a rigorous though covert inspection upon his arrival, from the time he alighted from his cream Daimler wearing that flamboyant cream-coloured suit, and gave his easy greeting by kissing Jack on both cheeks: from which Jack did his hostly best not to recoil, and covered his embarrassment with hearty laughter, *Ho ho ho*, like Santa out of uniform. Jacques, a Canadian from Quebec, is suaver than ever, *charmant* with the ladies, with perhaps a faint, urbane hint of contempt, from which however Maureen is and always has been exempt. Jacques honours Maureen with an extraordinary and beholden tenderness which has never, for some reason, bothered the possessive Jack a bit, though he envies almost everything about his old friend, especially that face with its shiny, supple skin, oddly nude of wrinkles. The passage of time is just not registering in Jacques.

'A cognac for you, Jacques. Tell us, what's your secret? A

portrait back home in your attic getting more hideously ravaged by the day?'

'Of course,' says Jacques, crossing his legs and picking an imaginary speck off the immaculate cream trousers. 'What else? But what's your secret, Jack, now that I've acknowledged mine?'

'*My* secret? Oh, good living, Maureen's cooking and a minimum of vices. Well – I fear I'm just an old seed-pod that's spilling about all over the place,' says Jack, patting his tummy self-consciously.

'He nibbles,' Maureen confides to the company. 'He is a nibbler. Hand always in the cookie-jar, the peanut tin. This is how he has come to resemble an old tub.'

'He does exhibit a comfortable roundness,' says Jacques in a temporising fashion. 'But that wasn't what I meant. Your music, Jack, You're composing again.'

'Just little things, Jacques. Nothing spectacular.'

'But I hear good things of these pieces. You must tell me more while I'm here.'

Jack transiently glows. What a discriminating fellow Jacques is: a man of taste and culture. He wonders if Jacques still has the seraglio of young men or whether with age he has narrowed his tastes. He remembers Jacques' heyday, his exquisite beauty amongst his troupe, the wit and elegance of the ballet world, which fascinated Jack and more than a little discomposed and even disturbed him. The sense of the power of Jacques coiled just below the surface smoothness and benignity of his demeanour, the calculated malice of his tongue on certain occasions, its cruel cadences. That had fascinated and enchanted Jack too, more than he understood. But then, a decade back, when he retired as choreographer, Jacques, they subsequently learnt, had twice attempted suicide. Jack never knew the details. Age, it seemed, had exerted its corrosive effect there too, beneath the surface of the well-preserved, cherubic skin.

'I have to go into hospital next month, as a matter of fact,' says Jacques casually. 'Rather a bore, but there you are.'

'My dear Jacques, what's the trouble?' asks Maureen.

'Oh you know, Maureen – humiliating tests, with hideous technical names. I'm having to cancel a Mediterranean cruise I'd planned with Ralph – Ralph Shore, a good friend, not sure if you've heard of him?'

All one's friends tagged with name, date of birth, hospital numbers; trundled in lonely state down disinfected corridors on stretchers by masked men, speaking with the Dutch courage of premedication to their captors, with thick voices from dry mouths; emerging with bits cut out of them, machines sewn in to replace the defective originals; pushed on wheelchairs in one direction, in boxes in the other: sheep or goats. One by one, drawing nearer to the end of the line. Making the best of it like Jacques, making the worst like Lewis.

Who now receives the Bourbon Jack provides and with shaky hand raises it to his mouth, where he imbibes its contents with difficulty. In two years, Lewis has fallen apart at the seams; has raced downhill at accelerating rate; all the familiar clichés occur to Jack as he regards the friend of his youth with eyes that have tenderly loved and now must abhor their object. Jack remembers with respect Lewis's choate, vigorous mind, the mind of a born academic: a mathematician with a humanist's concern for larger issues. They cycled across half of America in their prime, camping, swimming, meeting new people, learning their native land. Lewis was a champion of Indian rights, a high-minded democratic socialist and victim of the Macarthy purges: with a beguiling smile, rather boyish and uncertain, and an unexpectedly silly sense of humour. A pacifist in the Second War: that took some courage. *I loved him like a brother*, thinks Jack, *fifty years ago, or maybe more than a brother.*

Lewis has lost the ready use of everything except his tongue. His physical being has obeyed that thermodynamic law which has all energy tend towards immobility: all save his mouth, which has mutinously defied that law. Which would be fine, thinks Jack, with rue, with frantic boredom, if his topics of conversation were more variable and cheerful, and if his memory had survived the general ruin which has rendered Lewis an incarnate obsolescence.

'Did I tell you,' enquires Lewis, in the pause which succeeds Jacques's announcement that he is to be hospitalised, 'any of the details of my prostate operation?'

'You told *me*,' replies Maureen, 'in the kitchen just now. Have a vol-au-vent, Lewis dear – Nicki and I made them this morning.'

'Oh thank you, Maureen,' says Lewis, shaking his head plaintively. 'My doctor would certainly not allow it. It's my old duodenal ulcer, you see, honey: I have to be *very* careful. But you others – Jack – Jacques – have I told *you* about my prostate operation? The damnedest thing – '

Jack is somewhat harrowed to learn that the doctors at the Presbyterian Hospital, New York, when presented with the much-carved and now infamous anatomy of his friend, discovered upon opening up his insides to official inspection that they contained two of something undesirable and none of something else highly to be recommended: that Lewis had gone down in the medical books as a *lusus naturae* in the region of the prostate.

'Well I'm damned,' replies Jack politely. 'Fancy that.' He is still managing the drinks, pouring a complex and outlandish cocktail to Serena's specifications, which she learned, she explains, on Hawaii. She talks over the top of her husband's monologue with an experienced air, rather shrill for Jack's tastes, and keeping abreast of his emphases, so that when Lewis resonates, Serena shrieks, and they ebb and flow together connubially. Lewis has moved on to a frightful blow-by-blow account of the side-effects, urinary and otherwise, of the drugs they administer after the prostate operation; and promises to animadvert, in the course of this discourse, to a bladder infection he suffered in 1956; also gall stones, cystitis and a variety of parallel disorders which he feels must be of general interest.

'Oh Jack, you *are* such a sweetie-pie,' froths Serena, receiving her host's offering of a venomous orange liquid out of which peer several cherries on sticks, together with an olive like an aberrant eyeball, a garnish of lemon, and two straws. 'You don't mind my saying you're quite a *genius* at answering a woman's needs. Since dear Lewis – you know – *went*' (she taps her temple with one crimson-varnished fingernail) 'I don't mind telling you, Jackie darling, I've felt the want of a real man in my life. It's been tough.'

Jacques chokes. Jack stares at the girlishly lisping Serena with quiet amazement. The unfortunate misnomer of her allegorical name strikes him afresh as she begins to prattle to him confidentially, and with evident nervousness, about her new novel, in which it appears that a publisher in Detroit, her home town, has shown an inexplicable interest. Jack has skim-read several of Serena's manuscripts and made polite noises. In a real sense he admires Serena's conscientious refusal to accept discouragement from the rejections her novels have sustained; but she produces one a year, each aspiring to the length of *War and Peace* and this voluminous creativity even the most patient reader must deplore.

'In my latest work, two women rape a man in Manhattan,' says Serena. 'That's in Chapter One.'

'On separate occasions, or together?'

'Oh – one holds him down, of course, while the other – you know. In the interests of verisimilitude.'

'Goodness,' says Jack. 'Is that technically possible?'

'Certainly,' says Serena.

'One rather shrinks from enquiring how you know it's possible,' says Jacques. 'But how *do* you know?'

'Read my book,' says Serena pertly. 'And find out.'

'I look forward to completing my education, Serena,' says Jacques. 'But tell me, where do you get those wonderful frilly frocks of yours? I've never seen anything quite like them.'

'Yes, they are rather dolly,' agrees Serena. 'I like a girl to *be* a girl.' Serena foams, she eddies, with silky white lace and ribbons at the bosom, puff sleeves and swirling skirts. 'I think this dress emphasises my vulnerability,' she shouts, above the boom of her husband's excursus on the pancreas, which he is addressing to Maureen. 'I bought it at Maud's Modes, on 21st Street on our last trip to Washington.'

'Er hem, most becoming,' says Jack. He is galvanised by the sight of that blonded hair girlishly curling in careful fronds round an ageing neck, the thin braceleted arms with fleshy folds which gesticulate from Serena's puffed sleeves, the silk-stockinged knees which she crosses teasingly before her admirers. It is pathetic; but, more, it is grotesque. Jack has to admit that he cannot stand the thought of touching an elderly woman (bar Maureen of course, who is not elderly but Maureen), especially one who is impersonating youth. After all, a man lasts. A man is desirable for other attributes than beauty and child-bearing capacity – power, intellect, force of character. A man is never on the scrap-heap. But a woman, sad to say, becomes redundant at the menopause. Hard luck, but there you are. *Mutton dressed as lamb*, thinks Jack; and is dumbfounded while during these reflections Serena shoots him a most gentle, whimsical smile, which reminds him curiously of Jenny. The face he marred with his easily aroused contempt registers a wistful self-knowledge which shames Jack. *Who are you to cast judgment?* enquires the Jenny in his mind, with asperity. *You shambling turpitudinous old oaf.* And he bends over Serena and asks quite tenderly whether the drink in any way comes up to scratch; he will try again with pleasure, if it is quite undrinkable, but he has to admit that he is not an expert mixer, and may never rank amongst the cocktail *cognoscenti.*

'My dear Jack, it is a masterpiece,' Serena effuses. 'You *are* nice to me, Jack.' And again the soft humorous smile which is a trace or vestige of Jenny's smile, to Jack's questing eye. *You have nice eyes, Serena*, he decides.

But there is more to the comparison, Jack muses, than this. Playing the little girl in older company: could Jenny, with her winning ways and passionate, childlike responses, come to this? To the status of a dressed up performing monkey at a party? Jenny at sixty: how will she be? Impossible to imagine with any certainty, but Serena is a worrying mirror. It's not a matter of dress, for Jenny dressed with Quakerish austerity and disregard of appearances. It's more a case of the spirit – can it ripen? *Still, I shan't be around to see it*, concludes Jack complacently. Or if I am, I'll be more gaga than poor old Lewis over there, Lewis who has entirely lost the thread of his discourse and who is looking round vacantly to see if it might pop up among the peonies or sprout at him from amongst the beautiful hanging baskets of rare plants which Maureen so successfully cultivates. *She is so good with growing things*, thinks Jack with a sudden welling of emotion. *What a mother she was to our children.*

And looking at Maureen, he is suddenly back in their shared bed of forty-odd years ago and Maureen is nursing their firstborn, Josie, the pride of their eyes, propped beside him on the pillows, mouth working on his wife's full breast, beautiful, warm, blue-veined, milky-scented; and the child drops asleep and they lay her between them; and the world is there with the three of them as they drowse, his hand on the life-giving breast, his lips on the forehead of the child.

He stares fixedly at Maureen now, where she sits in her dark blue dress, its white lace collar fastened by a cameo, her back straight, her bosom still full and comely: and how lovely she remains overwhelms his senses, how dignified and pleasant her listening manner as she and Jacques converse. He would like to go across and raise her before all the company, and say: 'I did her wrong.' Too many times to enumerate. But once comes back to him now with an especial clarity. When she wrote him a long letter full of grievance and unhappiness, over fifteen years ago, and posted it to his department at the college. He was at the height of his career, chairman, teacher, composer (but his music was beginning to weaken and falter, he recalls that now): a brisk, hard man with a carapace, professional to the roots of his fingernails, hiring and firing, judge and jury and hangman and God Almighty. He read the letter through once, with irritation, thinking, *What's up with the woman?* and tore it into eight pieces. 'What was that silly letter all about?' he asked when he got home, late that night.

Maureen said nothing, she turned from him. 'I love my children more than I shall ever love you,' she informed him, with gimlet eyes, at breakfast the next day; which he has never forgiven, will never forgive, as long as he lives, and has bored his daughters by frequent paternal admonitions that they are not to say it to their husbands if they wish to keep them. *We are not thinking of saying it*, say his daughters' eyes, *but now you suggest it . . .*

He told Jenny about that letter. Jenny was bitterly shocked. 'When did your wife go through the menopause?' she enquired. Jack has no idea: in those days such things were strictly women's business. 'She was trying to tell you something; and you threw her letter away?'

'Oh Jenny, I was busy. I never really took women's things all that seriously . . .'

'Oh Jack, that's awful.'

'I know it.' When he returned, Jack asked Maureen what the letter had said. She doesn't remember, so she says. He has done her wrong and there is no atonement. Or is there?

Will he, won't he? thinks Maureen, glancing over at her husband where he stands at the drinks cabinet, enduring poor Serena's follies and the garrulous inanities of Lewis' converse. She is surprised to find Jack's gaze resting on herself with that rare look of searching sympathy, his head turned slightly away. His pale blue eyes would gaze intently towards you, focusing your image at the centre of his retina, doing you justice, assenting to the reality of your nature and needs. The just man peers out of the high and narrow prison-window of his gargantuan ego. This was the Jack whose children she bore and for whom she would have died, all those years ago. She has to look away quickly now to escape that lure. She has to readjust her mind to its habitual defensive cynicism: *will he, won't he?* For Jenny's lover has poured all his guests a drink, and is now abstractedly serving her with a glass of white wine; but as yet he has refrained from pouring anything for himself. *Give him time: he will.*

I won't, thinks Jack. *No. No, I won't. This shall be a sign. Of trust and faith-keeping, even though I have been told to 'Get lost'.* There is such a thing, Jack reflects, as making allowances for people who tell you to get lost; although he has had little practice at giving the benefit of the doubt, and somewhat inclines to wonder whether it is a skill that can be learnt late in life. It may be rather like hang-gliding or surfing, and require a certain muscular habituation.

Lewis, who has spent some time in a semi-comatose condition, now appears to jerk awake, a tremor goes through his bulk and he raises his bald and mottled head from its subsided estate. He groans. 'Oh my piles!' he cries, with genuine pain in his voice.

'Shift position, dear,' says Serena. 'That's right.'

'The agonies I've suffered from piles,' laments Lewis. 'I just can't begin to tell you.' And does. The arthritic disease which afflicts Lewis' legs (which can be wellnigh useless these days; he often resorts to crutches) also brings him subsidiary miseries in the form of haemorrhoidal disabilities, as he explains.

'Is there a soul amongst us above forty who hasn't at some time or other suffered from piles?' enquires Jacques, who has been surreptitiously consulting his watch during Lewis' peroration, and now stifles several yawns. 'Piles were a major part of God's curse on man when he first kicked us out of the happy garden – a stigma, so to speak, and a pledge of mortality.'

'That's as may be,' mutters Lewis. 'But my piles are special.'

'We all think that,' replies Jacques. 'Acute pain, like acute pleasure, is quite incommunicable.'

'But I'm telling you, Jacques, I'm *telling* you,' says Lewis with some desperation, and an admixture of resentment at the aspersion being cast upon his martyrdom. 'My piles are no common piles, as my physician will testify. I have to sit in a warm bath for a quarter of an hour each day, for the purposes of mollification. I hope that will be convenient, Maureen?'

'Of course, Lewis dear,' replies Maureen amiably. 'As many hours as give you ease.'

This too acts as mollification to Lewis' goaded sensibilities. But during the conversation, Jack has three times reached for the brandy-bottle, the last time grasping it by the scruff of the neck, thinking, with infinite relief, *I will.* However, he abstains at the last minute, mixes himself orange juice, soda water and ice, and goes to stand behind Maureen's chair, one hand on her shoulder.

'A toast! To old friends!' he proposes.

'To old friends!' and, with an efflorescence of tactful feeling typical of Jack, 'And to the not-so-old!' – raising his glass to the radiant Serena.

Serena's hour of indulged *gaucherie* is all too short. Jack tries to make it up to her, but in vain, for when Nicki is introduced, Serena enters a kind of doomed purdah and cannot be coaxed out to enjoy her former high spirits. No sartorial splendours can compensate, in Serena's self-mirroring vision, for the fact that the bronze-limbed, pagan-looking Nicki, all raw health and unselfconscious cheerfulness, has the edge by nearly twenty years. Here is an intruder whose less than four decades on the planet have not even exposed her to the imputation of piles. The axis of the party tilts downward to accommodate this ingress of what is, in their terms, blooming, primal youthfulness, though Nicki has teenage children and is accustoming herself to the challenges of middle age. But here Veronica is a babe-in-arms, a representative of the younger generation whom all must try to please with conversational gambits suited to her time of life, such as 'What do you young people think about . . . ?' and 'When we were your age . . .' Things cheer up remarkably, with the exception of the weather in Serena's soul, where low cloud gathers, presaging squalls, perhaps, for Lewis when they retire for the night. Canine felicity in the household, which has been at a low ebb on account of the three dogs' banishment to the yard, improves. Thoby, Paul and the senile Nancy, who have been scratching at the door and occasionally yowling, pour in together in Nicki's wake, and bombard the inmates with tongue and paws.

'Oh no!' cries Lewis faintly, at Thoby's bounding welcome; and has to be rescued, for it is his allergy to dog-hairs which has banished the pets. Nicki and Jack together heave Thoby out by the collar. His disgust is signalled by his determination to stand and make a fight of it, and, when bundled out of the door and told to be a good boy, flouncing off to the edge of the forest and there standing defiantly as if threatening to run away and seek his fortune in other worlds. Nancy limps into a warm corner and makes pathetic efforts to climb the three-inch parapet into her basket, which no one sees, as the human door shuts firmly upon her requirements.

Nicki goes over to perch on the arm of Maureen's chair, and saying 'How are you? How lovely you look,' kisses her softly on the cheek.

'Thank you, honey, I am fine. I've taken the sling off, as you can see, and I'm giving the arm what Dr Morgan calls "rational exercise".'

'Don't overdo it, Marmie,' says Nicki, and Jack watches her fingers run lightly over his wife's bare arm: soft, intimate, brushing the downy hairs of the arm rather than the skin itself. He feels a fascinated discomfort. And at the same time utter bafflement: what does a healthy young woman see in an old woman? There can't possibly be any sexual interest. (*What do lesbians do to each other anyway*? he's often idly speculated, and supposes that, lacking the necessary equipment, they just sort of lie around hugging and patting each other. Pretty tame stuff.) And in any case Maureen's not – one of *them*. Obviously not. Demonstrably not. No mother of five and grandmother of ten is going to turn (what's the faddy term these days?) Good God! – *gay* – overnight at the ripe age of sixty-four. Now is she? Jack stares hard at Maureen's rapt face, slightly uplifted to her friend's, a beautiful expression quite unearthly, lips slightly parted, eyes wide and bright looking straight into Nicki's without reservation. *She never looks at me like that. So vulnerable, so fearless. She looks aslant, or beyond me, she seldom or never meets my eyes*. Now if Maureen were a *man* of that age, of course one could understand Nicki's predilection – but, honestly, *Maureen*. What a fool she's making of herself, but no one except Jack seems to be aware of it.

'Come on, Nicki, let's go fix things up in the kitchen.' The chat flows on and Jack is part of it; but views in the double frame of the living-room door and the kitchen door his wife and their neighbour, their heads bent over a bowl; dark blue and silky turquoise dresses; a grey head and a gleaming auburn. They are tasting the blueberry sauce, sipping it from the same teaspoon, they nod, they chuckle as at some private but wordless joke. The world has drawn off them. *They are inside; we others outsiders*, thinks Jack enviously, remembering Jenny for whom he is moment by moment making eloquent allowances (her strain; her loneliness; her high-strung temperament) as against a denouncing voice within his own consciousness which emphasises her ingratitude, not to mention the disrespect to his white hairs: *Get lost.* He sees Nicki and Maureen as inhabiting the inside of a globe of glass, a perfect bubble of immunity, in which their shared, immaculate happiness communes with itself and revels. No need of words when one has recourse to such silences. Words are a cover for loss. He will drink champagne with his meal; why should he not? He will decant his aggrieved spirit into the glass of candle-lit bubbles, and there effervesce in his own solitary world of makeshift delusion.

Nicki takes his breath away now that he observes her at close quarters down the dinner-table. She has been placed at his left hand, Serena at his right; he as head of household must say the grace, carve, serve the wine, these were always Maureen's wishes. He pours champagne into all glasses, including his own. They are tasting fragrant game soup with many '*oohs*' and '*ahs*'. Nicki talks beautifully to his friends, draws Jacques out on the subject of the Ballet Rambert with which he worked in the 1960s; and appears to have worked a charm on Lewis, whose multifarious ailments have all tumbled out of the window like Christian's bundle – though no doubt they will not have rolled away too far to be collected at a moment's notice in time of need. Lewis is telling Nicki how he and Jack toured the Great Lakes as boys of eighteen and twenty-three more years ago than he cares to remember, and how in their twenties they hitched through America, as far as New Mexico. Does Jack remember that trip?

'I do indeed,' says Jack, with real pleasure, his hand pausing on the stem of the glass. It dawdles there and does not raise it to his lips. 'As if it were yesterday.' *How I loved you then.*

'And what was that evil cave called?' asks Lewis. In the transfiguring candle-light his face has lost its beefy hue and coarsely fleshy contour as he leans forward, spoon poised above the bowl, and seems in that eager gesture to have conjured back into sensitive life the boyish spirit Jack loved. 'You know the cave – with the stalagmites and tites, cave beneath cave, deep as an eighty-storey block, where I got the horrors. *You* know, Jack, I cried like a baby and you couldn't haul me out.'

'Carlsbad. The Carlsbad Caverns. You had a vision of Hades or a migraine aura down there, we couldn't decide.'

It is strange to consider Lewis the elder in relation to Lewis the younger: not least in terms of size. Lewis now is a gross bulk which would contain two of the svelte youth he has outgrown. And then as to wives. He was on Hilda then, number one wife, has multiplied fourfold in conjugal terms, but presumably cannot run to a fifth. Serena, who is eyeing her spouse with sepulchral sourness – for anything that predates her reign undermines it, and even a contemptible sovereignty is better than no power at all – enquires 'Did you take your pills, darling?' at which Lewis nods gloomily, and retires into his aching hide, which he feeds with soup.

Nicki is in turquoise, silky and sleeveless. Seated at Jack's left hand, she eats with her right, so that the arm which lifts the soup-spoon is open to his sidelong contemplation. He dwells on its beauty with pleasure. It is a powerful woman's arm, with well-developed biceps which flex as she raises the spoon to her lips. Its bronzed skin wears a burnish of candlelight; its finely tapered wrist is adorned with a single slender bracelet, made of plaited silver, which rhythmically falls slightly every time she raises her arm. He recognises the bracelet as one of Maureen's: the heirloom, very pricey, from her mother Bess, which went to the brother Robert like everything else in Bess' will, but Jack as soon as he could afford it bought it back from Robert, and gave it to Maureen, and Maureen wept. Now a stranger wears the precious token Jack scrimped for, bleeding himself to feed the hunger of his pelican wife. He stares at Nicki as at a sphinx. He looks round the table. Here is the fruit-bowl, piled with peaches and apricots; here two candelabra also from Bess via Robert, bearing green candles; here the cruet; two white and crimson floral decorations; and here is the owner of 'Shadows', the lover (one has to presume) of one's elderly wife, as opaque and irreducible as any mere object on the table.

Howls of mirth; unseemly boisterousness from Maureen's end of the table.

'What's the joke?' Jack wants to know. 'Let us in on it.'

'It's Serena's novel,' gasps Maureen. 'We've been debating how feasible it would be for two women to rape a man.'

'Really, Maureen,' Jack reproves her, shaking his head, drawing in his chin like a prude. The tone is mock-serious but his words express a gut-feeling which Jack could under no circumstances have repressed. He has had it on the best authority since his earliest years (his step-mother's, then the highest authority of all, Maureen herself) that women are to be regarded as custodians of chaste speech and propriety of conduct. The tongues of the mothers of the nation are seemly, and know no lewd words. The mouths of women outside the home may be as foul as you or they like but that's another thing: they are a kind of animal you would not bring indoors. Hence Jack is bound to say 'Really, Maureen' as he spies his wife wantoning at the other end of their oval dining-table of equal vintage, round which Josie, Frank, Tilly, Angela and Tom have in the course of things sat with egg-spoons, and been taught to eat with your mouth closed; how not to kick your sister under the table and what to do in common politeness should you find yourself choking on a crumb. Jack must continue, in the same vein of mock-seriousness in which his wife will recognise the veiled threat, 'What a subject for the dinner-table, Molly! I'm surprised at you all.'

'You're a good one to talk, Jack. You that brag of knowing by heart all the dirty bits in *Lysistrata* and denounce *Julius Caesar* as a bore in an otherwise admirable author for containing not one single dirty joke. Goodness me,' says Maureen. 'And *we* are simply having a technical conversation up here. Of course,' she adds, meaning the remark for Nicki, 'What Jack means by a "dirty joke" is simply anything that relates to the female anatomy. Have no fear, Jack, it's the male body we're mulling over at this end. Nothing dirty.'

She's had enough to drink: thank God I'm sober, thinks virtuous

Jack; he has not touched his champagne, whose fizz has lost its zest. *I'll set an example.*

'I happen to be a feminist these days,' he tells the company, which exchanges glances indicative of wishing to burst, but communally desists. 'I believe in a woman's right to her own body, and that her body must be respected. I do. I really believe this. I know I have a long way to go as regards my feminism – but we have a friend in England who tells me that she sees distinct signs that I am entering the twentieth century.' Further stirrings of risibility in the company are somehow discouraged by a note in Jack's voice which hints of power still extant: a power to put you down without ever raising its voice. It is as if the paterfamilias spoke from the head of the table, and the guests were at heart but the disguised wraiths of Josie, Frank, Tilly, Angela and Tom swinging their legs under the patriarchal table and mutely praying to the Mercy Seat to abort its intimated thunder. All but Serena appear somewhat quenched; but Serena is simmering.

'Never mind your damned airy-fairy paternalistic flirtations with feminism, Jack. What about my novel?' The little girl has bolted, leaving in her place the tigress scored. 'That is no dirty joke, Jacques, I must tell you, that is a deadly serious goddam literary questioning of sexual stereotypes. The world turned upside-down.'

'Forgive us,' says Jacques, fork in hand, urbanely toying with the fish course which Maureen is supplying. 'It wasn't your literary work we were making fun of, Serena. Not at all. I happened to remark that there are two distinct and ineluctable reasons why two of you here assembled could not by any stretch of the imagination hope to rape the three of us males here assembled: unless God is prepared to *raise* us (forgive me, Jack) on Judgment Day with new capabilities and, in my case at least, with new inclinations. I fear a certain decline, in the very nature of things, sets in and equalises us all into one big happy family – of eunuchs.'

'Speak – for – yourself,' says Lewis, grimly and slowly coming out of hiding, as if the rock in the pool should shift and disclose itself as a rhinoceros. Serena snorts; is still fuming with literary indignation.

'The character in my story is twenty-seven years old. And straight,' she mutters. 'And terribly virile. And handsome,' glaring at Lewis.

'Well, of course, Plato was said to have been potent well into his seventies,' says Jacques. 'And we hear wild tales of other nonagenarian ancients; but most of us, alas, lack an Alcibiades to fan our wasting flame, and unless like the poet Yeats we try an operation to renew our virility we must consent to decline into the condition of the Struldbruggs.'

'Did it work?' asks Nicki.

'What?'

'The operation Yeats had.'

'No, I don't think so. There is no cure, my dear young friend, for age. It is a matter of philosophical acceptance, they tell me, learning the art of patience; loving Wisdom.'

Never did a man advocating quietism to the dying look less disposed to take his own medicine. Jacques' baby-face, with its hardly receded hair-line and a good crop of silvery hair tastefully arranged to conceal a minor and localised bald spot (which Jack has observed, not without inner rejoicing) bears a sheen of candle-light; impersonates the face of a man knocking fifty. He has no bags under his eyes, no double chin, but a dapper, upright posture, a keen interest in life and a considerable acting gift: charm does the rest. *But is due for hospitalisation, so he said*, Jack reflects. The love he has for the gifted Jacques rues, but decades of envy relishes, this sign that the successful Jacques too is mortal; cannot escape his place in the queue. *But I can*, thinks Jack, *Oh yes. I can. I have. Please.*

'Or,' says Jack, 'we can live to the full, make some great change, in old age. Be free. Start over.'

'If one hasn't ossified – petrified – sure. A man is always free to start again.'

'And a woman,' puts in Maureen.

'Of course,' Jacques readily agrees. 'Woman is included in the term man.'

'Patriarchal point of view about language, that,' says Maureen, tutting. 'Jack's feminism will never stand it.'

'Leave me out of this,' says Jacques. 'I'm a simple guy. I know nothing about women except that I know nothing.'

'We live in a phallocentric universe,' remarks Serena, who has been drinking steadily, and nobody takes any notice. 'That's for sure. Thanks, Jack, this wine is awfully good. You *are* so sweet to me. Aren't you having any yourself?'

'Excuse me, won't you,' says Jack. 'I ought to go and see about the dogs. I can hear Nancy crying.'

He stands outside the back door before the black monolith which is the forest, and a sliver of moon is ascendant above the trees. Through the resinous, crisp air, the murmur of the dinner-party is conveyed as a muffled hum from a hive. Thoby is nowhere to be seen; has entered the skirts of the forest perhaps, but has probably remained within earshot. Sulking, no doubt, over his expulsion in favour of the rivals, the guests; nosing around amongst the scents of the night. Jack goes over and whistles into the void, calls 'Thoby, Thoby! home, boy!' expecting the dog to lope out and crowd round his master huffing and puffing like a gang of dogs rather than a single bundle of fur. There is nothing to be heard but faint rustles and the occasional snapping of a thin stick high in the boughs, intimations of the unseen bodies of squirrel or bird, and nothing to see but galaxies of fireflies breaking into light and going out amongst the trees like planets light-years distant. 'Thoby! come home!' he calls again, in a cross voice denoting anxiety; the dogs are children to them, fiercely loved compensations for the life that can be no longer bred.

He gives up and returns to the back door, hands in pockets. At last he notices that the feeble Nancy is still striving with a pertinacity both heroic and moronic to surmount the tiny wall that bounds her basket. He watches her lever one small, rheumatic foreleg up on the parapet, and push in her nose, raise the second foreleg so that the basket tips. Astraddle, she slips helplessly back and the toppling basket reasserts its centre of gravity. Whimpering, scratching, she appeals to Jack for redress in a world which has become obscurely resistant to the fulfilment of every need. Jack has never much liked the dachshund. She came from Maureen's mother at 'Shadows', one of the bequests he really could have done without. As far as he could see, the creature was constructed according to an architectural fallacy, squat pedestals to act as load-bearers to that sausage, her body, that *Wurst* rather, which with increasing age has become more and more obese. In all fairness, they should have poor Nancy put down. But Maureen has an attachment. Bess' dog must stay alive for as long as her human demigods require and can arrange. Jack bends with a twinge to his back and scoops her with one hand into the basket; arranges that mouldy scrap of tartan blanket which is Nancy's idea of home comfort around her body, and tucks her in for the night. He strokes her grizzled head absent-mindedly; squints around again for Thoby, who remains obstinately sulking (Jack imagines) somewhere in the forest daring him to venture in and have a look round.

Through the dining-room door, Jack glimpses the candle-lit group of old people, their huddled backs in shadow, those facing him illumined in a variety of characteristic gestures. Their conversation is in full flow. They are a quarter of an hour older than when he last beheld them and sat amongst them, their cordial host. Maureen's grandfather-clock in the living-room alcove booms out the hour with the sonority of a gong: midnight. It is followed shortly by the Queen Anne clock which peals the hour a fraction late with the timbre of a glass harmonica. Jack has always been rather fond of this concert; it makes for a home-like and eccentric music out of time.

He pauses; would rather stay apart, outside the group, and saunter in the grounds calling for Thoby and musing upon Jenny, than take his place round the table with the rest. But 'Where is Jack?' they are enquiring; 'Come on, Jack: carve the beef,' commands Maureen's voice, and they all turn in their chairs, and smile, and beckon. Jack goes back in and takes his place amongst his peers.

5
Wind

The Yorkshire springtime in a violent show of adolescent temperament assaults the landscape in torrents of rage and squall. Swarthy clouds come rolling in from the west; over Heptonstall, Haworth and the high moors down over Clayton they scud low to the ground and drop their pelting cargoes on the city in the cup of the valley. Lightning electrocutes two senior citizens in the civic park, and the railway line to Todmorden is closed for several days by flooding. Underground the new generation of daffodils keeps its own counsel in a prudent state of dormancy, reluctant to unsheathe its blades against such unequal conditions in the upper world. In this sleety apocalypse Jack's Cherubino, his Viola, cuts a sorry figure; huddles at night in sweaters and bed-socks and wonders if her lightly built attic extension will lift off altogether and sail up into the raving skies like Gulliver's doll's house. It creaks and seems to shift like a tent on guy-ropes; wind plays pan-pipes with the gutters and bellows down the chimney. Next door's chimney-stack collapsed the previous night, and all day workmen have been perambulating the terrace roof, adding to Jenny's sense of the bizarre state of things in the nether world by peering in at her window and waving enamel mugs in request for tea. They run like spiders over the rooftop with suckered feet, in defiance of sardonic small gusts which elbow at them and great blasts of air which threaten to toss them straight down to the coal-bunkers and washing-lines below.

Greasy-haired and sallow from sickness, Jenny saw off Oliver and Lawrence in Alexander's car on Sunday. Her burnished ex-spouse thanked her in a pleasant, business-like way for caring for them, in such a manner as to cast her as a baby-minder rather than the boy's legitimate mother. He leaned on the gatepost, superlatively tall, swinging to and fro on tiptoe slightly, his hair spiked in the latest fashion.

'You look pretty awful,' he commented pleasantly. 'You'll be able to rest up now that these two rascals are going home. See a doctor, I should, about yourself.'

To Alex's objective eye, loitering while the children arranged themselves in the car (faintly nauseous at the litter of infant coloureds which pressed in around them) Jenny now resembled a grotesque dwarf in the land of the full-sized. He surveyed the aberrant pigmy with something of sexual shame: whatever did the blokes at work think of him married to *that?* Whereas Renate – luscious, breasty, broad-bottomed Renate – a meal for a man; a six-course feast. He doesn't bother with his *Playboy* and his weekly photographic magazine now that he has Renate; has invested in a new Japanese camera and tripod, and at night when Oliver is safely tucked up in bed he poses her bouncing loveliness in all sorts of obliging postures, under the glamorous flowing light of his Anglepoise. And Renate will smile or sizzle or pout to order, denying nothing, though he occasionally imagines she responds to his desires with disconcerting coolness, as if the eye of her unblinking submissiveness stuck him on a pin of perception and had him squirming there like an ignominious insect aroused. Nightly he pumps his seed into Renate in a rage of possession and can't get enough of her; nightly Renate arises from his exploits with curious composure and cleanses herself thoroughly. Such fastidious cleanliness is almost an insult to the insignia of his potency; and it's as if for all her voluptuous compliance Renate retains a vestal purity which can't be touched. Her alien hygiene shares his bed, challenges and mystifies him. But then she's Teutonic, a foreigner, one mustn't expect to understand – and a female of course is always in some sense a foreigner in the tribe, speaking a strange dialect of our language. We don't understand them and they don't understand us and *Vive la différence!* thinks Alexander, gloatingly.

Renate, settled on the back seat of the car between whey-faced Oliver and the recovered Lawrence, looked on expressionlessly at the parental exchange.

'He'll sleep on the journey,' said Alex. 'Hope we don't catch the bug. We want to take him camping in Scotland next week.'

'*We?*'

'Uh huh. Renate and me. Nicer for him to have the two adults.'

'How many tents?' Jenny shot out.

'I beg your pardon.'

'Are you going to marry her? Olly says you are. If you do, I want Olly given back to me.'

'I'll be in touch.' Alex stuck his hands in his pockets and rattled the loose change in irritation; turned sleekly away. 'Any changes go through the courts. But there won't be any changes. Let you know my plans. By the way, I'm buying him a dog.'

'He hasn't got over his gerbil,' mumbled Jenny.

'He can't have his gerbil. The gerbil's dead. Once he *sees* the dog, he'll forget the wretched gerbil.'

'This gerbil,' pointed out Renate helpfully, craning her head out of the car window, 'Is not so human as the dog.'

Oliver, in the crook of the au pair's arm, sucking a Polo-mint dolorously, ventured no opinion on the canine issue. Having delivered his manifesto to his mother, he could offer no further guidance to the adults scuffling in their muddled battle for the allegiance of the young.

'He doesn't want a dog,' insisted Jenny. If she could win just one point against this blonde odious coinage, this counterfeit Kruger Rand . . .

'We're on our way.'

Alex sauntered round the Toyota, playing catch with the keys, inspecting the paintwork for signs of damage from grubby little Asian fingers. Family planning is what they need round here, thought Alex, winking to his son and heir through the smoky glass, that and mass repatriation.

Renate stuck her head out of the window again, beckoning Jenny nearer with her eyes. Jenny took no notice.

'Mrs Reinhold, I want to say, I will truly look after Oliver for you,' Renate blurted, rather quietly. 'I know you and he are missing each other. *Es tut mir leid.*'

Jenny stared as the car swept off, narrowly missing a skateboarding Khan as he shot down the cobbled incline. That was unexpected, the fellow-feeling when one had labelled and bottled a person in a solution of disdain; lined her up on a shelf with the rows of others to whom one's heart and imagination were implacably dead. That the hateful Renate could divine her trouble enough to sympathise with it was a soft shock to the self-defending ego. Not a foreigner after all.

Not foreign as Jack is foreign, in his maleness, in his time-traveller's zesty curiosity as he drops in on her generation and takes a tour of her gender and native land: *oh so that's how you do things over here – back home we –*. Jenny under the stress of the roof-raising Yorkshire weather and the shock of a redundancy notice that came through the door the day after Olly's departure, together with Jack's absenteeism, remembers persistent fits of hostility to Jack; and there are intimations of possible future strength in the recoil. Part-time art-helpers in the primary schools are being dropped as a response to government cuts and she will be on the dole queue. The unwanted and unwantable Jenny can punch back against them all, bring her mirroring left hand slamming into the adversarial world as once into the palm of Jack's great hand, to find her own bearings by turning against him into her own anti-clockwise world, her left-hander's vision. She takes the phone off the hook and leaves it there; gets out her oil paints and begins to daub, pictures of storm and blame, representations of *Get lost Jack* and *Come home Olly*. To summon the strength to throw Jack off is somehow, for reasons she imperfectly understands, to open the way for her child's return. There can be change, there can be ripening, even from congenital impairment, Jenny assures herself. Whistling through her teeth as she vigorously cleans her brushes and palette knife with turps and stands them in a coffee jar for the next time, she is translated to another Jenny, powerful and confident, inhabiting a lit space of her own. God kneels at Jenny's feet on arthritic knees, loaded with opprobrium. Moment by moment she counters the complexity of her own protective devotion that rushes in to mediate between her identity as Jenny and her affinity with Jack.

Tirades of vindictive weather make their case against the window-panes as Jenny leaves the flat and gets into the Escort. It's hardly a time for outings, as the home-coming commuters in raincoats imply, scurrying like Lowry figures over the black sleek pavements that reflect the charcoal skies above them. Heads topped with umbrellas or newspapers, coat-skirts pumped up and deflated by the anarchic bellows of the wind, they flee from bus-stops to the indoor world of television and premature artificial light. The yellow caps and sou'westers of cyclists glow; their wheels swish through puddles on the inside lane. The light is dimming dramatically as Jenny drives with the tide and makes for the open moors. She rises out of Bradford through the foursquare, millstone grit village of Clayton, grouped monolithically round its green like raw hewings of the moor. The clouds travel low to the ground as she passes under the viaduct. She drives elatedly and too fast down now deserted winding roads, keeping herself on the boil. Jack is being expelled like a parasite, like a virus, into the sour world with which the garish, sensual dream he fathers on her cannot coexist. *Yes, you, Jack, the Old Pretender, the Ancien Régime, the mockery king of snow – I mean you, your time has come.* All that was majestic in Jack, and what was silly and holy, and the taste on Jenny's tongue of his enduring sweetness and loving kindness, is out of the window and on to the plateau of the wilderness; and it's a relief, an amazing relief, to be quit of him and free. He wanders out there alone in the driving rain, wearing a confused, alarmed expression, eyebrows slightly raised, his white mane of hair raying about all ends on in the self-contradictory winds that whack forward and buffet back against his insignificant person. Albert Einstein cut down to size exposed on the immensity of his relative status. *What are you going to do now, Jack, now I'm cutting loose? Don't expect me to be sorry for you.* Madame la Guillotine navigates the crossroads above Haworth with a drunkard's panache, looking neither to left nor right, her car a regicidal tumbril that runs on pure air.

Between Heptonstall and Haworth she parks and gets out. Before her the moors are a forcefield of vehement light and shadow, stressfully fighting it out beneath extraordinary skies. A ray of sunlight like a wartime searchlight has penetrated the swarthy cloud-banks and cleaves the sky. The heathers crouch black and old, degenerate leavings of the old year, beneath repeated assaults of turbulence. Across to the west the grasses bear witness to their oppressor's coming by seething undulations where the gale stamps them down, releases and rides them down again. Doused in erratic light, they foam like a sea of sulphur, the ferrous acidic peat a repository of minerals that impregnate the vegetation in livid ochre, rust and orange-brown. Over hummocks of reedy grass and reefs of bilberry she swims forward, tears in her eyes from the scalding wind; angling against the blast towards the cairn at the centre of the moor where she and Rosie used to come and picnic on benign summer evenings to watch the lustrous sun sink down into the breast of the hill.

At the centre, crouched with her back against the cairn, arms folded, Jenny rests at the eye of the storm and her rage slackens like a balloon deflating. The wind, pausing in its persistent thumbing of the balls of her eyes, also thins and drops its interminable two-note dirge through the electric pylons and wires that bisect the moor, the dreariest of Aeolian harps. As the chambers of Jenny's mind empty of disturbance, Jack slips nimbly back in and installs himself inoffensively in a niche toasting his aching hands at a fire. The sheepish wanderer is home again, safe and sound, at least for the time being; and Jenny, rehousing Jack in his accustomed space, half faints with relief as she bears the burden of her love for him back to the car across the wilderness. Coming towards her from the road is a woman, lightly clad, stepping lightly, picking her way with care along the labyrinth of circuitous paths that web the heather invisibly. It's an Indian woman in a sari, a young and slender figure, her saffron scarf and skirts rippling and flowing out sideways in the wind. One arm is bare. *She'll die of exposure. What possessed her?* The woman comes level and begins to move past Jenny, smiling shyly, her eyes kept downcast.

'You'll freeze to death,' says Jenny. The woman shrugs and says something Jenny can't catch. Jenny stands and watches her as she moves further out on to the plateau: her braided hair all down her back, her sari flying, an occultly foreign figure on the great darkening landmass, travelling composedly God knows where.

Ten days ago, Thoby went and Jack has been inconsolable. It appears to him that that night was the turning-point, the end of that false dawn in which he received to himself the love of Jenny and the power to articulate, through her, his own swansong. Of the gathering of friends at the feast, Lewis and Serena remain ensconced and are liable to remain so until the Second Coming, so comfortable and cared for do they feel; but Jacques (whom Jack could well have borne to keep) left after a couple of days.

'My dear,' he said to Jack, walking out along the white silent ribbon of the hill-walk through the pines in search of the dog, 'I'd love to stay but I need to spend all the time remaining with Ralph. One feels the passage of time these days, the skull beneath the skin and so forth.'

Gentle spring breezes, soft as zephyrs and aromatic, blew their balm against Jack's tense face and lifted the hair from his forehead. He felt himself to be a walking slab of obsolescence, redundant in the mantling green of the tender season. Jack found himself unwilling to lose Jacques so precipitately: there were too many vanishings, fallings away. And besides, he felt he could have spoken to Jacques about Jenny – maybe – told his story and obtained the release of breathing her out in words. All that gave him pause was that hint of malice deep in his friend's silky manner. Even so: Jacques is a natural confidant – with all those *amours*.

'Ask him here, Jacques – your Ralph. We'd love to see him. He'll be more than welcome.'

Jacques shook his head; put a brotherly hand on Jack's shoulder. 'It wouldn't do.'

'Why not?'

'Because he'd see – me – too clearly in this context, Jack dear. I couldn't risk it.'

'How do you mean?'

'Jack, I'm sixty-nine years old. *Sixty-nine.*'

'You don't look it.'

'Quite so. But the fact remains. And my lovely Boy is not quite thirty. Bring Ralph into this hall of mirrors, Jack, and have Lewis blink his fish-eyes at him, and surround him with – what shall I say? – this old vintage-wine of ours, and Ralph will surely take fright. I never take that sort of risk. I husband time, Jack, I eke myself out for him, not quite a rouge-job as yet but I am careful with the façade. He thinks my age is – rather less than it is. At least, I *think* he thinks so.'

As Ralph will leave Jacques, so my Jenny must necessarily go. Jack is learning to repeat these elegiac formulae to himself, acquiescing in his own repudiation; thinking, *This will be best for my darling girl*, learning to mean that last, drawing on all the love that is in him. When Jacques left, Jack ran to him after all the palaver of farewells had been made, took him in his arms and kissed him hurriedly on the cheek, notwithstanding the probable consequence of a renewal of those profuse Gallic manifestations of affection which brought out all the Santa in Jack at Jacques' arrival. But Jacques' response was tentative, low-key. He retained his old friend's hand in both of his, and only his sombre eyes said, *I care for you my friend my brother.* He got into the cream Daimler, waved a hand out of the window as he started up and roared off up the drive.

Jenny's phone is permanently engaged. Jack tries her morning, noon and night, and interrogates the operator in America, the operator in London and the operator in Bradford, long and repetitiously. He then rings another operator to ensure that none of this rigmarole can be charged to his account. Jack thinks he knows why Jenny is permanently off the air. He dreams it nightly, and needs neither a communications expert nor an authority on Woman to tell him that Jenny has indeed, at last, after long and patient resistance, yielded to the Potent Young Man's importunities: and cares too much about Jack's sensibilities to be able to confess her lapse. By now the PYM, as Jack according to the current fashion of abbreviation labels his rival, has achieved such ascendancy in his inner world as to have trespassed the barrier between real and fictive. Jack forgets for long periods the fact that it was his own jealousy and insecurity which dreamed up the PYM in the first place and bestowed his tumid flesh and flexed musculature upon the unfortunate Jenny. The PYM assumes the facial characteristics of a glamorous identikit, and (the more to torture his creator) is beginning to graduate to other forms of potency, in which Jack had, till now, conceived himself uniquely qualified. Jack is operating the dishwasher after an enormous breakfast, and stacking away in a cupboard Lewis' packets of life-enhancing dietary fibre, when he distinctly sees the PYM nudge open Jenny's bedroom door and approach Jenny in bed carrying a tea-tray with a silver teapot, a cup, a plate of biscuits and a specimen vase containing a single red rose. Jenny's bare arms reach up to receive the tray from the PYM who kisses her tenderly and retreats to afford her the peace and privacy to enjoy her tea. Now the PYM puts on a record of Beethoven's First Piano Concerto in an adjoining room. Jack is utterly dashed by this vision. The beautiful youth has learnt the twin arts of nurture and culture. Then Jack's occupation's lost. He has no more to offer. He stands at the kitchen sink while the dishwasher rumbles and the two remaining dogs lap water from their bowls. *Yes I have more to offer. I can let Jenny go, with my absolute blessing, to someone who will care for her.* He picks up the phone to tell her so, but her phone is still engaged. With many tears he writes her a long letter on this subject.

But it is Thoby's continued absence which really lacerates Jack, on a day-to-day basis. He had not realised how he had depended on the creature for warmth and companionship. Jenny with her intemperately affectionate and demonstrative nature has taught him to depend on that kind of warmth which is not sexual but a form of animal comfort, holding, hugging, rocking, leaning, stroking: all those unmanly intimacies which busy Jack and equally busy Maureen somehow contrived to avoid throughout their married life, rushing past each other with a greeting, a good word, or conversing across the table. Their family life had been verbal and active, rather than close and intimate, and he never felt a lack. Now there is a void like a withdrawal of necessary sustenance, very hard to bear. He constantly finds himself searching round for Thoby, dangling his fingers from the arm of the easy chair and expecting Thoby's moist muzzle in the palm of his hand, the slobber of his genial tongue. His legs miss the pressure of that warm weight, the go of its heartbeat; even Thoby's annoying demolitions of necessary articles, his berserk magician's trick of dragging off the table-cloth together with its cargo, his appropriation of Jack's bedclothes when he judges it time to wake up. Every spare hour Jack is in the grounds, alone or with Nicki who helps conscientiously, scouring the underbrush, calling 'Thoby, Thoby' into the echoing columns of tall timber, to be answered by the repartee of the jay, or the far-off delusive yapping of another dog. Jack visits the stream and lake where they swam on his return, and tramps along the bouldery, fern-fringed edge, his heart thunderous. The fast-moving icy water, as it pleats and ripples over the stones, appears to Jack's brooding eye to exhibit a quality of fatality. With each bend of the shore-line, he falters in his intention to make a thorough search, lest it should find its quietus; and determine in a stiff mound of clogged and saturated fur cast up on one of the numerous inlets. But no: but no – Thoby couldn't die by water. Newfoundlands have slightly webbed feet and are good in water. Think of the long tradition of their rescues of men from shipwreck on the east coast of Canada. But nothing seems as safe any more: the drift of the current flows past his feet like a fast-flowing grave.

With loss comes Nemesis. Jack has had to break to Maureen the news that Thoby did not come home. He told her in the kitchen the morning after the party, having come in from the first of his fruitless expeditions. Maureen was polishing crystal wine-glasses from the previous night, before arranging them on the dresser. She was wearing her housecoat, a purple kaftan, with its golden cord tied at her narrow waist, and she was singing. He heard it from way down the track through the open window – years now since she had stood there singing to herself over the dishes:

> Did you not see my lady
> Go down the garden singing?

A wedge of cool, early sunlight composed a triangle of light which caught the brocaded and beaded sleeve of the kaftan, her slender wrist and hand, the blue and white check towel and the glass that winked in and out of the slice of light.

> Blackbird and thrush were silent
> To hear the alleys ringing.

As Jack spoke to her of Thoby, she averted her face and moved into the shadowed part of the room.

'I blame you, Jack,' said Maureen quietly, and that was all she would say. She continued to polish relentlessly.

'Molly,' Jack pleaded. Maureen replaced the glass with care upon the shelf of the dresser. She reached for another. 'Molly, please.' He could not see her face. But he knew her lips were thinly pursed, her brown eyes practically null. All he could see was the wispy grey curl at the nape of her neck, escaping from the roll in which she bound her hair. How inexpressibly he longed to go to her now and, taking her shoulders in his hands, bend his head and kiss the nape of her neck, there, where the stray hair flowered and one vertebra of her spine, slightly arthritic, cast a tiny shadow; and, keeping his head bent to the body of his wife, let down the skein of hair that falls, almost, to her waist, turn her and press her to him, shielding and comforting her with his own body. How impossible that he should command that one atoning step into communion. She was a world distant, across a lifetime's gulf of *I blame you*.

'You have no reason to blame me, Molly,' he said reasonably, clearing his throat, his voice husky and constrained with the churning misery of it all; his constitutional anxiety about offending her. *Offending Mother. Mustn't do it.* 'We *had* to put Thoby out last night, you know that, because of goddam Lewis' goddam allergy. I wish we'd put Lewis out instead.'

'Hush, he'll hear you. Would you bring that tray of liqueur glasses over here, please, Jack?'

Jack did as he was told. But behind the obedient façade, his own resentment and irritation were growing; his own disposition to carry on that quarrel that began prehistorically, a dispute of fabulous complexity, predicated on offences, verbal and active, issuing from prior offences, each one minutely chronicled in the memory of both parties, like a long-running case in Chancery. Jack flicks through his minutes; Maureen hers. *In 1848 you stated . . . , In 1954 you refused . . . , In 1959 you remarked. . . .* Maureen lined the glasses up in a mathematical row on the correct shelf of the oak dresser. Jack stood with his great hands dangling uselessly at his side. Sometimes he could imagine one of those hands being raised to strike her, lethally, so undeviatingly implacable was her will to his.

'Thoby will come home,' he said. 'He probably just got involved with some scents and one thing led to another. He will come back.'

'I hope you're right,' said Maureen.

He heard her phoning round to the neighbouring farms: 'My dog is missing . . . Let me know if you see my dog.'

My dog. Thoby her dog? thought Jack. Does she really see it like that? He has always thought of Thoby as his own pet: fed him, walked him, loved him. He realises how much it would have meant to have heard her say *our dog, Jack's and mine.* As the days passed and Thoby became more quintessentially lost, Maureen retreated further and further into her capsule of betrayal. Nicki was away for a few days taking her class on a school camping trip, so there was no one to support Maureen. Only Lewis, carping and querulous, enlivened the tense hours of days that acquired a ghastly longevity from Lewis' habit of arising when Jack does, with the dawn, and insisting on being, in that peaceful time in which Jack is used to composing himself and distilling a few drops of music from the untenanted air, grossly conversational. Like a monstrous hurdy-gurdy, Lewis grinds out the same grating tune, of 'oh my gouty toe' and 'nobody loves me'. He gives a worm-eating display that puts Jack's amateurish exhibitions of self-pity in the shade. As Lewis drones on, polluting Jack's air with pipe-tobacco, Jack rests his head in his hand and the grave invitingly beckons.

On the Tuesday, the aged Nancy gives a high-pitched yelp in her sleep, her body spasms and buckles, and she dies in her basket on the back porch. Thank Christ for that, Jack inwardly feels; and he buries her beneath a copper beech tree which was a particular haunt of hers, believing that Maureen will be happy at this sensitive funeral arrangement, and glad to have it done for her. But as usual Jack has miscalculated. She marches out to the beech tree, flourishing her limp, and stands in silence with her hands on her hips accusing the mound of damp earth which houses Nancy with her whole posture; and rounds on Jack as he pants up, sweating from the spade-work.

'I buried her here, Molly, where she used to come. I thought it would save you pain, if I just laid her to rest here, and told you after.' He puts his arms round her, offering her comfort, but it is as if the malefactor should seek to inveigle the hangman into illicit embrace. Maureen's arms are tight to her sides; she is a stone lady at the graveside of her favourite.

'You never liked Nancy, Jack,' says Maureen evenly. 'Because she came from my mother at "Shadows". You never liked my little dog and now you've buried her.'

Jack has taken a step back from his wife, whose eyes convict and sentence him on a charge of something more wicked than culpable homicide. This is too much.

'Don't be ridiculous, Molly. She was my dog too,' he snaps back. 'And what's more, *only* a dog. Not a human.'

But Thoby is *only* a dog too; and he loves Thoby with a more lavish affection than any human creature at the moment, especially that thorn, that briar, Maureen. His look now frankly returns her hostility. The old punitive rage begins to swell within him, that pleasurable, tumid heat and pressure rising in his skull, the hardening of the tongue into a weapon of maleness before whose whiplash strokes Maureen over the decades of their union learned to feign dead, lying helplessly supine, a dog in a basket. *Oh the relief*, Jack feels, *to shake off the emasculating yoke of Jenny's sentimental feminism, to go after*

Maureen again in time-honoured fashion; give her something to smart about. He glares down into Maureen's eyes from his red, distended fortress.

Is put right off his stroke to see Maureen's severely authoritative eye looking right back into his, with no tremor of relenting, much as to say, The king is dead, things have changed, royally, once and for all.

'I'm sorry,' Jack hears himself mutter.

'You never mean it, Jack, when you say sorry,' she replies, moving off towards the house.

'I do.' He follows.

'You do not. You just say it to keep the peace. One of my dogs is dead. One is lost. I asked you to keep an eye on Thoby that night.'

Oh damn you, you cackling nagging relentless bitch, Jack shrieks falsetto in his mind. He hates her like wormwood, like poison.

'*Our dogs*,' he mutters. And he recalls that this was how it was with the children, and remains so still, the fight for possession: *my son, my daughter*, never *ours*. Which each feels the other has obscurely won, by double-crossing and seduction. Hence it is that Maureen turns away from her husband, telling him without a qualm, *I blame you*, and rehearses to herself trivially anachronistic grudges which Jack views with incredulity. How could the woman be so petty? His own grudges of course are of a different calibre: tragic, meaningful, replete with pathos. Hence it is that when Maureen is baking cookies and the fragrance steals out so luscious that the hovering Jack can hardly bear to wait a second more for one of the delicacies, she slaps with the flat of a knife at his fingers prowling above the cooling tray and says, *They're not for you;* and turns her longing, famished eyes towards 'Shadows' and Nicki in search of the passionate cherishing they have all neglected to supply.

Now Maureen limps indoors, and Jack stomps along in her wake. In the house furore is loose. The schnauzer Paul, whether over-excited at finding himself *fils unique* in the household or for another unspecified reason, is whirling in hysteria on the kitchen floor, chasing his own tail and violently barking. The voice of Lewis can be heard roaring, 'Shut up that goddam noise you flea-bitten son of a rat or I will personally choke you to death on your goddam chain'; and the voice of Serena is urging, 'Shush, Lewis, quiet – they're in the house for Godsake. Oh hi you two,' she purrs. 'Dear little Doggie seems to be having a slight turn.'

Rescuing Paul, their last extant pet, from his own dementia on the one hand and that of the house-guest on the other, Jack snaps on Paul's lead and takes him out in search of Thoby.

At the perimeter fence between their property and 'Shadows', Jack sees his neighbour fiddling with the engine of her car. She straightens up, yawning, then claps her hand over the yawn and laughs to Jack in greeting.

'You look worn out,' says Jack. 'Don't let me disturb you. We're tramping around on our usual expedition.'

'No luck?'

'No luck. Quite honestly . . . ah well.'

'Let me come with you. I brought the class back safely last night and deposited each child with its proper parent. I could do with a *quiet* ramble where no one says "Please Mrs Fairburn".'

'Please Mrs Fairburn . . .'

'Don't you *do* that to me, Jack. Shelley – Pete –' she calls back into the house. 'I'm off to look for Thoby with Mr Middleton.'

Since they began these mutual searches, a kindness has grown between them, Jack likes to think. He respects the reserve she shows in relation to him; her resistance to his charm which warns him off from the tempting reflex of trying to poach her from Maureen. *Keep your distance*, she warns him. *This is one child she shan't lose*. And a deep part of him wants that, too, against instinct and habit, that Maureen should have this kingdom and hold it against himself. Half a century's flawed but abiding allegiance, through thick and thin, health and sickness and his own crude selfishness, is in that notice to himself staked into his own heart: *Keep out, Jack*. In the end he wants Maureen's good; and her good is Nicki, who refuses to let Jack flow in around her like the recreant amoeba he is: protean, absorbent.

'Why don't we try the Scott estate again, Jack?'

'I dread to.' John Scott never recovered from Okinawa. He has mined his land with gins and traps, barbed wire and booby traps. He tours his boundaries letting off a twelve bore. 'But okay. If you think so.'

While Nicki is driving them the five miles over the undulating track to the Scott estate, Jack tells her that Nancy died.

'How did Marmie take it?' asks Nicki. Jack winces at the nickname. It still astounds and not a little unsettles him that Maureen has a life and a personality apart from himself, as if a central oak tree should put forth whimsical shoots of revolutionary beech; and have to be rechristened, in the name of its bastard liberty. As if the planet's axis should take it upon itself to tip, with a sudden energetic self-assertion, without consulting Jack Middleton. *Who is this Marmie of yours? Her own person. Not Jack's docile wife. Not loving mother to five, doting grandmother to ten. Someone overwhelmingly free; alien; aloof.*

'She took it real bad,' says Jack. 'She blames me. She has always blamed me.'

'That's true,' says Nicki, causing Jack to look at her sharply. This woman must have been told all about him – Maureen's version, anyway. She is the voyeur of his inmost privacy. Is probably familiar with his love of Jenny; is doubtless on intimate terms with the condition of his underwear.

'Why, do you think she's right to blame me, Nicki? *Am* I to blame for the world's ills in so far as they bear on her?' he flings out defensively.

Nicki shrugs, as at an irrelevance. 'It doesn't matter whether you are to blame or not,' she says, swinging the car off the track, to park in the shade of a great over-arching birch tree. 'Who is to judge you anyway?'

'Well, Maureen does, for sure.'

'Let her,' replies Nicki. They slam the car doors and start together into the forest, which is thick and tangled here to the south-west, its soft fibrous floor falling away to the lake at the edge of Scott's estate. The air carries the tang of the minerals in that dark, peaty, seldom-visited pool, a strange dark odour like a sour taste on the tongue. Nicki's words are heavy, to Jack's jaded sense, with incomprehensibly gnomic implication. He cannot follow. He is tired of it all. Tired of Maureen, Nicki, Jenny, Serena, the whole nagging, badgering lot of them.

They reach the bowl of the valley. Here the deer-herds travel at twilight, treading with delicate steps down the sheer slope, heads and ears erect, nostrils working, to drink from their reflections in the pure waters. The breeze has dropped and the pool is a still mirror.

'Jack, has it ever crossed your mind,' says Nicki, breaking into his peace as if a stone should ring the glassy surface of the water into a flurry of concentricities, 'that blame may be an aspect of love?'

'No,' says Jack, with candour. 'It has not.'

'She loads you with all that she finds difficult to bear, and trusts you to bear it for her. After half a century she thinks she's earned at least the right to beat upon you.'

'Like a disreputable old camel or a superannuated ox?'

Nicki smiles. 'Exactly like a camel or an ox. Or maybe a certain species of goat resident in the wilderness.'

Jack the atoner passes on through the criss-cross bars of shadow in the temple of pines, bearing all the iniquities of the children of Israel and all their transgressions in all their sins. He feels heady with an obscure sensation of enlightenment as if he had been drinking; though it is over ten days since he touched a drop, much to Maureen's irritation, for she is not averse to seeing him wallow in his own manifold indignities. In his mind there is the relief of clarification of this, as of so many other, details. He does not expect his life to gain in comfort, but he begins to divine a meaning in the thistles.

'Jack, look. *Look*, Jack.' Paul is throttling himself on his lead, shooting forward and yapping in agitation. Nicki is charging through the undergrowth, breaking twigs, grazing skin. The Newfoundland pup lies alive, with his eyes open, much emaciated, bloody and devoid of bark, in a coil of barbed wire at the border of the Scott estate.

'Oh Nicki, Nicki, Nicki, you've brought him home to me.' Maureen is beside herself, embracing her friend, tending Thoby, who is enthroned in honour on a bed of blankets upon the best settee, a proximity which even the allergic Lewis is, through his sneezes, bearing with fortitude.

'Oh thank you, Nicki, thank you – my dear, *dear*, girl.'

She offers no thanks to Jack, though it was Jack who, at the limit of his strength, carried the great maimed creature in to her, with many tears; who conveyed the vet over, bathed the wounds, fed Thoby's thirst with water; who said to Maureen, with all the love that was in him, 'Here's your dog back, my darling,' in a voice so husky with emotion that it came out like a croak. She extended no thanks in formal terms, nor did she return the pressure of his hand; but after the rumpus has died down and she is sitting with Thoby's head in her lap, rhythmically stroking the fur back from his eyes, sipping a glass of gin and tonic, she looks out of the window towards the distant hills and informs Jack quite casually, 'I got through to Jenny, by the way, dear, and prevailed upon her to fly over to us at the weekend: I pay. I understand she's been unwell, so we'll have to take good care of her.'

Part Two

1
Primavera

Jenny awakens to the vision of a humming-bird at her window, and thinks she must have died, or be dreaming, at any rate it is clear she is elsewhere than Bradford. The morning is so still that she hears the creature whirr out there as it hovers, a tiny vibrating life with its long beak and sitting up posture, a foreigner coming close. Then the humming-bird is gone, and there are just five windows framing rectangles of glowing turquoise and lemon-green light. The light washes through her mind, and the world is quiet, quieter than it has ever been. At each window hangs a basket of plants or flowers, whose tendrils wander freely in the air beneath in an expeditionary manner. Jenny lies and considers the loops and curves of the plants, their curlicues like those of an Elizabethan signature. She considers the brilliant light and the sabbath lull in the sanctuary.

She kneels on the bed and looks around. Everything is unvarnished wood within as without, and old, and exquisitely turned in accordance with the nature of the wood, as if the carpenter were one with the gardener who set the spindles of the tall chairs and the fluted columns of the four-poster to root in the outdoor world. Slipping out of bed, she runs her fingers over the bedposts with their twists and bevels, their flow of wood which ends in – nothing at all, for there is no canopy, the ceiling being too low to admit one; hence the four posts, defying utility, impersonate exotic tree-stumps, planted in the floorboards with their few woven Indian mats. On the mantelpiece, two silver candlesticks repeat the undulations of the bedposts, and the immense dog-grate is piled with logs; it contains traces of the cinders of an old fire.

Jenny's eyes travel the walls which bear, she now perceives, dozens of portraits – both oils and photographs – of Maureen and her aristocratic family from 'Shadows'. Many Maureens bridally attired look in through as many windows from the past to the present, and scan the latterday visitor in her white cotton nightgown with mild perplexity. Jenny moves to the window and throws up the sash. An expansive lawn runs up the slope of a gentle hill on this side of the house, meeting with a line of larches, oak and pine which fringes the horizon and throws forward an oblique line of early-morning shadows slantwise from the summit, like eyelashes. The forest behind is thickly, darkly green to the point of umber; and beyond that 'Shadows' is visible from this window, white timbers bosomed high in tufted trees; and beyond 'Shadows' the breasts of further hills to the west, and to the south-west a falling away of the land to the invisible lake in the deepest lap of the valley. Jenny's eyes adore the creation.

Just at the summit of the lawn, on the threshold of the forest sits Jack on a camp-stool, half in, half out of the dappling shadows, with a dog luxuriating full-length at his feet: a small figure casting an improbably long shadow down a third of the slope in the early sunlight.

Jack, wearing a red tartan shirt and his best pair of jeans, rather tight as to the middle (but he holds in his breath for the sake of fashion and beauty, and hardly notices the discomfort) sits in the sunlight cracking walnuts. This is one of the list of tasks he has blithely undertaken for Maureen, promising to resist the temptation to make a meal of them for himself and Thoby. He shatters the woody shells with relish and scatters them on the ground, letting fall the wrinkled nuts into the bowl and occasionally sharing out a handful between the two of them. Never were nuts so good. Never did the sun rest so warm on the back of one's neck. The air has never smelt so good, the fume of resin exhaling from the forest in waves, mingling with a waft of pine-smoke from a neighbour's bonfire. Jack has been alive, he calculates, for a total of 25,233 days precisely; today being the 25,234th. You would think that the glum conclusion might have dawned in that time that one has done it all before, seen it all before; the sense of taste should coarsen, the eye be filmed with residue of routine, the ear tick like a clock in one's head telling the time which is always the same time, interminably reproducing its antecedents. But, no. This is the first day of

Creation. Jack is a new-made man. He has never set eyes on any of this before today.

Jenny is asleep under his roof. He looks back over the lawns to the house that holds her. He has her in his care and protection. He has her safe. This is enough. This is the moment toward which his life has tended. It is the clasp on the bracelet closing; it is the garden-gate swinging shut. He has her. He has her. Over and over it reverberates like bird-calls under his own eaves with the renewal of morning. Her presence is felt through every leaf and ray and breeze; in his own body at ease on the camp-stool shelling the nuts, knees apart, ankles crossed; in the sun on the gnarled old hand that flicks away the shells with a squeeze of finger and thumb, or a fingernail levering the kernel; in the taste as he crunches the illicit walnuts; in sharing the haul with Thoby – though Thoby since his late misadventure is indisputably a little gone in the head, wages pitched battles against harmless slippers and wanders nocturnally baying anger and defiance at the moon.

The staggering joy as he met her off the plane: he thought he'd drop. Then there was a different kind of shock at thinking the shadows under her eyes were bruises. She didn't look her old self. 'You look so thin and drawn.'

'Can't say the same for you,' said the Jenny who was her old self, 'you melon.' He drove her home, out of his mind with excitement, and Maureen fussed her, and fed her, and put her to bed, where he dared not go to kiss her goodnight, but tiptoed about on the landing in his bare feet at various stages of the night outside her door, listening for her breathing; and the dogs came padding to join him, chinking their chains, and sniffing at the stranger's door.

Jack in his delirium is prepared to love everyone under his roof, not least Lewis, the old friend who still peeps out in flashes from that moribund hulk who is not the true Lewis. Through Jenny he can bless Maureen and Nicki, Serena, even the wraith of Maureen's mother, the rancorous old queen of 'Shadows' whose posthumous presence he still entertains as a ghostly gate-crashing house-guest. He blesses the five children, the grandchildren, dogs, squirrels, deer, all, there is no creature to whom he is prepared to refuse a place in the circle of reconciliation. Looking down the sunlit lawn to the white, ivied house, one could imagine a ring-dance of all these characters, stately, comic, a celebration of eternal amity somewhat after the Elizabethans. With this in mind, Jack begins to compose, whistling the theme of the round through his teeth and seeing it all, so clear it might be a film: Maureen, Jenny, Nicki, Serena, Lewis, Bess, Jacques, take hands and dance to the far-fetched music of his flute, and around them the family gathers in a greater encompassing ring, the parents and grandparents and all their retinue of loves and friendships, his children and his children's children take hands. The dead and the unborn take hands and dance.

All things are possible, his euphoria tells him, *in or out of season.* He looks towards 'Red Earth' and waves, for there is Maureen at the door in a blue dress, standing with her arms folded, just standing there, uncharacteristically doing nothing.

She hardly notices Jack as anything other than an aspect of the scene, like a crimson berry on an autumn bough. When he waves and calls, she is faintly nonplussed and would like to say, *Hey, don't do that, you're spoiling the pattern, flapping that red tartan arm of yours about*, as if looking out from the porch to the hills and forests were like the feeling when you have completed a rather complex jigsaw, and sit back to survey the way in which the pieces fit together. Eventually, she raises her hand and waves back, to restore the pensive harmony of the vista to its prior condition. Jack resumes his passive place in the configuration and leaves Maureen free to muse.

It was a good night, for once in a while: a long, dream-swept (but not turbulent) night of deep and easy sleep. Since old age set in, Maureen has not slept as well as she used to do, but in a patchy, shallow manner, dipping and bobbing like a duck in water, got through the frustrating hours in fits and starts. *Yes, that's right, Jack*, she thinks now, watching him bend to tousle Thoby's pelt, *you be happy, bad old creature, out there in your dream-world*, and she hears (so quiet is the morning) the nuts he is cracking pop and ting into the bowl with a tiny metallic echo across the high lawn, *I'll let you.* He is like a rascally dog on the end of a fully played-out leash, whose tether she elects not to tug: *though I could bring you running home any time I choose, tail between your legs, head low and fawning. Be free, you have your Jenny now, enjoy her while you may*, thinks Maureen looking towards her husband with a beneficent smile, as who should remark, *Fiat lux*. Jack goes back to being a red berry on the great hanging bough of her thoughts.

This well-being; this singular marriage of composure with possession; the illusion of all things being in the right relation, and oneself an intrinsic and necessary part of the whole design. She sighs with the sense of plenitude. Last night she dreamed that Mother revoked the will that left everything to Robert: a new codicil, *To my beloved daughter, Maureen, my house and lands, and to her daughters in perpetuity*. It is still so hard to believe, after all these years, that Mother left her nothing, no keepsake, no token of regard, not one word. All to the boy, nothing to the girl. Yet *here is my world*, she thinks now in the glistening morning light; she has built her own house, planted her own garden. Here is her forest of box-hedges planted thirty years ago according to her own plan and cut with her shears into a miniature labyrinth: the grandchildren run round screaming in there tipsy with excitement veering to panic, and there poor old Nancy would wander, and keen a dirge, her fuddled old wits and nose not equal to the task of escape. There is the tree-house built for the elder children in the 1950s; there the rose-garden, somewhat unkempt now, the roses ten foot high, the stock as thick as small trees; there her rock-garden, her pool, her bower. And over there at 'Shadows' – Maureen raises her eyes to the slice of white roof which is all she can spy from the back door – is Nicki, sleeping in, the restorer of the estranged heritage, who for some inconceivable reason has entrusted to this superannuated scarecrow, this parcel of bone, this barren mother, the paradisal gift of her self.

Serena, waking, turns over on her back and stretches out her left arm to embrace the lover of whom she has been dreaming, who was, of course, not Lewis but a rather younger version of Jack, minus the pot belly and his face purged of that expression of polite incredulity with which it is wont to confront and parry her charms. 'Oh darling,' the Dream-Jack was just saying before she awoke, 'I can hardly keep my hands off you. Dear, dearest girl': he was so tender, and so knowing, and he called her girl and she fainted under the compulsion of his touch. And now, awakening, she feels like a young person again, confident that she counts in the world and unashamed of those anatomical defects which preoccupy her some days to the exclusion of all other thoughts. On such hagridden mornings she cannot see her self in the face in the mirror, with its wrinkled throat, the many lines age has rudely scrawled across the null, unlettered loveliness of her original incarnation. She makes the best of it with costly creams with hormones and extract of embryo and God knows what foul witch's brew. With light upward strokes of her fingertips she smooths in cream, staring at the sad, offended face of her shadow, thinking *You are not myself, I am somewhere else.* She nourishes the skin of the poor creature, and rouges its cheeks in the recommended manner, with just a hint of natural colour: *You painted clown, how can you bear to exist at all?*

Today she can more than bear to exist, she would recommend it to anyone, although the hand that reaches out to her lover across the pink world of sheets and pillows meets with no fellow being, not even Lewis; and her body's starved, neglected condition immediately upon waking asserts itself. For she has the hallucination, an afterglow of the dream, that somebody badly wants her, with as naked and ruthless a passion as she needs to be wanted. It's a good thing, thinks Serena, that my breasts are still full and don't sag in that regrettable way some older women's do: that's because I never had babies, a point in my favour. She determines to wear her most *décolleté* dress this morning, to make available for public inspection these enviable appurtenances. She is sure that Jack, who is a real man, prefers a bouncing buxomness to that broomhandle bean-pole boy-girl they let in like a stray dog last night; who was embarrassingly gauche in manner, and clearly did not know the first thing about how to dress. Serena is willing to offer a few tips to the bean-pole on how to pad out and flounce itself up into a semblance of femininity.

Serena sits up in bed against the pillows and, oh heavens, here is her image in the full-length wardrobe mirror: but, really, not too bad a shock today at all, in its white gauzy negligée, low at the breast and lacy and strung round with ribbons, so pretty, and her hair not frowsty but interestingly disarrayed, and her skin in the generous dim-gold light from the closed curtains not raddled but firm and taut. *I'm not really so terribly changed*, thinks Serena, *not really. I'm the same girl*. She was father's girl fifty years ago, the apple of his eye, then the college girl with a writing gift. The beauty of her year, she was never at a loss for dates. Then she was Ed's wife, who adored her but couldn't keep her, who bought her everything, the swimming pool, the yacht, the exotic foreign holidays. In the Californian sunshine, how wives shed husbands to her, brown as a berry all over – but how her skin aged, with terrifying rapidity, until she seemed to go invisible, suddenly, catastrophically. Lost Ed to a dowdy little thing in a pinafore dress; caught a beachboy of eighteen at Rehoboth and lost him before the year was out, aborting his child; came north, caught Lewis with a hook right through the gills, but honestly and truly was he worth the bother? She was father's girl again ten years ago, forty-seven to his sixty-four, and how he babied her and made much of her, but even then he did not know how to love and satisfy her, so ashamed at his impotence, so uncomprehending of her needs (of her basic anatomical composition, she is inclined to think), and even when she has said to him 'Now, look here, Lou, you are getting nowhere fast' (the books all say you should be assertive) 'put your hand here; and then do this; and this', he seized up like a clam, twitched and rubbed like someone well-trained in skinning new potatoes, enquired politely, 'Are you finished, dear?' and, turning over with a sigh of relief, fell fast asleep. *Geriatric, palsied old fool*, thought Serena in her bitterness, and used sometimes to awaken him by yelling in his ear, *No, mister, I am not 'finished' as you call it, I have not even begun to start*, to which he would limply reply, *Oh dear*, before relapsing into coma. She sometimes wondered how his first three wives had got on with this degree of handicap, and how it was that they had succeeded in teaching Lewis nothing, just plain nothing. It was hardly fair on the next-comer, almost a conspiracy, to leave the guy in a state of such abject ignorance.

Now she crosses to the window and pulls the curtains; and the world is lovely in her eyes, and full of promise, the dew scarcely evaporated from the lawn, the birds declaiming; and the world is lovelier than ever because there is darling Jack who touched her with worshipping fingertips in her dream, who said *Dear girl*. Jack, to whom she now will show herself by throwing open the casement with a flourish and calling *Hi*! and seeming to beckon. But first she unties the ribbon at the breast of her negligée and lets the gown fall to an almost indecent extent; and as she fiddles with the hasp on the window she wishes Maureen, lovable as she is but watchful as a hawk, could somehow be got rid of; couldn't Lewis take her and Bean-pole on some kind of expedition, leaving her and Jack . . . surely it can be arranged? Christ, this window . . . she struggles, it springs open, and Serena greets Jack with a big, coy come-on in her smile and wave, only to witness her husband, advancing across the lawn towards the far, red figure of Jack and the black blob of the dog. 'Hi, there, Lou,' she calls, and there is a note of reconciliation in Serena's voice which she had not predicted, for as he turns and meets her eyes, his face carries a look which remembers someone from long ago, and which contains in it something of valediction.

Lewis steps into the unknown with the reckless spirit of the pioneering settlers who founded Pennsylvania in the first place. For he has decided to travel across the lawn to join his friend without benefit of walking-stick. *I shall not shamble, neither shall I groan, not even once; no; I shall walk upright God-like erect and tall; like a man.* Today Lewis feels more like his old self – his young self, rather, who neither wears out nor metamorphoses with the years, but who is somehow retained within the bag of the body, or wears that decaying outside like a cumbersome diver's suit it can never slough. Or like the bandages in which H. G. Wells bound his Invisible Man to make him detectable. Some days, and this is one, the Young Lewis makes himself felt within the desuetude of the old carcass so persuasively that it is as if his energy can motivate the rotting organism to feats of miracle. *Take up your bed and walk*, says Young Lewis zestfully, and Old Lewis agrees to try. Was it the sight of Serena sleeping that so engaged him – one hand curled at that pretty breast he so longs to cradle and kiss, or it is just the enigma of body-chemistry, the blood rinsing away the deposits of calcium and phosphate crystals in the joints, the murk from the brain? He has been a scientist and would favour the latter solution; but the Young Lewis argues for the former, most vehemently. But he does not dare to touch his wife. Surely her youth is revolted at his mastodon's bulk, a creature by rights extinct, from whose sensual desires all right-thinking young persons must turn in disgust. *Monster, not man.* Lewis sublimates his sensuality in the celebration of bodily ills: and certainly he has plenty of twinges, distresses and aches to squeal about. It never once crosses Lewis' mind to conceive that his wife is ageing too, or could be conscious of loss in this respect. To him she is the epitome of youthfulness and charm; when he sees and hears her flirting with other men (as she does whenever a pair of trousers appears in the room) he cannot blame her, but like a dying elephant he trumpets all the louder of the chronic pains rooting around in the core of his mortality.

She waves to him, and she is beautiful in the sunlight. More beautiful than he can bear, or has any right to expect to be bestowed on himself. As she raises her hand, he sees the veiling white sleeve of her nightgown ripple down over her arm; her full breasts are revealed, one more than the other as the gown slides from the left shoulder, and *oh Christ, oh Christ*, he stands there in the centre of the lawn without his walking-stick, and stares, with a jealous ache in the very sockets of the eyes that see her. And he would like to go in there (but that he is to the earth as a rooted piece of immovable timber, stockstill) and pull her away by the arm from the window that lends her beauty to any voyeur; and say to her *Wrap your body up decently*, though he would rather say, with appropriative tenderness *You are mine – mine – see?* But what has he left in his sapless frame to offer to her loveliness? There is no way to enter her, and he might as well go shuffle round Maureen's box-hedge labyrinth as claim his own wife. He is the monster at the centre from whom she must be saved, bellowing and grunting in his languageless pain. And yet he distinctly hears the lady call to the monster, 'Hi, there, Lou!' and the arm of the monster waves back cheerily, and answers in human speech, 'Good morning, sweetheart!'

She retires into the bedroom; hasps the window. He imagines her scent, it drifts across his senses in remembrance, as do the rows of bottles, jars, compacts and unguents, how that excites him about her: just to watch her paint her fingernails with such exactitude till they are like crimson talons, and then her toenails. She is like a gilded creature of prey, so magnificent, watching herself in the mirror. If he only knew the secret of how to approach her without excoriation, this bird of paradise nominally his: who just then was a diaphanous vision, Venus arising in Jack's garden. Perhaps Jack would know; could help – if one could find the words, beyond *ahem* and *er, well* to communicate his need. But significant words, listening, sharing words, are hard to find these days. Oh he can talk; he hears himself at it, droning on and on like a pianola plucking at the same set of strings, execrable tunes of *I remember*, vile, self-pitying dirges of *my peptic ulcer, my strangulated hernia*, and he sees all too well how his listeners itch and yawn and fidget, and how their eyes go dead. With a malevolent pertinacity he visits on them more and more elaborate and long-winded torments, thinking *This will show them.* For this is a last stand, the power of Thermopylae perhaps: to refuse to subside into silence. Perhaps after all he is most comfortable in hospital in these latter days, where he is encouraged to exercise his favourite topic of conversation without restraint; where persons in white coats come and poke and discuss your organs as an object of serious study; and the dear little nurses express interest in the state of your urine, and are salaried to pay attention to your stagiest groans.

And yet there are days, like today, when Lewis cuts the cackle. The balmy weather forbids it. The vision of his old friend like an English pillar box across the lawns reminds him of early ideals and allegiances. Lewis summons his legs, those refractory spindles built on the principle of a collapsing deckchair, into use, and, complying, they propel him forward in an oddly scurrying motion, as if they surrendered to an independent panic about something behind him. *Slow down, slow down*: Lewis, breathing rapidly, seeks means to put the brakes on this high-velocity locomotion; and feels somewhat hysterical as he hurries over the grass uphill, for to maintain this pace will mean to capsize forward whereas to decelerate may precipitate his brittle body down the slope, to certain fracture of vital portions. *That's it, that's it*: Lewis totters nervously onward but he has lost the violent momentum which gave a sense of casualty to his endeavour. And here is Jack, swooping downhill, one great tartan arm fathering his frailty, saying, 'My *friend*!' and leading him to the deckchair.

'Nothing to it,' replies Lewis. 'Perfect morning.' Still grasping Jack's arm, he squeezes intermittently, much out of breath.

'The first morning of the world: Jenny's here,' says Jack in a revelatory manner, and the two statements can be construed as cause and effect by the listening ear.

'Uh-*huh*?' says Lewis, and Jack is sure he listened.

'And how about you? Did you sleep well? How are you

feeling this morning?' *Here we go*, can be read all over Jack's face, *a dose of diseases coming up*.

'I slept like a baby,' says Lewis. 'Did you see her at the window?'

'I did,' replies Jack.

'She was beautiful.'

'She was indeed.'

'Breakfast in the garden, I think, Jack,' says Maureen, bustling. They have barbecue tables of weathered pine-wood which Jack and his elder boy Frank felled, sawed, planed and hammered together when Jack was a capering youth of forty. He is especially fond of these eccentrically fashioned, lopsided and battered tables, which stand on the eastern side of the house; and at evening likes to sit and drink a can of iced beer out here, notwithstanding the gnats which plague the sunset hours, which he snatches out of the air, or in the days when he used to smoke a pipe, would keep at bay with his tobacco.

Jenny sits quietly at Jack's old table with Jack's old friends, in a state of sweet shock. Yesterday she was in Bradford where the smoke of neighbours' coal-fires lay heavy on the air and even the green of the hills was a derivative of grey. Now she has climbed up into a painting, stained with jewelly colours, azure, emerald-green and lemon-gold. One's eye can hardly take the change. It feeds the libido like a sensual film. She accepts a waffle from Maureen and cuts into it with a fork. Nothing has ever tasted so good. The benign old man across the table offers more syrup. He looks upon his wife so adoringly; his wife the fantastically adorned Serena, who is loaded with bright-coloured Indian beads, from her ears and throat and her wrist they hang, and like a child's baubles, compel attention. And then there is Jack, in ruthless red, whose eyes skid about all over the place rather than alight upon her; and Maureen who keeps looking round as if she missed some link in the necklace necessary to clasp it shut.

'Are you tired, dear, from your long trip?' Serena asks Bean-pole, who is not so bad, it seems to her, on closer inspection, sitting there in her white shirt and black trousers and with a nervous mannerism pushing the short hair back behind her ears; and of course if she is more like a tomboy than a grown woman, that effectively rules her out as a challenge.

'I am tired but I slept well,' says Jenny to this rainbow lady, who reminds her of a brave country-and-western singer of considerable vintage. 'When I woke up there was a humming-bird at my window. I thought I'd died and gone to heaven.'

Jack is a high bubble of hope, rising above himself. His eyes are brilliantly blue and lively. 'Who is to say,' he insists to Lewis, 'when the time of creativity is finally over? I think of Milton in the season of his blindness. I think of Haydn in his sixties bringing in his winter harvest – *The Creation* of course was written then. The seventies could be our best decade yet.'

'And Sophocles, of course, and Aeschylus, and Segovia and Horowitz.'

'It's worse for a woman,' says Serena. 'Age. I feel that.'

'How would you know?' asks her husband.

'Excuse me?'

'How would you know? You haven't the slightest need to feel anything of the sort. You're a child.'

'Lewis, I am not a child,' says Serena, very quietly.

'Serena – '

'I'm growing old. I know it.'

'Oh come on.'

'And wrinkled and shapeless and hideous as a gargoyle. Did you honestly think I didn't know?' she exhorts the company, none of whom has a word to say.

'Oh *sweetheart*.' He is stricken, and almost lets out a groan according to his habit of publicly mourning his own decrepitude; but, swallowing most of it, expels the rest as a cough.

'Don't you sweetheart me. I've got a mirror, haven't I, and the use of my eyes – well, contact lenses anyway.'

'But you're so *damned* beautiful.'

'Oh go *on*, you old fool.' He has covered her hand in his, and she does not withdraw. 'And the worst of it is – ' says Serena, and can't go on.

'What, darling, what?'

'I'll never have a child. Okay, Lewis, if you want to know, never have *your* child. You have three sons, Lewis, by a miscellany of wives, none of them me. Maureen has five children and goodness knows how many dozen grandchildren at the last count. All our friends have littered the world with prodigious quantities of offspring. I have no children. Do you have children, Jenny?'

'I have one son.'

'You see, even she has children. I end in me.'

'But I never knew you felt like this.'

'You never asked. And besides one doesn't go around advertising one's deficiencies.'

'Children are such perishable commodities,' says Maureen sympathetically. 'They don't stay long. I too end and begin in me.'

'You think so?' asks Serena wonderingly. She has always thought of Maureen as the mother-dove, fulfilled on her nest.

'Oh yes,' says Maureen matter-of-factly. 'Oh yes.'

'Mirrors tell lies,' says Jenny. 'You have great beauty, if you don't mind my saying so.' She blushes hotly and wishes she had not spoken. But Serena begins to glow, and somehow the telling of undignified truths, *I am old, I am ugly, I feel dearth, I need love* releases the group round the table into a feeling of freedom. The table tilts between them, with its ancient grained holes into which some long-extinct child has stuffed pine-cones, and on summer afternoons the ants run in busy tribes. Venus, presiding in the person of Serena, turns to Lewis and favours his mouth with a swift, soft kiss, out of the blue. The pressure of her breast warms him to the cockles of his heart and induces certain sensations in a long-moribund portion of his anatomy so astonishing to himself that he pushes her away and, holding her at arm's length, announces, 'Good God!'

On the evening of the first day of Jenny's visit, they walk in pairs into the forest. The late sun runs slantwise through the lichenous pines. The forest is full of scents, tangerine and balsam from the resins of the trees, as if one had entered a plantation of healing herbs. Jack and Jenny drift along arm in arm over the pliable floor which is composed entirely of dust of bark, needles, leaves, seeds, spores. Ahead, Nicki and Maureen walk together in the cool of the evening. Behind, Serena and Lewis come along with the aid of a stick, and Serena keeps up a terrific prattle, with Lewis doing the unprecedented thing of listening: of which rigmarole nothing can be heard but a sort of rhythmic murmur, like the muffled patter of rain on a forest floor. They pass the beechen grave of Nancy, which Jack points out; and the tree-house which thirty-odd years back Maureen and Jack built with their bare hands for the vanished childhoods of their brood. As Jenny looks up, she sees that the whole structure is overrun by red squirrels, whose bodies ripple along the branches like coppery waves. The squirrels shin up and down the ladder and sit up on the boards of the tree-house floor to gnaw their pickings. The moment is perfect. Only poor Thoby, who has never been the same since his traumatic experience of loss, seems unable to share the common rapture, and shows a neurotic terror of squirrels which reflects ignominiously on the spirit of his species. He creeps along at Jack's heels with his tail low to the ground, and his weighty head pendant as if gravity constrained it; and when the foreign squirrel world is sighted, will not under any circumstances proceed. 'Come on, my boy,' Jack coaxes him; but Thoby sticks. 'Then we must circumnavigate,' Jack says, and drags him round by the collar: an energetic procedure the labour of which makes Jack's own heart race and knock rather painfully so that, straightening up, he pauses in momentary alarm to regain his breath.

'Are you all right, Jack?' asks Jenny concernedly. He is always so hale.

'Excess of joy. Surplus of ecstasy. Too much Jenny for this old heart.'

2
Shade

There is a scattering. Maureen and Nicki are going touring together in Nicki's car; Lewis and Serena are off to visit friends in Washington before returning for a few days more at 'Red Earth'.

'I've been helping Serena pack,' Jenny tells Maureen and Jack, accepting coffee. 'She has an awful lot of clothes. Cases and cases of the most astonishing frocks and skirts. She made me try some of her things on.'

'Now *that* I wish I'd seen,' says Jack.

'I looked like a female impersonator,' says Jenny. 'She also wanted to make me up, but then Lewis came in and started to look rather fascinated, so she bundled me out and decided to tell him off instead.'

The voice of Serena can be heard from her bedroom, imperative, directing operations and uttering words like 'useless' and 'can't you tell a petticoat from a brassière?'

'Poor old Lewis,' says Jack. 'He's really coming in for it today. But she has a lot to put up with. My goodness, but ten years ago when she married him, she was still a gorgeous woman, wasn't she, Molly?'

'She was absolutely lovely.'

'On the plump side, but delectable,' Jack licks his lips. 'Looked fifteen years younger than her true age, absolutely chokingly, head-turningly stunningly luscious. You could have eaten her.'

'Cannibal,' says Jenny with distaste.

'No, honestly, it's true.'

'Why did she marry Lewis then?'

'Oh Lewis wasn't always like this, Jenny, with his Godawful piles and his miseries. He was a person of enormous sensitivity and mental power. He and she sort of caved in together. Now they're shadows of their former selves. It's what we dread for ourselves, isn't it, Maureen?'

'I have done. It's receded lately. Go and help out in there, would you, Jack?'

Lewis has finally had enough, and begun to answer back. The female voice is muted, the scold silenced. His monologue rasps through the house like an electric drill, and is again in action hours later while Jenny phones Oliver, uttering its immemorial afflictions as an indignant denunciation of Mother Eve.

'Hang on, Mrs Reinhold, I'll get Oliver for you,' says Renate, with a bland absence of inflection and a considerably improved English accent.

'Could you hurry, please? I'm ringing from America.'

'Here he is. It's your mother, Oliver. Come for breakfast as soon as you're finished, I'll keep it warm in the oven.'

'Hello, Olly, it's me.'

'Where are you?'

'In America. Staying for a while, you knew I was coming, love. Getting better from my illness.' *Should I be here?*

'Oh. Are you having a nice time?'

'Yes thank you, darling,' she answers lamely. *Does the guilt crackle along the wires and give the poor child ear-ache; or does it stop with me*? 'But I'm thinking about you, sweetheart, all the time.'

'Oh,' says Oliver and can apparently rise to no further response.

'I saw a humming-bird at my window this morning.'

'What was it like?'

'Tiny little fellow sitting up and begging in the air, with a long thin bill. And I've seen raccoons, deer, squirrels, fireflies – you wouldn't believe the wildlife here, Olly,' Jenny pleads. 'The forest smells of menthol and oranges.'

'That sounds nice. We have a dog.'

'Good, love. What species? What's its name?'

'It's a red setter called Heidi. Named after Renate's sister. It pees all over the best carpet, Renate was not thrilled, she says it turns her stomach clearing up after Heidi. She keeps on being sick.'

'Who – Renate or the dog?'

'Renate. The dog just pees.'

'Oh. Did she catch the bug?'

'She and Daddy both did – on holiday in Scotland, and it poured with rain, and my sleeping bag was soaked, we had to strike camp and go into a hotel in Braemar. I played with some boys there. They just stayed in their room being sick. I had a good time though.'

Jenny has trouble suppressing her malicious delight. 'Bad luck,' she says cheerfully.

'Yes, but now she's just sick in the mornings, it's not the bug.'

There is a rustling on the line which sounds like a small scuffle or altercation, then Renate's voice unexpectedly replaces Olly's with, 'Mrs Reinhold do not credit Oliver here, he miscalculates. I am just slow in recovering from this damn bug.' Renate's rising tone and deteriorating English signal panic.

Jenny surprises herself by her cool command: '*Ich verstehe wohl*, Renate. Please could I speak to my son in private.'

'Hello, Mummy.'

'Is she listening?'

'Yes. No. She's gone away.'

'Are you all right, Olly?'

'*I*'m all right. Renate isn't. All my six stick-insects hatched. One – Moses – got away while he was supposed to be climbing up my trouser leg and accidentally crawled into Renate's nightgown. She and insects don't get on. Daddy was furious. Renate threatened to – '

'Mrs Reinhold,' comes Renate's voice this time on an extension. 'I have never smacked your boy. Though he is becoming impossible. Please ask Oliver to treat me with more respect. And also he has blacked his friend's eye. His parents were most distressed. His father just laughs, says "Boys will be boys" but for me this is no joke. *Ihr Sohn würdt ein Rowdy, Frau Reinhold*.'

'You can always go home to Germany, I take it, if you don't like your position,' says Jenny with acerbity.

'I can't, I cannot,' weeps Renate. *I'm going to marry your husband*, she does not say, but Jenny hears.

'Would you get off this line, please. This is a private call. Does she hit you, Olly?'

'No. She threatens when she's mad.'

'Do you dislike her very much?'

'No. She's okay.' *I'm getting rid of her, and you can come back,* he does not say.

'Did you bash someone in the eye?'

'Yes. Lawrence. It was just – normal. You know.'

'Do you think you could try not to punch Lawrence in the eye, Olly, as a favour to me? And maybe if it comes over you to put creatures in anyone's bed, you could think of Cruelty to Animals or something, and desist.'

'Okay, Mummy.' Olly laughs right out, joyously. 'When are you coming home?'

'In a fortnight. Then I've got you for a whole week. What shall we do? Think about it. Can you put Renate on the line now, for a minute? Renate,' says Jenny, very tense, her hand clenched hard on the receiver, so that the knuckles whiten. 'Please be kind to Olly. He needs an awful lot of kindness.'

'I *am* kind to him. But you are his mother.' So much is unspoken; the girl's voice is querying, it is like being stroked with antennae.

'You know I want to have Olly to live with me, Renate. Can we meet and talk when I come back, just you and I?'

'Certainly, Mrs Reinhold. Nothing would please me more.'

Oliver's mother sits opposite to Maureen's husband, ill at ease in the wake of the departure of Maureen, Nicki and the house-guests. The early afternoon sunlight pouring through the great window catches the dim gold of the wedding ring, which was Maureen's grandfather's and then her father's and has grown into the flesh of Jack's third finger so that it would have to be cut out if one wished to tamper with it. Looking up, Jenny's eye is led to the mirror on the wall behind him, in which is reflected the portrait of Maureen under which she sits, which dominates the whole room. The portrait was made twenty-five years ago, when Jack's wife was a ripe matron not very much older than Jenny is now. With the eye of omniscience, the severe sitter gazes out with a judgmental aspect from a world of paint which is making a feint at modernism by affecting to reduce her to a system of triangles. The real Maureen appears softer, more contingent than this; the mirrored mimesis has a terrible air which touches a key-note in Jenny. She does not like the picture. She does not like the Maureen it refracts, whose eyes are, without equivocation, telling her to depart. Not in anger, but because there is no place for her in this house. There exists no corner of 'Red Earth' which is not packed with shades of Maureen. She is the stitches that seam the curtains, sewn by her decades ago; the orchids in the great hanging bowl which her hands planted in peat and nourish daily; she is the light in the chandelier and the glass in Jack's hand from which he now drinks, looking down at her, swirling the nearly melted ice-cubes, wondering at her silence. Jenny can hardly breathe for the plenitude of Maureen's suffocating presence. It crams the air from wall to wall, it fingers Jack's face with melancholy mockery from every atom of the containing air.

'I'll never have another child,' she suddenly acknowledges to Jack. 'It's the first time I've ever recognised that. Do you realise I'm thirty-four next birthday: almost middle-aged. Now fancy that. Amongst you here one feels like a child, rich in new beginnings, but I have wrinkles round my eyes and mouth, and a frown-mark where I scowl, and a few grey hairs.'

'You've no grey hairs.'

'I haven't *now*. I plucked them out with tweezers.'

'Oh Jenny!' he laughs. 'You may well have another child.' He saddens. 'But not mine.' With how painful a twist of the knife one made those acknowledgments of the obvious and the assumed. The thought of the possibility of a child from his old blighted seed was almost lewd. 'Not mine.'

'Of course not. You're old enough to be my father. It would be – '

'Unnatural.'

'Yes.'

He almost hates Jenny for agreeing straight out like that, *Of course not* and *Yes*. Yet what could she do but agree? The extent to which he has retarded her from her own generation's life by attaching her to his waning self overwhelms him now: self-gratifying, sordid, so to appropriate her in the Kingdom of the Shades.

'Jenny. I'm so sorry.'

'No. Don't be. You've been heaven and earth to me, Jack.'

'It sounds like a – valediction.'

'No . . . no. Jack, I might get Olly back. Renate is pregnant with Alex's child. She seems eager to be rid of mine now that her own is on the way.'

'But, Jenny, that's too wonderful for words.'

A cold shadow seems to creep over Jack even as he says so, for he knows the boy's retrieval signals his own decline; a chance to make Jenny free of himself and his unwarrantable detention of her in a false past. The seed detained overlong in the underworld of winter: Pluto holding Persephone. There is a piece of music in this revelation, he hears it on the rim of his mind, haunting, thin – two oboes, solo flute.

'I want you to see a proper lawyer when you get back, not that cretinous little creep you saddled yourself with last time – someone effective, which probably means expensive, who will take the bastard on. Will you promise me that?'

'Yes I will. I'll get a woman this time. But, Jack, maybe it won't be necessary. Alex might be prevailed upon to hand Olly over, if he has another infant on the way.'

'God, I hope so. Whatever I can do to help get him back – just say the word.'

'I will. Don't worry.'

'You sound so much firmer.'

'I am firmer. I am.' She looks at Jack with such a direct challenge that he quails. 'You won't leave Maureen, will you, Jack, and come and make a home with us?'

'– No,' Jack hears himself reply, at one remove from himself, as if he'd thrown his voice to the other side of the room, so insufferable is the message he is honour-bound to give. '– No, Jenny, I couldn't do that.'

'Good,' says Jenny. 'That's fine.' She flings him off as once with anger she trounced him in her heart of hearts that windy day on the moors above Haworth; and marched off free of him, the old heavy man buckled to her nervous system with the dead weight of the whole past. '*That*'s okay then. We know where we are.'

Getting up, she rubs her hands together in a gesture of washing. She moves towards the door, brushing past Jack, her head high. *I can manage this. I can get free of you.* She does her best to keep breathing. Her eyes are brilliant with unshed tears. They pierce Jack through.

'Cherubino – Cherubino,' he bursts out. 'You're no more bound to me than I am to you. Would you leave Oliver for me? Choose. Go on. Choose between us. The old man or the boy? The past or the future?' He has both her wrists in his grasp, and he squeezes painfully. *Say my name. Say Jack I choose you.*

'I choose Oliver. Of course I do.'

The blind man learns to read the black pane of the world through fingertips, echo, guesswork, intuitions. The whole darkened body becomes at times lit up like a visionary peacock's tail instinct with eyes. Seeing through his pores he navigates the unmediated loneliness of his world. The stroke victim finds a compensatory periscope in the right lobe of his brain, for seeing round the blanched wall of language's erasure. Springtime will come to left-handed, right-brained Jenny too, she knows it, in the least expected fashion, learning from scratch how to see without the aid of Jack, how to feel her way in the deep privation that will come when his breast is lost to her head, his powerful hand to her blind, beseeching fingers. The decisive phase in Jenny's metamorphosis is already felt at work within her, like the quickenings of imaginary pain in the raw stumps of an amputee, before they heal and quieten enough to bear the crutches. She feels a surge of future strength as she and Jack move out of Maureen's house together, at peace, companionate, now that the worst has been said that can be said, and thread the labyrinth of young saplings and the parent tamarack on the short cut to the lake. She never before felt quite as close to him as in this recessional through the resinous sanctuary of the forest.

So it is over, or on the verge of being over. The freak plant bastardised of opposites does not expect longevity but buds, flowers and perishes in five minutes of eternity. We knew that – but it's still a shock, Jack thinks, leading the way along the margin of the stream where it bends sharply west; and she is following so quietly she seems to stalk him like an Indian tracking deer, one cannot be sure of her presence. He does not look behind. Their joint infraction of the laws of nature links and parts them at the same time; they are part of nature but have nothing to give back to nature. *An albino boy* is what he called her son in his mind: but, no, the albino is Jack, sterile Jack with his white head. A flying fish, a black swan, a cross-breed. It is the child that settles things, Jack feels, the conclusive child. The boy of Jenny's runs into the space between them, and the space is taboo, it is no man's land, and the flaxen boy exerts a forcefield like a reverse magnet, pushing Jack off, tugging Jenny in. And that is right. That is just. How cruel to array myself against a mere child. But Jenny's albino boy is David to his Goliath; he stands there at the margin of the stream with his sling drawn back, Jack can almost see him on the bank, and his hair has darkened as it was bound to do with time and maturity, and he draws back the sling with the stone, with practised, flexile hand, taking aim at the colossal shadow Jack has flung across his mother. *Yes: do that: don't spare me,* Jack encourages the boy. *Come on, why do you delay? See the old beggar off.*

The reeds in the inlets cast exquisite reflections in a linear tracery exact as the proof of a geometrical theorem upon that upside-down world dreaming down there. As do small birds that stand on legs like parallel stems alongside the reeds and have their own inverted counterparts below; and as the bird stabs its prey, it meets its own bill like a pouncing blade coming up to meet it. The old man, epicene, amphibious, wanders along beside his shadow at the water's edge, and Jenny rambles along behind him.

'Are you still with me?' he asks, not turning.

'Still with you.'

'Here's the pool.'

The path around the pool is spongy with powdered filaments of last year's trees, scrolls of birch bark, shavings of pine. Her feet sink into the absorbent mat, she is assimilated into the silence of that green place as into the round of a thinking mind. The water is hemmed with pine and larch whose boughs reflect upon themselves above that answering mirror. Fishes mouth the surface. Peaceful whirlpools from their nosings grow and die. In this sanctuary only poor addled Thoby is an estranged element. He creeps along at Jack's heels and seems obscurely troubled by the pool, second home though water is to Newfoundlands. Suspicious of his own shadow, Thoby has taken to barking at the very things that should give him comfort – his basket, his bit of blanket and his rubber bone. If you throw a stick for him to retrieve, Thoby hares in the opposite direction. He has given Maureen a little nip when she called him to heel, to her reproachful grief; has in effect departed from himself into a canine wilderness of paranoid anxiety. Only Jack is sure of him, and has his measure. Now that great black snout insinuates itself into Jack's flapping trouser-leg as if the creature were in search of the quickest route home. Jack stops and Thoby leaps up at him, paws scrabbling on his master's chest, so that Jack almost topples. Grasping his legs, he levers Thoby to the ground, crouches and holds the great head between his hands, enquiring 'What's up, Thoby? What's the trouble, boy?' his face up close. He receives an impassioned licking from that rough, wet tongue, and a whiff of powerful fear. He strokes back Thoby's forehead with firm palm so that the whites of the eyes show; Thoby pants fast, alert as if for dangers that might find loopholes even in Jack's guarantee of shelter. 'Come on now. What's the problem?' Through the language of the eyes Thoby explains to Jack that the falling skies are the problem, and striding trees and level planes of water, and bodies that scuttle beneath ferns, and barbed wire coiled in dappled shadow where the scents are most potent, and Jack, understanding the sum of this all too well, signals back in the same code that he has no easy answer to the foreign character of the creation. *I am not God*, he says to Thoby, *but subject, just like you.*

'What's wrong with Thoby?'

'Goodness knows. He's never been the same since he got lost that time.'

'He bays in the night.'

'I know he does.'

'I hear you talking to him. You talk to him like a human.'

'Do I? I never thought of that.'

'He really matters to you, doesn't he?'

'Of course he does. You jealous or something?'

'You can't be jealous of a *dog*.'

'You don't like dogs, do you, Jenny?'

'They've scared me ever since I can remember.'

'Why? He's gentle. Stroke him – go on, Jenny, stroke the poor old boy.'

Jenny's inexperienced hand on the creature's head masters its own fears, and unexpectedly has the effect of soothing and comforting Thoby.

'Jack, could I swim?'

'Of course, sweetheart, but I've no towels.'

'That's okay. I'll dry off on my sweater. Are you coming?'

He wants to come, is jealous of the very water that has her. But lately – he couldn't date it but it's been creeping along his arteries, lodging in his marrow – he hasn't felt all that well. Nothing you could name: a liverishness, fatigue, the odd pain or two in his chest, the sort you close your mind to the minute it's gone. A few years ago he'd have let everybody know about it, *Mother I've a pain, what are you going to do about it?* Now he leaves all that to Lewis. He wants Jenny to think he's a man until the last possible moment.

'I won't come. I'll watch. And paddle. And nurse poor old Thoby out of his manic phase. There's a little beach down here, Jenny, if you want to come, which we and the children always used for swimming in the old days.'

In the circle of silt, sheltered by dense shrubs, Jack sits down on a stone in the sun to remove his shoes and socks, and peeps while Jenny peels off her shirt and jeans; and her slender, white, vulnerable flesh enters the natural scene. While she tries the water, he approaches but does not touch, though her skin hurts his senses as if she both stroked and refused him. The dark wedge of pubic hair, her nipples erect with the cold, there is such a yearning to take hold of her and such an awe of her defencelessness which must not be profaned.

'It's icy.'

'Thought better of it?'

'No.'

For a moment as she takes the plunge, smashing the age-old tranquillity of the pool, he sees the cold white dive of her body as that of a boy, not a woman, and as she comes up, sleeked hair darkly plastered to her head, her body with its small breasts and narrow hips is that of a stripling youth: the youth he first sighted at Florence, and so wanted, and had to have, and now must forfeit. Pain; pain. He'd rather rip her to pieces than let her go. Death would be far far more desirable than the loss of that pale, cool water-spirit who now takes off for the centre with a thunderous wake.

She is a good swimmer but more bold than she is strong. She should not go too deep.

'You're too far out!' he gets up and calls. 'Come back to shore now.'

A white arm waves. 'It's great! Come in!'

'Come – back – out – now – Jenny. *Now*,' he roars; and it is like calling in Frank and Tommy when they had races over that treacherous area thirty years ago; and going back beyond that it is like calling out in his need and desire to some other child – who? – decades since. Old radio signals blur and crackle with interference in his *déjà vu*; but here it comes again, an image of a forbidden boy tangled in water-weed, and he reaches out –

'No!' calls Jenny. 'You come in!'

'*No*!' call Frank and Tom mutinously to their stranded paterfamilias, and crooked arms thrash the water as they sprint across the diameter.

No, implores the boy decades old, as Jack's underwater hands clasp his narrow, bony hips.

Jenny lies back relaxing upon the cold quilt of the water. Her hands feather the water on either side. Her head is well back, her breast gleams through the swirl in the sunlight. From her near-still body, concentric ripples glide and die. It is now that Thoby, obeying in a confused trance the ancestral promptings of his tribe, elects to save Jenny from drowning. With a furious charge he enters the water, conveying himself with thrusts of his webbed feet towards drifting Jenny.

'Thoby! Get back!' calls Jack. 'What in hell do you think you're doing?'

The great black body steers powerfully through the water, making nothing of the journey. She hears nothing till the dog is almost upon her. A massive black head looms upon hers, its eyes are staring, its muzzle drawn right back over the teeth. She panics, smacks at Thoby, is grazed by his claws and goes under. Bursts up above the surface and shrieks, pushing, spitting. Thoby dives for her. Underwater, wrestling with his black power, the lungs are bursting, a shout's caged in the top of her head. Breaks the surface for the second time, hollers at the top of her voice, then gives up. Jenny's panic ebbs, she pushes off from Thoby's chest and breast-strokes a lame couple of yards. Thoby cruises companionably beside her, his soft wake fanning out behind in a great smooth V. But she is tiring; the cold reaches into Jenny's muscles, they spasm in her leaden body. Time slows; slows again. The roof of the sky is low to the water. Compressed in that narrow chamber of air, Jenny hears her ears boom like a drum, the forests collapse around the pool and the deluge of their needles on the water breeds a million floating splinters of light which perforate Jenny's eye as she flails for home. The figure on the shore roars like an animal in pain. Only the fellow swimmer is free from the terminal state of pandemonium into which all other existences have entered. Jenny grasps at Thoby's coat with perishing fingers. He angles himself obligingly so that she may loop one arm around his neck and with one fist grasp a wad of long hair, and be dragged to land. The black well-meaning villain sails like a dolphin into shore with his white salvage; and shakes his saturated waterproof pelt with satisfaction at the inimical trees and skies who implied it couldn't be done. Jenny, bundled up in Jack's clothes and her own, has taken no harm.

'He was only trying to be friendly,' says Jack, thinking, *If he goes on like this he'll have to be put down*, and this thought brings such a drilling pain that he speaks quite sharply to Jenny. 'It was entirely your own fault, you shouldn't have been showing off out there so deep, and you shouldn't have panicked when you saw Thoby.'

'I'm sorry, Thoby,' says Jenny. She puts her arms round the dog's wet, bewildered face. The fear has entirely gone.

'I thought you were a boy out there, Cherubino. As I did when I first set eyes upon you in Florence under the *Primavera*. A shivery feeling of recognition. Goodness, whatever does it mean about me?'

Hard-faced, reactionary, virtuous Father comes crystal-clear to Jack's mind: John Middleton the First whom the young Jack lovelessly obeyed. His heavy hand thrust Jack up to declare himself a converted Christian at the Revival that time, when the boy whispered 'But I'm not converted' and Father whispered back 'Oh yes you damned well are', shoving him between the shoulder-blades towards the pulpit. Niggers and queers were 'human trash' to Father. Even Jack's musicianship was reckoned a nancy trade. 'Hey there, Pansy, help me out with this . . .' How he winced. 'Come on Lady . . .' More kudos in the honest trade of piano-removing than in the effeminate fingering of suspect keys. Jack did not dispute with Father; prided himself on being one of the few musicians of his day who was a straight heterosexual male.

She turns her head. Jack sees the boy again. *Go back, go back down, I don't want to know*. But the boy won't go. He is Christopher, Jack's young stepbrother, killed at Salerno at twenty, which Jack in the midst of his mourning registered with relief: for now nobody would ever know. He himself would cease to know. It never happened.

Chris, Christie. The child is nearly eleven years old, Jack fourteen. Christopher's eyes are an unusual navy shade of blue, too dark, his lips so full they seem to pout; his face is white and rather angular, and he has a shock of chestnut hair, cut short at the back of the neck but elsewhere luxuriant. Jack's stepmother scissors it twice a month, the child high up on a kitchen stool, parting it severely and plastering it down with water. But the hair is wildly animate, it mocks kempt usage. Now in a characteristic gesture, Christopher carries his fallen locks to one side, left to right, snared between index and second finger of his right hand. He looks Jack straight in the eyes, queryingly: *Yes? Yes, Jack?* Jack's heart beats up. *It is really you. As if I saw you yesterday, not fifty-five years ago. Follow me: you always did.* They are going to swim in the little pond at home. Christopher strips off, dives in; Jack too. They racket about; churn the muddy waters which are really quite disgusting when you think about it – you can quite see why they are out-of-bounds. A cesspit, a quagmire. All round the pond a kind of algae like chickweed breeds, lime-green and slimy if it gets on your skin, and emanating a smell far on the bilious side of unwholesome; but distinctive. Even when you've showered, there is still the aroma of green stuff left on your body – which is how the stepmother knows if you've been trespassing there. She sniffs you. It is a guilty smell. As Jack and Christopher, years on, romp in the murky waters, that stink is in his nostrils again, horrible and exciting.

Your skin, white, let me, let me, you know what I want to do, let me do it to you.

his nipples small delicate like little pink buttons made of puckered flesh, or seeds, hard on the tongue as he licks them; thin thin shoulders in Jack's maturing hands, he turns the child around and around in the water, mouths the beautiful shoulder-blades with the cleft behind them, collar-bone, ribs through the skin, and the soft depths of his stomach,

oh Chris let me let me,

his own erection is so hard it hurts, and he will hurt Chris if Chris won't let him, he's so big and Chris so fine-boned: perfectly made, Chris is Jack as Jack would have wanted to be made flesh if anyone had consulted his wishes at the Creation, so

Chris you had better let me,

but Jack is quite unclear about what exactly he wants to do, the child's eyes say

No, please, Jack, no

but his body is permissive; is swaying clay in Jack's searching hands. The excitement of Chris' soft belly, he reaches into it with blind hands, what is in you Chris? What are you? Beautiful between the hip-bones whose slick surfaces Jack's hands flow on, and the small handful of Chris' unready manhood which he finds out with his fingers and rolls in his palm, down there where the child's mud-polluted body vanishes in the soup they swim in. Hunger; hunger; violence; ire; burning compulsion, it centres in the stand of Jack's prick that points out its prey. But he doesn't know what to do; how to appease.

Please Chris touch me

and imploring he steers the child's hand, treading water, stirring the brew; and the boy's wet face is up close to his expressionless but as if he would kiss, and his hand meets Jack's rage of need and then like a fish that flicks from carnivorous jaws he spins from Jack, kicks off furiously from Jack's chest through the green slime to the edge; lopes off fast with his clothes, without a word. Jack in the shameful pool of filth eases himself there in a fit of violent self-loathing and incomprehension.

Mother's boy, he thinks, and he notices at table that Chris, the true son, gets the steak without the gristle, the larger of the two baked apples with cinnamon and honey; that Jack the infiltrator gets to dry the dishes she washes, while Christopher's presence is known solely by the echo of his boot on his ball as he plays football against the paddock wall.

Fifty-five years on the graves all open and their occupants arise: the boy's face, waif-pale, just as it was, seeking acknowledgment, asking atonement. *Forgive me*, begs Jack of the wronged child, *I was young and brutal, you had your mother; I had none.* He would have been, what, let's see, sixty-six or thereabouts now, how impossible that seems, and has been for more than forty years a thing of the past, the deciduous leavings of the family tree, swept away long ago. Look at his face so angular and definite, hint of a cleft in the chin giving the illusion of blood-kinship; the pretty lively child, always on the run, fleet of foot, unrepeatable dark blue eyes. The complex of emotion: pitying love and envious rapacity, the wish to own that face, peel it off like a rubber mask and possess it as his own. Beside that fey, graceful, tightrope-balancing body, Jack's own was lubberly, his face a peasant's. Surely all the mortal sins collected in Jack beside that filthy pool: envy and greed, concupiscence and cruelty.

'Why are you crying Jack? All is well, I'm here.'

He opens his eyes upon the clean place and the dear eyes in their clemency. He has never deserved this late remission but here is the assurance of Grace, who tells him but in no actual words, *Mother never left you, you were mistaken about that. Understandably so, but mistaken nevertheless.*

Later, lying together in Jack's bed in the still of the evening, Jenny dozes but he is wide awake. The sense of healing is so strong; the scar tissue become tender and supple again, the strain relaxed over certain areas of his consciousness. He would like to see Jacques again soon and call him brother. When Lewis returns they must discuss their early affection, he will tell Lewis how he loved him, and loves him still, clarifying the past and sharing the present. He takes Jenny's drowsy head to his breast in a gesture of maternal cherishing.

3
Rage

'She's a devil, that woman, an incarnate goddam sex-mad she-devil – I'm telling you Jack she's a filthy slut of a whore of a bitch on heat and that's a scientific opinion.'

'Good gracious,' says Jack mildly. Lewis is brick-red, swallowing neat bourbon as if it were coke, and looks fit to have a seizure. He and Serena have returned early from Washington, the latter in storms of tears, the former apoplectic.

'I'll throttle her,' promises Lewis. 'Pour me another for Godsake. Never trust a woman, my friend, never trust them, keep a man-eating shark or a praying mantis, keep a skunk or a squid rather than a human woman.'

'What happened?' asks Jack. 'I wouldn't have another just now, Lou . . .' Lewis heaves himself to his feet, lumbers over to the cabinet and fills his tumbler to the brim. It slops over Maureen's mother's best Indian wool hearthrug as he lowers himself back into his seat. Jack wipes up the mess; Lewis gulps some more fire into his belly; Jenny is upstairs hastily changing the beds around and removing the traces of herself from Jack's room. She is weeping quietly, continually.

'What happened? What do you mean, what happened? What do you think happened?' demands Lewis quarrelsomely, indicating that it would be no challenge to his ingenuity to seize on something of which to accuse his old friend.

'I haven't a clue. Tell me if you want to. Meanwhile I'm locking the drink away. You've had too much.'

'Bastard,' mutters Lewis, with evil eyes. 'I suppose you've had her too, have you? *Friend.*'

'I am not following you.'

'Had her. Her. Up there. Had her for dinner and spat her out. The whole lot of you. *Yes, you,*' he suddenly barks at the top of his voice, *'you dirty little trollop!'* and all at once subsides into tears, weeping a copious volume in a short period.

'I assure you, Lewis . . . I've never even considered . . .'

'Oh!' says Lewis, bridling again. 'So she's not good enough for you, is that it? I tell you, Jack, she's a beautiful woman, abeautifulwoman.'

'She's *your* wife!'

'Oh is that so? Really? It's news to me, let's tell her, she might like to know – the bitch the slut the – '

'You're drunk. I'll put you to bed.' Jack is at the end of his tether.

'Oh yes Randall Jack what'syourname that's the idea, pin on his diapers, give him a bottle, tuck the old fool up in bed, and then go screw that whore my wife – '

'Are you saying that Randall – '

'Randy Randall, aptly named. Denise takes me off to see the sights – pushes me from Memorial to Memorial in a wheelchair, the goddam Folger the National Gallery the whole damn boring lot – and where is my wife? In bed with Randall that's where.'

'Oh come on, Lou. Come on now. It strains credulity.' Randall, Lewis' host and a real estate dealer, is a dapper, impeccable, churchy little man, of the utmost respectability and piously right-wing opinions.

'I *saw* them at it. I watched for five minutes from the open doorway. A real edifying sight.'

'Oh dear.'

'You see, you just don't know, Jack. You don't know – how gorgeous she is, real gorgeous. Just plain gorgeous. There's no other word.'

'That's true, I don't,' says Jack nimbly, claiming diplomatic immunity.

'And she throws herself at everything in pants.'

That's true too, thinks Jack, who found the experience embarrassing but recalls liking Serena's eyes a while back; and now, for her sake as well as Lewis', draws up his chair and says, 'She's maybe lonely, Lou?'

'Why should she be lonely? She's got me.'

Quite so, thinks Jack. *Enough said.* 'And she feels her age?'

'I give her everything she wants,' Lewis grumbles on, but less aggressively. 'Clothes. Holidays. Outings.' He weeps. 'I never really reached her.'

'It's not too late,' coaxes Jack's blithe springtime.

'It is,' desponds the ancient wreckage of Lewis.

'If you love her, you may have to let her – be free.'

'No.'

'Can I come in?'

'No, go away,' says Serena, but the key turns in the lock and Jenny enters to find Serena hunched in her petticoat on the bed, her face red, puffy and blotched. There is a bruise on her cheek.

'Is Maureen there?' she whispers. 'I want Maureen.'

'She isn't here,' Jenny whispers back. 'I'm afraid there's only me. What can I do for you?' She kneels at the bedside and offers her arms. Serena, bursting into a new flood of tears, falls upon her neck. 'Things may not be as bad as you think,' Jenny suggests, but her wishful thinking is at once contradicted by the human earthquake below the timbers of their floor, which is dementedly cataloguing the attributes of female dogs.

'He hit me by accident. Flailing about with his walking-stick.'

'What's the matter with him?'

'Senile decay,' answers Serena with better spirit, and blows her nose passionately. 'In combination with sexual jealousy. An odious mixture. Pass me those tissues, dear, I'm obviously in for a long bout.'

Having never held a plump, soft body before, Jenny marvels at the fullness and give of it; is both repelled and interested. *So this is how a real woman feels?* Her own bony little body is a handful of twigs by comparison with this ripe fruit. *How can Jack prefer this stick-insect, this bean-pole who is me?* 'Is your husband always like this?'

'Oh no,' sniffs Serena. 'Usually he just sits moaning and groaning about his bodily ills. I take no notice. But then he's never seen me in bed with anyone else before.'

'Did he – *see*?' asks Jenny pruriently.

'Oh yes. I'll never forgive him.'

'For . . . ?'

'For looking, of course. At his age he should just be getting on with his raffia-work – or cultivating radishes – or whatever old people are supposed to do. What does he expect of me? Tied to Methuselah. I'd rather be married to a pickled mummy in Tutankhamun's tomb. A pickled goddam mummy would be much more fun.'

'I can understand that.'

'I like you. You are a real human being.'

'I like you too.'

'You see,' says Serena, gripping Jenny's hand so that her rings dig into it. 'I feel I am a ridiculous spectacle.'

'You are anything but,' Jenny says, squeezing the hand back, cutting rings and all. And receiving these confidences from the poor face, she feels it too, an emanation of warmth from the vulnerable inner world.

'When I was a young girl in California, I used to sit in the garden and watch the next-door neighbour in hers, she'd sit out there under a parasol suckling her baby. It was a pretty sight. But she had a milk-production problem: too much. She was overflowing. Far more than any normal baby could be expected to cope with. She'd show me her tits – hard and overflowing, she'd have to draw it off. The tenseness was so sore, she used to say, that she'd be dancing from foot to foot with pain. I touched it once, rock-hard, and then the milk just violently spurted – quite a jet. I never forgot it. That would be forty years ago, I don't recall her name – just the agonising surplus. And it's how I feel, I have too much affection in me, too much need. I don't *want* to stay with Lewis but I've nowhere to go. If only Father were alive – but he'd be a hundred and . . . what would he be? born in 1887, he'd be a hundred and two. Still technically possible, but . . . ah well.'

'You haven't lost your father, if he is still alive – *in* you,' suggests Jenny. 'He hasn't aged in there. Time is different.'

'Do you really think so?' Serena pathetically clings to this light spar. 'Do you?'

'Of course.'

'But how do you know?' *How do I know? Because of Jack I know it*, Jenny suddenly realises. *Nothing is lost, all within is in safe-keeping, even if I never see him again, there is strength in me for the road, growing, growing.*

'One feels one has – outlived oneself – and that the past, being dead, rejects one – he rejects me, he has no mercy, he throws me off.'

'He doesn't. Your loneliness says so, it lies to you.'

Throughout their conversation the rumble of the altercation

downstairs has been playing a bass line. A loud chant now arises, and Jack shouting 'Oh shut up for Godsake – you'll give yourself a rupture!' in a tone of terminal exasperation.

'When is Maureen getting back?'

'We don't know. Now look, I'll go down and speak to him. He can't go on like this. Okay?'

'No, don't . . . What'll you say?' Serena is a child in Jenny's hands. Jenny, from compendious experience of the infantile, garnered both from Olly and from Jack, feels (to her own surprise) fairly confident about tactics.

Serena's husband, like some antediluvian spectator at a football game, is still muttering and bouncing his empty tumbler on the arm of the chair, as if cheering on a team. His legs are splayed, his face red, he appears to be enjoying himself.

'Shut up,' says Jenny, marching in. He stares, Jack stares. Jenny stands over Lewis with her hands on her hips.

'How dare you behave like that? How dare you? It's a disgusting exhibition.'

Lewis, glazed, has no response to hand. 'Er . . .' he says, looking round for support, but his roving eye happening to meet the glacial gaze of the portrait of Maureen in her matriarchal and judicious aspect, is gorgonised, and he is silent.

'I'm asking you. How dare you?'

'She's a slut,' drawls Lewis, laying hold on his refrain and growing bolder now that he has caught his own drift again.

'You should be ashamed of yourself. All she wants is a little love and care. Just because you're old, you don't have to be a drunken cantankerous self-pitying brutal old bore. Do you? Come on: *do* you?'

'I'm not a bore.'

'Yes you are. And the rest.'

'Jack. Take this woman away.'

'Don't you appeal to Jack. How dare you treat your wife like that?'

'Not my wife. Whore. Slut.'

'You don't deserve her.'

'I don't. I know I don't. I never thought I'd keep her – even this long. What do you want me to do?'

'I don't know what you *can* do,' says Jenny, deflating at the old man's sudden capitulation. She sits down on the settee and regards him in perplexity. 'Do you still love her?'

'I don't know. I've forgotten,' says Lewis, and falls fast asleep.

Maureen and Nicki return late that afternoon to a quiet and orderly household. Lewis has been tucked up in the games room, where his condition can be monitored if you check his rhythmic snoring outside the door. Serena has been put to bed with two sleeping pills, and as she has had little rest during the past week with its calls to erotic exertion, she went out like a light. Jack is in the kitchen, frying pancakes; Jenny, curled up on the hearthrug with one arm round Thoby, is reading a book before the logfire. She scrambles up and embraces Maureen.

'How lovely to see you – but you're home early. Did you have a good time?'

'Very good.' Maureen is in an uncharacteristic check shirt and jeans; she does not look quite right in this attire, and seems a trifle uncertain of her bearings, as if to enter her own house and find such a state of domestic peace reigning called her into question.

'What's that smell of cooking? Who's doing it?'

'Jack is. He's making pancakes for my tea. Are you two very hungry? He can do some for everyone, there's loads of batter.'

'Jack can't cook,' says Maureen definitively. 'He never has been able to. He can't boil an egg. He eats raw spinach cold from the can.'

'He can now,' says Jenny.

'Jack and cookery just do not go together,' repeats Maureen, not really arguing; just reaffirming the axiomatic. 'They never have done and they never will do. I don't let him in my kitchen normally, Jenny: he drops things. Soup-stains appear on the ceilings. Silver spoons dive down the waste disposal.'

'Jack hasn't done any of that. He's made me beautiful meals. He must have been doing secret training,' *a sort of culinary resistance movement*, thinks Jenny, digging in against the returning regime.

'You English and your politeness . . . Jack, what *are* you doing?' Maureen is upon him.

'Molly, *hello*. I didn't hear the car. Had a good time? I hope you're hungry – ?'

The pancake keeping warm under the grill is undeniably an example of perfection. It is golden and succulent, with a garnish of lemon ready to add, it has been flipped with panache; it steams and is fragrant.

'Oh *Jack*. That's not how you do it.' Maureen looks at him with her head on one side, her mouth pursed. 'Here, give it to me.' She takes her apron from the peg.

'No, no, let *me* feed you.'

'Pass me the batter. Let go of the pan.' She chivvies him to one side. All Jack's cookery skills fail him. He stands there in his pin-striped apron in which a moment ago he had been confidently humming to the sizzling music of the pan. The spatula with which he had been conducting the Pancake Divertimento now wilts at his side, in foolish impotence. If Jack essayed a new pancake, it would turn to instant carbon or escape the great iron pan altogether and hurry to a destination in the dog's bowl.

'We went all the way along to Rehoboth Beach – a junky place but the condominium was so nice – bumped into two friends of Nicki there – yes, go along, out of my kitchen with you, Jack . . . no place for a man – '

'*Marmie*,' said Nicki, and that is all she says, but Maureen colours up, and looks flustered.

'Oh all *right*,' replies Maureen. 'but he really can't cook.'

'Sit down, Marmie – come, shoo. Jack and I will organise the meal together and we will try not to burn anything.'

Maureen retreats but looks extremely unhappy, and her gentle figure in the denims and shirt, sitting beneath her own imperious portrait, calls to mind an abdication-scene.

'How are my plants?' she asks Jenny, rather faintly. 'How are my dogs? I hope Jack didn't accidentally exterminate anything in my absence.'

'All alive but waiting for you to you come home.' Laughter rings out from the usurped kitchen. Maureen looks close to tears but is diverted by the account Jenny can give of the arrival of Serena and Lewis earlier in the day.

'A thoroughly ill-matched couple,' judges Maureen. She can do little more than pick at her pancake when it comes, though it does look appetising and smells so good. She has never felt so undefended. Plans keep misfiring in every possible way. She comes home to find little Jenny and her husband in harmony, the former not at all disillusioned with the latter, as far as can be made out, but rather the reverse: secure, infolded to one another. She senses their peaceful joy in one another. It hurts; it hurts: so that she would like to rage aloud like an infant or an animal. She remembers having that with Jack. In the bright hinterland of early days.

And the holiday with Nicki did not go well. Once out of sight of 'Shadows' and 'Red Earth' she began to feel exposed, uncertain. She kept swallowing. She perused her own scared eyes in the vanity mirror. Nicki drove. The further out they got, the older and more self-conscious she felt. Nicki's bare, sinewy arms twisted the wheel. She drove fast along the Interstate, too fast Maureen felt. Her heart raced. Her mouth was dry, she licked her lips frequently. And because of her tension Nicki's behaviour became more and more domineering, cocksure. She harassed Maureen to say if she wanted coffee, was she hungry? tired? – pestered to find out what was the matter. Was it anything she'd said or done because if so, for goodness sake say and she'd retract whatever it was, or make amends. Maureen looked down at her own arm with the turquoise bracelet, reclining in a patch of sunlight along the window-edge of the car-door, and it was an old woman's arm, *parchmenty old skin*, she thought with disgust, *loose, flabby flesh dropping away from the bone*; and though it was the same arm which she had wound round her friend with careless joy the previous day, with its soft-skinned hand Nicki loved to kiss, now she saw it otherwise. *Leathery old throat, tired breasts, legs like brittle sticks*: she saw it all. Away from home, the kind light that obscured her blemishes was replaced by the indecent eye of day, lifting the film of illusion from her person like a membrane. *Old old old old old old* was all the tune her mind could toll, then *fool fool fool*, 'Oh let me alone!' she burst out at Nicki, just outside Rehoboth, her eyes tight shut and longing for the decent anonymity of home. At which Nicki was silent for a full period of three hours and a quarter, carrying in the cases to the condominium, making up the beds, showering, shopping, taking a dip in the pool. There, the unexpected appearance of the lesbian couple Clara and Sandy put the finishing touches to Maureen's misery. Kind, voluble, youthful company, they sat in their swimsuits by the nearly deserted pool and prattled of mutual friends, of Marguerite the actress and how she'd had a nervous breakdown, and 'My God,' said Nicki coarsely, 'she is one hell of a desirable woman – but brittle. I must have her to stay.' Brazenly staring at the blonde female lifeguard flaunting her daring crimson bikini; raffishly strolling round the rim of the pool, hands in jeans' pockets, and chatting the girl up like a man, shooting Maureen a look as if to say *What's up, Marmie? Don't you like me after all? This is how I was before you house-trained me, I could be again. No, I don't like you one little bit,* thought Maureen, *but I dislike me more.* 'Are you coming for a swim?' wondered Clara and Sandy, but no, the grey woman thought she'd stay put, it was too cold for old ladies in the pool at this time of year. She pulled her skirts down over her knees and tied a headscarf against the breeze while their sleek porpoise bodies flowed darkly up and down the tiled and turquoise shimmer of the human aquarium. Nicki took them all on and beat the lot, even the lifeguard, with those powerful thighs and shoulders, and on her wake bobbed helplessly two gossiping old ladies in yellow costumes and matching caps holding what seemed to be a lifelong conversation in the shallow end. Out came Nicki, and Maureen towelled her dry. Her body, streaming with water, was an athlete's, imposing; she seemed taller, seemed somehow to tower statuesque and uncompromising as a Florentine sculpture, beyond reach. She was in a sulk. Maureen had the memory of her children in that state. And though she treasured even the footprint her wet sole left on the warm concrete, she was already beyond the extravagances of Eros. Nicki's friends came everywhere with them. The very respect with which she was treated saddened and demoralised her. Her limp came back, her bad arm twinged. The three went walking at sunset for miles along the Atlantic. Maureen stayed home and watched television. At night, Nicki slept the long, deep sleeps of the fit and active; Maureen lay awake, thinking of the children, and how she must invite the grandchildren, and what she would cook them for treats. Then, when at last she arrived home and sought to restore her household to its former order, Nicki said *Marmie*, just that, and ousted her from the hub of her own world. She cannot eat the pancake. It looks good. The crisp part around the edge is a delicate web of lace. The tang of the lemon on the sugar granules stirs her appetite. The plate on her lap goes cold.

'You don't like it, Mother?' asks Jack in consternation.

'It's very good. I can't eat it though,' says Maureen, putting down the fork, bending her head. She has never cried in front of Jack: she is not going to start now. All she wants is that Nicki should go home; Jenny vanish. Jack can stay. He is part of the structure: a timber wall, a door she can shut and lock, a window with curtains.

Nicki removes the plate from her lap, setting it quietly on a side-table. She rests one hand softly on Maureen's shoulder and bends her head to Maureen's bent head.

'I'll go now, Marmie. Give you some peace. Forgive me.'

'Is she not well?' asks Jack in the hall, showing Nicki out.

'It was an absurd fiasco from start to finish. My fault entirely. I'm sorry. Give her some space, I should – just let her be.'

Jenny has put on another log, and is riddling the fire with the poker. Maureen may be feeling the cold, if she's overtired. The pine-logs being slightly damp spit and smoke, emitting a pungently resinous scent. That brings in Thoby in a rush, scenting danger. Catching sight of the stranger, he bares his teeth and snarls, then barks a warning to his shadowy owners.

'Hey – Thoby – stop it *at once*! It's Mother come home. For goodness' sake!'

Jack drags Thoby off by his chain, but the great animal sticks foursquare in an attitude of aggression, battening his claws into the weft of the carpet. Raising his head, he barks deafeningly at the trespasser. Maureen's tears well slowly and overflow.

'No, Thoby, no.' Jenny taps him on the snout with two fingers; his bloodshot, confused eyes focus on the face of quiet authority above him. He submits to be led out of the room, his tail low.

'Damned schizophrenic dog,' grunts Jack. He straightens up. Maureen's face, awash with tears, is tilted slightly upward, her eyes closed, her mouth pulled out tight; she sits bolt upright, the palms of her hands flat on her jeans like some hieratic figure. She has not cried since Mother's death, and then never in front of Jack; and before then not since childhood. The shock of seeing her break is total. The walls tilt, the ceiling slips. Jack has no precedent for dealing with such eventualities. He takes the knowledge gleaned from loving Jenny and offers to Maureen all the latterday tenderness of which he is capable.

'My heart failed me, and I felt so – bygone.'

Maureen forgets her pride and his catalogue of cardinal sins and lets him hold her to his breast; and there weeps, his great hands clasping her head, swaying against the substance of Jack, carried nearly off her feet.

It's finished, it is finished. Jenny watching from the doorway is beside herself with grief. She knew and he knew it was over, but they never said goodbye and she didn't want to see it. There is a polarity between knowing and seeing. Out in the yard with the dogs she marches about, up and down, up and down, biting her nails, wringing her hands, saying Jack's name, calling Olly's, under the billion falling atoms of the skies. Clouds scud in from the Atlantic, over 'Shadows', and discharge their cargo of cold and wet over trees and lake, over Jenny and the dogs, over the roof and windows of 'Red Earth'.

The faces around the supper-table late that night all have red eyes, with the exception of Serena who has one red and the other a livid blackish-green. The drunken rage has died in Lewis who sits blearily opposite his defaced spouse at the oval dining-table drinking Perrier water and nibbling crackers, and communing with the deep pain which is scrabbling like a trapped crab in the lumbar region of the back. He does not distinctly remember having called Serena a 'filthy bitch, slut and whore' though he knows there was an altercation of some sort in which he gave voice rampantly; and he knows she slept with Randall but what the hell? The bony little nancy. He recalls Randall's bare backside revealed to public view as the little guy did all he could to bestride the voluptuous Serena – a white scrambling puny fellow much like a skinned mouse. He doubts if Serena got much satisfaction. *And she sure isn't getting it from me.* He is sorry he caught her with the knob of his walking-cane; he wishes he hadn't, though a part of him rejoices that he can still assert his manhood despite his reduced condition. But he has begged her pardon. Whether Serena accepted his apology was unclear; she offered none of her own. But she cheered right up.

Serena sits between poor little Bean-pole and her dear Maureen, and feels (despite the hot distended ache under her eye) a return of comfort, and assurance. Lewis is vanquished.

She has made her point. If he wants to retain her services as nurse to his old age, he is going to have to accept her new life of freedom. She enjoyed it extraordinarily with Randall. Though he is not a massive man like Lewis and Jack, he is a wiry one, and a witty. Lewis and Jack, they are like great panting dogs, adoring, idealising, possessive, coming down on you with a heavy weight (she surveys them now, picking at her Brie and black grapes) but ultimately she suspects they hold you in contempt. But Randall now: Randall. Teasing her, calculating thrills to offer, nimble, amusing. Serena found she liked that. His blue jokes and salacious stories had her roaring with laughter. It did her good, she just lay there and wept with laughter, and he lay on top of her like the least ponderous of paperweights and laughed with her. She liked the flighty levity, the absence of demand. He bought her negligées and marvellous underwear with holes and frilled transparencies, black suspender belts and tights – she has them now in the case upstairs, and means to wear them often. Denise his wife is a deaconess of the Presbyterian church, a model of piety: a stringy, rigid lass, riddled with inhibitions and with God. Serena saw her brassière and stays drying in the laundry room; thought their elasticated modesty said it all. When Lewis and Serena departed, Denise was already making preparations for a full-scale forgiveness of her back-sliding husband: a trial which he could meet with better fortitude in that he and Serena had already agreed on an assignation in an hotel in New York renowned for its water-beds and Jacuzzis. Fornication is to become Serena's new way of life, and she commits herself to it with the dedication of a nun to her convent. If she cannot attract affection, she can at least enjoy her body, and now reflects that an elderly lover is a real advantage in this day and age, as being less likely to pass on AIDS, in view of his insuperable difficulty of entry. If Lewis doesn't like it: too bad for Lewis.

Maureen quietly presides over a household of which she is queen. But her sovereignty is built on the impairment of several surrenders, her own as well as those of her husband and guests. It is over with Nicki: the impossible, anachronistic joy has quit her, like an over-staying beloved house-guest taking a final leave. She does not know how she will adapt to the clock in this time-zone where she must again be accounted as an old woman without a future. But she is suffused with renewed gratitude for the gifts Nicki brought; and she knows there is a benefit from this magical transformation which will last the remainder of her life. Quite what is nebulous, but real for all that: an energy, a sense of self, like a figure stepping out of its place in a group portrait – the *Primavera* perhaps – to assert a wayward autonomy in the human throng. Now Jack shaves a slice of delicious smoked Swiss cheese for her, butters a roll, and she accepts his offerings lovingly; and can eat at his hands; and has apologised for her rudeness about the pancake. She has asked him to share her bed again when Jenny leaves: just for holding one another in warmth and comfort, she explains, not for sexual sharing, which she does not want. His tears then were hard to bear. He has very occasionally cried before her in the past but his eyes were always dry, he went through the motions merely, like an unproductive mechanism. But now as she has wept before Jack, so Jack has replied with his own sacrifice; and she knew the double source of his anguish, the joy at reclaiming something of her love, the farewell to Jenny, who now sits white-faced between Serena and her husband, and to whom her own heart goes out uselessly in a complex of ways.

Jenny sits very still and tries to chew and swallow what she has in her mouth, which impersonates a helping of ash. Her tongue pushes it from side to side but wherever it tends it binds, sticks to the roof of her mouth and when she forces herself to swallow, her throat tightens and wants to gag. Serena pours her a glass of white wine, it does the trick. She carries on drinking, this seems best. *I give her back to you, I give you now.* There has never been a pain like this, never since the beginning of the world. Never since God aborted her into this void below, where there was no kin waiting to welcome into being this anguishing knot of membrane, jelly of eye, whorl of soft bone, this God-made mistake, has she known such pain.

'Let me fill your glass again.'

Fill me, fill me.

She is a honeycomb of vacant caves and cavities – orifices of mouth and ear, sex and lung – the soughing heart that pumps the obligatory blood. To think of how she is going to leave Jack behind who filled her full and whole, who was comfort and blessing and jester and father, is so frightening.

The skin lifts right off her back at the thought of it, her scalp crawls. She holds the glass to her mouth and looks sidelong to where Jack's hands crumble a roll to a mass of leavings on his plate, his silver knife a gleam dissecting the circle. The cave of her sex cramps in upon absence, his future deeper daily absences. The current of sensation runs wild around the circuit of her nervous system from end to end of her body, from clitoris to instep to bared wrist and inside-lip. There is no one to govern it now, she can't, never could. She can't be anyone without Jack. She will be at the mercy of this pit of need: her unaccommodated self. She can't imagine feeling such pain as she is knowing now and not crying out. Wants to hold herself between the legs like a child and shriek for help.

On her last night she dreams of Oliver and Bradford; that they are going to set up house together on the open moor above the city. In her dream, Olly is insanely zestful and positive about the advantages of their new residence. He points out the healthiness of the good fresh air that whacks in across the scudding heathlands; the undrinkable peaty stream-water with its ferrous tinge reminds him a lot of orange juice, he remarks, as he scoops it up appreciatively in a billy can. He has woven an impromptu tent of the fibrous heather-stems of the old year and implores his dubious mother to lie down and rest in this hand-made, hard-won accommodation. Settling her head on her reedy pillow, Jenny drops off into a deeper rest, untroubled by dreams.

At the airport the following evening, Jenny is quieter and more assured. Jack alternates between jollity and oppressive solicitude, organising for Jenny a seat on the side of the plane nearest the moon – non-smoker, window-seat of course, only the best for Jenny – a view of the Northern Lights laid on. Enough cash? Would you like a newspaper? And ice-cream? Jack has been drinking sherry and is red in the face. If he swallows enough sherry he blanks off to everything save the material claims of the moment, erasing the activities of at least half his brain. A tricky balance: one drop too much, and he becomes cussed and lachrymose, and there is the danger of Virgilian recitation, *Tum pater Anchises . . .* , Dido on her pyre, *Memora me . . .* , eloquent in broad Pennsylvanian Latin. When he gets home he will pour the remainder of the bottle down his throat and crash out just like old times; won't feel, see or recall a thing in that Elysium where Jenny recedes across the ocean, her distress-calls smothered in illimitable distances. He will switch her off; put her out like a cat at night. Jenny will be cancelled; and Jack will swim through the torrential dark in a sea of alcohol, oblivious to the bedlam of his own snores, and awaken tomorrow to the headachy first morning of a new world, bending to fondle Thoby's pelt, to accept a cup of English tea from his wife's hands and that night to welcome into his embrace her anodyne body in their shared bed.

Now he becomes argumentative with Jenny over the carrying of her suitcases. Let me take it for you, dear. No thank you, Jack, I can manage myself. Come on. No. Please, I said please. No Jack, I can carry my own luggage. 'Let her be,' says Maureen. 'She knows her own mind.'

Jenny kisses them goodbye quite calmly, *goodbye goodbye, take care, write soon*, Maureen first, Jack last, inconsequently as a duty-visiting offspring at the parental home who cannot conceal the sense of release. She turns resolutely to go through customs, determined not to turn round and look again; but finds that she does so anyway, and witnesses the retreat of their twin figures across the concourse, two-dimensional under the artificial glare, an elderly couple, the husband rather bent, supporting the wife with his palm beneath her elbow. Jenny shows her boarding card; embarks; the plane taxies, ascends into the roaring void between worlds. As they level out, the pilot calls passengers' attention to a panorama of electric storms crackling below over Delaware, black filthy-looking mushroom-clouds far down beneath her godlike eye, which shoot forth intermittent lightning upon the colonies of earthbound mortals in that gaseous incinerator. The sky above this maelstrom of many black storms is a velvet ocean of navy-blue. Jenny observes with a touch of irony as she flies towards daybreak that, while Jack had indeed commandeered the moon, which rides steadily at her window in milk-white isolation, he has had no luck with the phantasmagoria of the Northern Lights, which remain aloof from his high-handed wizardry.

Part Three

1
Fall

With the fall come the grandchildren, the offspring of their two youngest: Angela's twins, Nicolette and Richard, and Tom's three, Rachel, Matthew and James the two-month-old baby. Maureen now has twelve grandchildren, with yet another announced as pending, and is beginning to feel like a dynasty. The house is full of rough and tumble, they racket about playing table tennis in the games room where Lewis snored in his affliction: Lewis who has now been admitted to an old folk's home where he seems unexpectedly tranquil, enjoying all the lavish care and concern that money is able to buy. He has taken, he tells her, to water-colour painting and to moulding clay models; is surrounded by ancient widowed ladies who all pet him outrageously and are sitting for portraits. He obliges his sitters by blurring their images to a semblance of half their ages, and is grateful for their attentions, though he confides to Maureen that he finds their constant rehearsals of ills and infirmities a little trying. There is one special lady whom he likes, a gentle, smiling soul . . . Maureen will visit there, next month: Nicki has agreed to come over as a baby-sitter for Jack.

On the forest verge, up at the summit of the lawn where in high spring the master of the house sat like sunrise in a glory of blood-red tartan, cracking walnuts, their son Tom has erected a village of tepees for the little savages. Last night they slept out there under the canopy of the stars, one of the mildest Octobers they have ever known, and now Tom and his wife Emma are organising breakfast over the campfire. Maureen can see the billowing smoke from where she sits in the window with her weaving, and hear the halloos of the braves as they fry their sausages on toasting-forks over the flames. Yesterday came a long letter from Jenny, with a postscript from her boy, whom Jenny is almost sure now to retrieve from his father. Maureen takes a real interest in Oliver, and now re-reads his contribution, admiring his clear, well-trained handwriting and immaculate spelling. Jenny recounts a visit from Serena and Randall who on a European tour dropped in on Bradford, much to their and its surprise. The poverty of Jenny's surroundings did not come within Serena's category of 'quaint'. 'How can you bear it?' she kept asking; and Jenny found two fifty-pound notes on the table when they had gone. It was odd how Serena took to Jenny, and Jenny had seemed to return the feeling. Maureen bears Serena no ill will for her wild fling, none in the world, for didn't she herself, eight years the senior, a happy staid old grandmother, indulge a passion of her own and take leave of her senses for almost two years? Now it seems hard to believe. Nicki has her new girlfriend installed at 'Shadows', the brittle, dark-haired Marguerite, in her late twenties, calls everyone 'darling' and seems rather unbalanced to Maureen, though that – to be candid – may be just her own sour grapes. She wishes Nicki well; she wishes all of them well, and is relieved to have travelled through that odd phase out of character, to rejoin the continuity of her historical self. She feels more reconciled to the matrix of life for having stepped rashly out of it. Jenny has asked her to read part of her letter out loud to Jack, which she now does, twice over, slowly and distinctly. He gives no sign of having comprehended, though his eyes seem to rest on the paper in her hands.

The Indian population has evacuated its village and now swarms ululating down the slope to the house, bursting in at the back door. The tribe bears hot sausages as a tribute to Grandmother, all except the four-year-old Matthew, whose exceptionally wild whooping and gyrations of the fork sent his sausage flying in the direction of his fellow-camper Paul the schnauzer, who ate it. The heartbroken Matthew inhabits Grandmother's lap and, sucking his two middle fingers between sobs, glares with bitter personal animosity at the trio of sausages which advance their steaming carbon upon his grandmother. Matthew's sausage was infinitely superior: a king amongst its kind. Upon his father's remarking that big boys don't cry, Matthew's tears immediately cease, but he plunges his head deep into the bosom of Maureen's sweater and won't come out. No one offers Grandfather a bite of sausage. They know he wouldn't reply. The little ones trample over his feet in their carpet-slippers as if he were just an extension of the furniture. The two elder girls, Nicolette and Rachel, take care to skirt his form; have an unacknowledged fear of him. They know he's human but he doesn't act it. He is no longer like a real grandfather, but a strange and inanimate replica of someone they used to recognise. And what if he suddenly started up and roared *Boo!* in a huge mocking voice and laughed like the child-consuming giant in the fairy-tale (as who knows he might) what a shock they'd all get then.

'Come on, you guys,' says Tom as his wife Emma brings in Jamie the baby to nurse. 'Back to the big pow-wow.'

Matthew digs in and makes it clear he won't go.

'It's all right, Tom,' says Maureen. 'I'll fix him a sandwich and he shall have some of Grandma's best honey cookies, shan't he chickabiddy?'

Matthew peeps to ascertain that the siblings are out of the way and instantly cheers up. In a grandiose concession he even forgets his fratricidal rage at the dribbling spotty baby's contumacious refusal to go back wherever it was he came from.

'You're amazing with them,' says Emma. 'It never fails to astonish me.' She suckles the hungry baby, which makes an extraordinary noise over its feed for one so small before settling down to a contented rhythm. 'So uncoercive. They drive me nearly crazy, especially with Mattie's being so difficult. Yes, *you*, you little varmint. I only have to clap eyes on them first thing in the morning to be set off yelling. But I've never heard you raise your voice, they just come to you, they quieten.'

Suffer the little children . . . forbid them not. That was what echoed when Mother held out an arm, patted a lap, and converted a blood-curdling rout of hell-raising villains to a clutch of innocents, mild as their natal milk and eager to please and be pleased. Emma recalls a Dutch painting of Christ and the children whenever she sees Mother making this gesture of invitation: the opening arm that places no obligation on anyone to do anything, but lays bare the heart like a magnet whose terrifying power of conductivity draws in its kin along an invisible line. There is no hint of envy in Emma's admiration. You do not envy a force of nature. And anyway the gesture of welcome is quite inclusive. She too is in there somewhere; and when she hears Maureen *shan't-he-chickabiddy* her rebellious son, she sighs and relaxes her tense shoulder-muscles, and is rested, and the milk flows more easily for the child she nurses. But it's odd: after the child reaches the age of eight or so, Maureen's power seems to wane, Emma notices that. The teenage grandchildren scissor the cord and spring away, almost angrily. *What makes Grandmother think we feel at home in the kingdom of heaven anyhow?* She watches Mother let go, with perfectly uncoercive equanimity. And whether this quality of powerful quietism is related to the Quakerism in Mother's family, or is just a wisdom of her own heart, Emma occasionally reflects but cannot decide. If one had known Mother's own mother, the legendary Bess (whom poor Father so hated) this might be clearer; but all that was before Emma's time.

Chickabiddy is wolfing honey cakes. They are small and succulent, and he crams them in two at a time. Grandmother's house is a place of largesse and superabundance, where there's usually another batch baked 'just-in-case'; and where they don't *no more* you as they do at home. Matthew takes advantage of this, as any sane and prudent boy must do, in case of blight or usurpation.

'I saw the big round milky moon from the flap of my tepee,' he confides, mouth stuffed with cake, and one in either hand.

'I saw it too,' says Grandmother. 'It was a glorious moon. Did you make a wish?'

'Yes, I – '

'Don't tell me, honey. It has to be your secret.'

Matthew is arriving at the point of surfeit. He is glutted not only with food but with sensations of well-being and goodwill. These feelings gain ground to such an unspeakable extent that the sight of the back of the baby's pale downy head as it is lifted to its mother's shoulder to have its white woolly back rubbed for wind summons in Matthew a rare desire to succour rather than slap. With an air of martyrdom he gets down from Grandmother's lap and takes the plate with its two remaining cookies (one of which is broken and doesn't count) round to the gap between his brother's and grandfather's chair. He offers Jamie a cookie, with a rather sickly smile; and Jamie as usual possets gently and looks in a shifting variety of directions with his unfocusing eyes, and Mother says 'Good boy, Mattie' but explains that Jamie isn't quite up to the cookie stage as yet. Matthew, balked, will try Grandfather instead. At least Grandfather has teeth; and he knows he eats, for he has observed Grandmother feeding him, placing the food in his hands and coaxing him to raise it to his mouth, chew and swallow. Grandfather is clearly, in some ways, a more advanced kind of baby than Jamie, not only judging by size but also in terms of mechanical aptitudes. And Grandfather has also the incalculable advantage of remaining entirely mute, despite Herculean family encouragement to linguistic endeavour. Matthew is not at all afraid of Grandfather, for he interprets him simply as an immobile extension of Grandmother.

'Granpop have a cookie?'

He extends the plate, planting his sturdy little body between the old man's legs. He watches his grandfather peruse the cookies which tend to slide about the heavy china with its flower-pattern. Matthew intuits that, though he really would relish a cake, there is some difficulty about transportation. Putting down the plate, he personally conveys a cake to Grandfather's hand, politely adding, 'Excuse fingers.' The rest really has to be up to him, there is a limit to what can be done by way of intervention. The cookie reposes quietly in the great, gnarled hand into which it was deposited, lying quite still and half open on his knee. But when Grandmother tries to remove the cookie, explaining that Grandfather, having just breakfasted, is not hungry at this moment, they are surprised to find that he clenches his hand around the gift, so violently that it disintegrates. And then he weeps several tears. Matthew does not like him to cry; it is frightening. He runs out yodelling and joins the campers round the barbecue.

Of all the recent sadnesses and changes, perhaps the one which (somewhat to her surprise) most affected Maureen was the suicide of Jacques back in August, the month after Jack's stroke. She often finds herself sitting at the window and playing her mind over his memory. Now with the fall, with the birch golden and the few maples crimson upon her eye, the ground beneath the deciduous parts of the world a flamy maze of gorgeous dying, the full reality of his departure is known. She conjures his face into being, its aesthete's cultivation, its charm, the hint of slyness and malice in his temperament, the soft manner which could be extraordinarily tender. In relation to Jack, Jacques was always uncharacteristically chaste and charitable: they seemed to touch one another at an oblique and difficult angle, but the friendship went deep. She has no idea whether Jack ever registered the loss of his friend. She doubts it. Jack's mind seems pretty well gone. In relation to herself, Jacques' habitual misogyny was in abeyance, and became more so. He bore towards her an almost childlike veneration; once told her, twenty, thirty years ago that if any woman could have persuaded him to marriage, it must have been herself. That was not realistic but it was touching: no doubt he turned to the mother in her. The physical reality of a woman would have aroused his fastidious aversion.

How sane to choose the hour of his death, how characteristically resolute. On his last visit he must have been looking his death in the eyes. Everyone, of course, thought it was AIDS, but that was not so: it was cancer. So his lover, Ralph Shore, posthumous emissary of Jacques, insisted, straight out, when he visited in September. Maureen had just brought Jack home from hospital. No one was yet used to his hunched form over there in the corner, one arm straight and almost useless, the other foetally retracted to his chest, head slightly to one side, as if cocked and listening. No one was habituated, most of all, to the thick slab of silence which was the indwelling presence in that body which had been the home of such a warmly garrulous spirit. The lack of motion and the thick padding of silence. At first the sinister implication of that brooding, non-committal shadow of something which used to be Jack had made even Maureen anxiously afraid, like a haunting; or as if some contemptuous alien visitor were silently planted to judge your most casual utterances. She wanted sometimes to squeal when she saw him there, huddled. Then Ruby the specialist nurse came and took over the household, and that too required adjustment, but she normalised Jack, his foetal arm uncurled somewhat, he ate and drank and passed his waste products at Ruby's command. But she remembers when Jacques' Ralph arrived, how Jack was new-returned, and how he seemed to lurk there in the background, while that tall and elegant young man (the principal dancer of Jacques' new troupe, and what a surprise he was black, there had been no suggestion) told her the manner and rationale of Jacques' death.

'Jacques asked me to bring you orange-blossom as his last gift, with his love; and there's a note in there.' She took the flowers quietly and stood with their heavy burden of powerfully scented bridal white, saying nothing: for whom should one thank, air? The dark Mercury himself, with his superb self-containment, fulfilling orders, a mediator solely.

'And I am to tell you and Mr Middleton it was a good death. Jacques took a rational decision. He had cancer. He took his freedom and gave us ours – didn't want me to see him in the obscenity of suffering, didn't want it for himself.'

'That is like Jacques,' said Maureen. 'I honour him for it.'

It was a measured, gracious exchange. She was glad that their old friend had kept his young lover till the very end, preserving his own glamorous and lovable image intact, keeping control. When Ralph had gone, to fulfil his trust as messenger to Jacques' legion other friends, Maureen opened the card which accompanied the flowers.

My friends – I shall see you both in the next world.

Could Jacques have meant that? Could he have believed that there is a threshold over which we step; a country in which to repossess our loves? Maureen pondered it and could not say. Jack sat in the corner beside the door like a sentinel or janitor, and it seemed to Maureen turning from the fume of perishable orange-blossom and Jacques' cryptic farewell note, that he sat as a kind of outpost of that empire, medial between here and there. His funerary state; her bridal flowers. His silent bulk; his eloquent tongue that conversed perhaps even now over the border in that other land where *I shall see you both;* laughing at the top of his voice, timelessly holding forth, somewhere other than here and now. Maureen put down the flowers, went over and knelt by Jack, looking into his eyes. How much of him is left? Nothing? Wisps? Chaos? The whole Jack but incommunicado? The doctors could not guess. It goes beyond the limits of science, they say, to surmise the workings of the inner soul. It is reckoned that large sections of Jack's brain are pretty well destroyed, and they can say for certain that he is unlikely to survive another attack. She ran her fingers through that wild white hair, the lion's mane; the lion did not stir.

But with the fall, a certain minimal regeneration has set in. Jack is learning to hold his head upright and is observed to focus his eyes upon persons and objects. He is being trained by Ruby to eat, using his left hand, and to scan the words in a child's reading book, which is turned away from him and reflected in a mirror while the sounds are articulated by the nurse. He appears to be seeing in reverse. It is not known whether the signs and sounds make any sense to him; but it is mental activity. This phenomenon the indefatigable Ruby explains she has observed in a small number of other stroke victims: brain death is compensated by the activation of other parts of the brain, it is just a case of assisting this transfer of function to take place. A curious sensation of peace and well-being flows over Maureen with this adaptation of her husband's psyche and bodily functions to the terms of his imprisonment. Ministering to Jack and intuiting his needs brings a satisfaction which seems to recapitulate an earlier halcyon state of things between the two of them, though with the initial elements realigned. She tries to catch the echo, but what is it? It flits like a dream before her waking mind. Then when Tom and Emma introduce the new baby, James, into the household, and the other grandchildren pelt round the grounds hallooing, and chase the squirrels from the tree-house, she realises. The lobotomised Jack, his aggressions excised, is her new baby. She is free to mother him. She feels ashamed. Poor Jack, his lost powers, his undignified immobility. Always he said that this was what he dreaded above all fates: the loss of control. *Put me out of my misery if I ever get like that, Molly.*

And she laments it too, on his behalf. Yet now she recalls with a quite shocking current of joy, as Ruby guides Jack's power-assisted wheelchair out past Nancy's grave into the pine-world, the bringing home of their firstborn. And how Jack ran crashing out into the sun-dappled glade and announced the baby to the bird population and the breathless trees, and whatever peered down from the heavens or up from the fern-masked earth: 'Molly and Jack have a baby girl! A baby girl!' Joy volleyed from tree to tree, it echoed and rang through the resinous wilderness as Maureen carried Josie out in her arms, the milky-mouthed slumbrous face bound in Bess' grandmother's great carrying blanket which was passed on to the bearer of Bess' first grandchild.

'A baby girl! Yes! Yes!' roared the youthful father, beside himself, 'And her name shall be called Josephine! Wonderful! Glorious! The princess of peace!'

Forty-four years on, Josie's father is wheeled out with difficulty across the soft forest floor, over odd knots of root, down gentle furrows in the spongy, living earth; Josie's father swaddled in a green and blue tartan blanket; Josie's father who no more than a mite of a week's age can be reached in the sealed twilight of the interior world. And Maureen for a grotesquely idyllic interim this fall has a newborn baby home to nurse: one who will never grow up to quit the nest.

They are all gathered with the fall of dusk in the living room, Tom and Emma with their threefold brood; Angela and Keith with the twins; Jack and Maureen in easy chairs at either side of the logfire; Nicki and her girlfriend Marguerite over from 'Shadows'. The standard lamps are on; the fire shoots raving up the chimney, drawn by a high wind outside; they are all drinking cocoa. It is the picture of family bliss. Mattie with crimson scorch-patches on his cheeks drowses on the hearthrug, one hot hand stretched out and clasping Grandmother's moccasin so that she will not be able to get away, and in order to guard him against the unpredictable impulses of the big basking dog Thoby, with whom he is sharing the fireside. The room circulates with conversation, it swells and falls on comfortable topics, reminiscences of places visited, recapitulations of the doings and sayings – always so much more pithy and eccentric than our own – of the characters of the last generation, that of the legendary Bess and Jack's father John.

Out come the family photograph albums. Here are the great-uncles with their penny-farthing bicycles; here Bess in her strapping prime and her obscure and hen-pecked husband William; here is – whoever is this, Mother? Angela wants to know. It is a head-and-shoulders portrait in black and white of a lady in a high-collared blouse caught with an oval brooch whose thick gathers ray out over a magnificent bosom. The face is august, square-jawed, but its expression belies the imperial cast of the fashion of the day by a whimsical, querying softness around the lines of mouth and eyes. Masses of brown, lustrous, prodigious hair are piled like the superfluous abundance of the princess in the doorless tower. The hair is excess of beauty, ravishingly disproportionate to that of the ordinary mortal measure; and soft as well as thick.

'Oh Angie, you know who that is, darling. That's your grandmother – Dad's mother, Florence.'

'No – I've never seen her before.'

'Of course you have. We used to have that picture up in the den for years and years – you must remember.'

'No, I don't. Do you, Tom?'

'Vaguely. My goodness, what a head of hair. Quite a crown. Look here, Rachel, that's your great-grandmother. Rather wonderful, isn't she? Is she the one that died, Mother, when Dad was seven: not the stepmother?'

'No, not the stepmother. Dad would never have kept her picture, I doubt if one exists, he *hated* her. No, that's Florence. He worshipped her, right up to, well, July of this year I suppose – she died, maybe you could say, before he was able to find out she was human and fallible like the rest of us. She was God to him.'

Angela passes the photograph to Maureen, directly across Jack's line of vision.

'Goodness me, yes,' says Maureen, putting on her reading glasses, for the print is quite small and unusually detailed for that period. 'What a figure of a woman. I often wonder what she was like, I mean apart from Jack's understandable idealisations. A strong-minded woman? A tender? Bright? This is the only sign we have to go by. He kept it in the den for years and then took it abroad to show Jenny last year – I guess it never found its way back up. What do you think she looks like, Mattie? I mean, what kind of person?'

'Nejjy,' says Jack.

There is a silence, everyone stares, as if caught out. It was a dark room, now someone has snapped on the light. It was a private party, they have been gate-crashed. Jack is looking at Matthew, who holds the photograph, and his eyes follow his grandson's face as he rises on the hearthrug.

'What did you say, Grandpop?' he enquires politely. There is no reply.

Angela kneels at her father's feet. 'Dad, Dad. What is it? What did you say?' She holds both his hands and kisses them repeatedly. 'Dad, Daddy.'

'Did he really speak?'

'It's his first word, he said his first word. The doctor said he might regain some language.'

'But what was it he said?'

'Sounded like *neige*. That's French for *snow*.'

'Was it *Nicki?* It could have been Nicki. Nicki, see if he's trying to speak to you.'

'Jack, dear, it's me, Nicki. If you wanted to say something to me, could you squeeze my hand?'

Jack looks blankly at Nicki. It is clear he does not recognise her. There is something inexpressibly poignant about his person, which used to be so sloppily homely in its clothes, just an old sack tied round the middle he used to say, which is now dressed up by Ruby as if for its first day at school, in collar and tie, and immaculate hand-knitted sweater.

'It was probably just a sound, not a word,' says Keith. 'Not meaningful as such.'

Angela glares at her spouse in detestation. Why she married such a crass lump of civil engineer in the first place she cannot conceive. She is planning to leave the insensitive clod as soon as the twins are old enough.

'Shut up,' she hisses.

'What have I said? What have I said?'

'Could it be my name, all garbled?' whispers Angela to her mother. 'Dad, squeeze my hand if you mean me.' She desperately wishes that he did. He does not.

'This is pointless – *is there anybody there?* – like a séance. It was just a random sound, like I said,' remorselessly continues Angela's apparently computerised other half. 'He probably didn't even know he was saying it.'

'Nejjy,' says Jack to Maureen, quite distinctly. 'Nejjy.'

'You want Jenny. Of course, my lamb, of course you shall have her, my dear one, of *course*.'

Tom and Emma exchange significant glances. They had heard, of course, along the family grape-vine, that the old fellow had been involved in some unlikely affair with an unstable European girl half his age that Maureen took under her wing; but they didn't know how much, if any, to credit. One never imagined one's aged parents having a private life, still less a sexual one. Still, they speculated; and Emma pointed out that Dad had mellowed out of all recognition in late years; had grown his hair and kept ringing up all the available daughters and daughters-in-law to tell them he loved them; had made up the obscure quarrel with Frank their elder brother and written him back into the will. Only a happy man dispenses with the allowable compensations of age: grumbling and taking offence.

Later on, getting ready for bed, Tom says, wrinkling his nose, 'I think it's rather obscene. The old guy ought by rights to have been past such nonsense by now. And by all accounts Mother positively encouraged it.'

Emma disagrees. 'Don't you think old people have a right to their feelings?'

'God! It gives me the creeps. They ought to just – subside – and leave it to us. C'mhere.'

'You're wrong, Tommy. Love is *always* a good. *Always*. Never anachronistic – never ridiculous. Love –'

'Suffers long and is very kind. All right, nursing mother, okay, I won't argue with your milk and water. Come over here and educate me.'

'You need it.'

'I know it, I know it. Mother is a saint. Would *you* get *my* mistress to my death-bed if I asked for her?'

'Don't say that.' Cold fingers sift into Emma. *Death-bed?* Jack's son thirty years on, with a secret liaison? The very words make her catch her breath. 'Oh, don't. Dad will get better, he will. Take it back.'

'Baby. Baby. You're nothing but a little fish, smallfry. You take the hook every time. Come here, minnow, and be baited.'

Tom, like Frank, has inherited his father's predeliction for the cruel, taunting jest, the manipulative retort. The patriarchal carapace creaks about Jack's two sons' hearts and may in time harden about Mattie's and baby Jamie's: and whether there will be springtimes vivid enough to crack the carapace of the creature in time is quite unsure.

'Dad won't get better, Em. You know that. It's just a matter of when he goes, not whether. God, I've hated that man in my time. The autocratic bloody-minded bull-shitting tyrant.' He lies back with his head pillowed on his arms and reflects on Jack's past crimes, whistling softly through his teeth. 'Jee-sus.'

'He will get better,' Emma insists stubbornly.

'He won't.'

'Please say he will.'

'Okay, Em. He will. He will get better. Satisfied?'

2
Time

Oliver is in a state of giddy, scintillating excitement. He has a tempest in his head such as has never been brewed in a child since the world began. Today he flies to America. With Mummy. Without Renate. He practises aerobatic manoeuvres on the staircase, which is uncarpeted since he and his mother have only just moved in to Rosie's terraced house in Clayton, just above Bradford. Bare floorboards conduce to sound-effects such as the breaking of the sound barrier and the aimless pursuit of noise in general. Rosie, back from Lesotho and starting a demanding social work job, likes to sleep in on her days off, and, having no children of her own, groans at the thunder of Oliver and wonders if it was a good thing to take in Jenny and her boy. But *yes, yes it was, wholeheartedly it was*, she thinks, snuggling up to Jenny's warm back and muttering, 'Come on you, get up – you've a plane to catch and your personal alarm clock's going off on the stairs.'

'Shut up Olly. Rosie's trying to sleep in. There you are, go back to your catatonic trance.' Rosie already has.

'We're going to America today. Hurry up,' Oliver informs her with a frenzied air.

'*No*. You don't say. Are you sure?' She puts the kettle on. Oliver, fully dressed, is fighting to strap on his backpack and depart.

'Yes. Come on. You're not even dressed.'

'It's not time. Calm right down.'

'I can't be calm. I'm going to America.'

I'm going home, thinks Jenny. *At long and dear last going home*. All her thoughts for the past three days, since Maureen told her Jack was asking for her, would she please please come? have taken the form of secret messages transmitted in Jack's direction. Finally he is grounded in her mind, made safe there like terrible beautiful lightning earthed. He is sure and certain and centred within her mind. She feels guided by an astonishing peace. She talks to Jack as to a presence abiding in her own spirit, and hence not capable of loss: *till the close of the age*, he used to say, and that has been attested. When Maureen said *he spoke your name, it is all he has said*, this feeling of indwelling began. And what if he did say it backwards? and what if, as Maureen warns, he is baffled by all external reality, in a fog, not himself, a wanderer in a labyrinth, and may well not recognise her face when she presents it to his eyes? Still she can't rid herself of the conviction, or passionate delusion, of home-coming.

And now she's not going to him empty-handed or alone. She can take Oliver. He has consented to divest himself of his pack, sit down and eat a piece of toast and honey; finding his eye transiently beguiled by the robot competition on the back of the Shreddies packet, he forgets to remind her about America. *I have you*, she says to Oliver, drinking him in with her eyes, still unused to the security of possession: the darkening blond of his hair which she is letting grow as a token of Samsonian release from the regime of his father, the thin fine face with hectic eyes and cheeks, the slender fingers. *I traded Jack for you.* That had been the crossroads, the appalling crossroads at which she had chosen to stick with Olly and forsaken Jack. In July Jack's stroke had coincided with the crisis in the delicate negotiations between herself, Renate and Alex which resulted in the mutually agreed release of Oliver into her custody. In July she thought she died. She never cried one tear, though she had been raining them since her return from America, knowing that Jack had in a measure returned to his wife. And though she had freely helped him to this happiness, it crucified her every night afresh, to know that he slept with Maureen 'for warmth, for comfort' as he put it. *But where's my warmth, my comfort?* she howled into her pillow like a demented child, *where's mine?* She believed Jack meant it when he wrote in his daily letters that he loved and needed her entirely, still, but she could not derive benefit from his love. It stopped short by a few inches after its far-sped journey of thousands of miles, deflected by her invisible armoury of grief and extrusion. She wished him happiness because she loved him, but the tearing vacuum of need in her sucked back at the blessings she urged herself to send. Her tone was remote, haughty; she bled.

Renate burgeoned. She was like some luscious and very exotic fruit coming to maturity. In her radiantly pregnant state, her value soared for Alexander like some rampant commodity on the stock market. At the end of July she and Alex were married at Harrogate Register Office, in the company of Renate's parents, two colleagues from Alex's firm and Oliver, who failed to smile throughout the festive day despite the inducement of manifold coaxings both in the English and German tongues, the telling of 'Knock knock' jokes by the two colleagues, and finally his infuriated father's hissed injunction to *Bloody well cheer up, you miserable little brat.* That evening the couple embarked on their honeymoon weekend leaving Olly with Renate's parents. Olly began a campaign of bed-wetting, lying, small thefts, expensive breakages and runnings away. 'I cannot and I will not cope with him,' said Renate to Alex. 'In my condition. Either he goes or I go.' Jenny sat and waited for Olly to drop through the machine into her arms. She was sharing with Rosie now, and had a really warm home to offer her son. And Rosie gave affection too, lavishly, tenderly, and seemed to need her friend in the cold northern hemisphere in the manner if not to the measure of Jenny's own need. It seemed there could be a new life. Then Jack had his stroke, just on the cusp of the signs; just when she was not free to go to him and offer her care.

'Can you come over, Jenny?'

'Oh Maureen, I can't leave here just now. I can't.'

She caught her child falling; she let the man who was son and father, brother and God fall past her into the void. She struck herself then out of the book of life: she had no name, no kin, no origins, because no deservings. But Jack has said her name; has called her back into being from where he has fallen, over the edge of the world.

There is the huge steel wing over the patchwork of October fields, dun, ochre, brown, the floss of clouds as they climb. Oliver opens fully to the fact of his soaring altitude. Always there had been the wish for wings, praying nightly, badgering God and tempting Him to prove His reality, *Please God make me able to fly:* white like a gull he would cruise over the rooftops, and all the neighbours and schoolfriends below, and

Mummy and Daddy, would point open-mouthed: 'Isn't that Oliver Reinhold up there? Hey what's your secret?'

'We won't crash, Mummy,' he reassures her. The clouds engulf him, then fall away from the plane into a dazzling polar world below this turquoise lagoon of the heavens, in which the plane levels out; and the stewardesses come with head-sets in plastic bags, and orange juice accompanied by bags of twelve peanuts to each of which Oliver accords an individual respect. He likes his little plastic table which is let down from the seat in front; on which he arranges colouring books and felt tip pens, and assiduously joins dots until his meal comes, and he likes that too, on principle. And always beside him as he draws or as he dozes, the great pale ocean travels, and he laces his fingers with Jenny's and squeezes, surcharged with pleasure, as the earthbound crane and point, agreeing, 'Yes, that's definitely Oliver Reinhold up there flying. Did you know Oliver could fly?'

'Are we nearly there?'

'No. We have a whole continent to cross. But we're over Canada. Look out.'

'How long?'

'Oh – three hours or so yet.'

'Three *hours?*'

'Yes, there'll be another film, I expect. It won't seem so very long. Well, it will, but we'll get through it. Shall we put our watches back now?'

They have to lose five hours. Olly ponders this, whirling Time on his dial-face in giddy loops backward and forward, playing God with the winder between finger and thumb. Up here in the roaring void they are at no time and any time, so he is told. They are at a standstill and the earth is revolving. They are temporarily immune from Time, exempt. It doesn't make a lot of sense to Olly. It seems like forever they have been sitting here in cramped rows travelling forwards into the past. Eternity. And he is hungry again. He can think of a fairly spectacular Tarzan game one might play swinging along the narrow aisle, *aaaieeee*, and has observed a smaller boy equally bored and squirming, and well suited to the role of Tarzan's chimpanzee.

'Can I walk about, Mummy?'

'No, I don't think so. Look, here come the stewardesses with the tea.'

'I don't want tea, I want coke.'

He has his coke and three cakes. He subsides. Thrashes on with Time. How can you lose five hours? You ought to be that much younger when you arrive.

'If you had a newborn baby,' he points out, 'and took it on a plane to America, it would have to be born all over again at some stage in the journey.'

'How's that?'

'Because when you turned the clock back it would not have been born.'

'Ah well – only technically speaking. *We* don't change, Olly, only the time-zones change. Time is a – fiction. Relative. Or something.' Jenny feels to her discomfort she doesn't understand it very well herself.

'For instance, what's the time now?' asks Olly.

'Whatever you decide it should be. Or, whatever time it is down there in Newfoundland.'

Olly looks out to inspect Newfoundland. It is a mass of pitted and wrinkled coppery-grey rocks jutting in promontories like fingers out into the blue seas; the rocks are scored with rivers and fjords, and appear to have folded into themselves as if crushed by some immense force. They appear to Olly's eye immeasurably old, like the claws of some prehistoric monster petrified at the edge of the terrestrial world. No one lives there. Olly could not go down and enquire of a native 'What's the time here please?' It is a bizarre world he is entering with his mother, where the clock-face would tick backwards, if there were a clock.

'Newfoundland,' he ruminates. 'New Found Land. I like that name. There would be giants there, and kings. Labrador. It would be full of great dogs coming out of the mist at you. No humans.'

Newfoundland. That echoes too in Jenny's mind. Jack was that land to her, ancient and original, a zone out of time. In that Cloudcuckooland, Never-never, old and young were, for a brief eternity, one.

'How are you, my dear dear Oliver?'

Maureen greets Jenny's drooping, tired child like long-lost kin, and, putting forth her natural magic to him, crouches with open arms to enfold the little stranger, his backpack and teddy-bear. The weather has turned bitterly cold; she wraps

Oliver up in one of her grandchildren's scarves, mittens and a bright woolly hat. Jenny has the ordeal of meeting Jack's younger son, Tom, who is exceedingly tall and rather inclined to premature baldness (how it tickled Jack that his sons' hair fell out while his own burgeoned wildly into old age); and about her own age. Tom is polite but eagle-eyed, coldly curious.

'You will find him much changed,' says Maureen in the car, Tom driving, Oliver under her arm. 'Don't expect him to recognise you, dear, will you? His mind is almost completely gone. He lives in his own world.'

Newfoundland. Cloudcuckooland. Never-never.

'Didn't he always?' says Jenny unexpectedly. Tom's startled, all-too-familiar eyes meet hers like a bolt from the blue in the driving mirror.

3
No

Behind the soundproof glass in the other world, Jack Middleton sits and hears himself respire. The bag of his body fills and empties, fills and empties. Eyes stare with neurotic anxiety into the fishtank where he lives, mouths work in manic physiognomies, with forced smiles, up against the glass. Their world, seen through his fisheye lens distends into convexities and concavities very disagreeable to contemplate. At times it comes up close and faces like creatures of the deep nose and bat against the vulnerable film that guards his eyeball, seeking to penetrate the globe of his brain. Jack bears it out with more than Trojan fortitude till they draw off. The air is filled with muffled booming, *la la la* of singsong, *tic-tic-tic-tic-tic*, round and round we go, and they come and they go, *swoosh flap*, ballooning of skirts across the prairie of carpets to and from where he sits bare-headed in the wide-open mouth of illimitable space. And doesn't sag and doesn't whimper but like a much-visited freak of art and nature, a human statue, impersonates Eternity and holds his pose behind the pane (one arm foetally retracted, one hand on his knee) through aeons in which the lash can fall from the eye, flakes of skin have time to settle. The eighth wonder of the world is housed in the aquarium, he sees the fungus on the gold finny backs that rise bloated past his eye to decompose on the surface, sees all, reveals nothing.

The house Jack built is stripped bare. It contains not one single named item of furniture, nor a covering for reality; its shelves of books have been censored; the unknown room is both windowless and doorless. Language rips off every surface like a plaster and takes the skin off all reality. As soon as Jack lays eyes on any item, its label peels off and curls up.

The fire-warmed, lamp-lit room in which he sits so profoundly secluded is a system of vanishings. *Candle, plant, clock, bridal photographs:* he stares, enquiry gathers and *déjà vu*, but not the words for these things. At times something is on the tip of his tongue, there is a ticklish, fluttering, maddening sensation in his brain as if clues were about to surface. He looks at the clock and the word *clock* hovers just behind it, in its shadow: he would need a periscope to rise in his brain to locate it. Language has made a tricky escape, he trails it, with devious crabwise motion scuttles at words sidelong, but words skip round corners always just ahead, or they bury like shoreline creatures in soft sand. The world is nude of designation, terrifyingly, obscenely free of meaning.

Jack has just awoken, or Jack has just fallen fast asleep (for the two are no longer distinct) with the apprehension that someone has been and gone from his bedroom. The moment he opened his eyes she latched the door behind her; was checking up on Jack, her face bending over him.

Once – when? – there was such a face – but whose? – came in from the void and hung over the side of some – what? – high grating or fence or prison bars stretching dauntingly high, he'd tried to scale them and he knew; came in from the world beyond the net of vision and hung there like the moon or other milky planet. Once from that face came tumbling a huge slide of darkness, slithering round Jack's face in a rustling mass it poured on to his pillow. Curtained in that solicitous darkness, her face and his face, wellnigh one. Question and answer delicately adjusted, the tough equation poised in a neat solution. He wrapped his hands in the sanctuary of her fallen hair and he crowed out loud. But who – who?

Remedial light is implicit in the room where he lies, which she has just vacated, like the time-lag of a vintage fluorescent strip with its jaded flickerings of electricity, the never-say-die of an old lamp trying to do its duty. Who? The name will surely catch. But it doesn't, and motherless Jack floats on, anarchically free of his human heritage. The languageless world is so pure. Utility has been scoured off the chair whose outline against the bars of the window makes itself known, now that morning light intensifies, as a shadowy irruption of matter: revolutionary, violent, like some abstract painting by a mad Teutonic artist expecting war or death-camps.

Undenominated space alarms Jack by its corners and edges; it curves away from his eye, or, worse, it rebounds on him in coils or protuberances, and all he can do to confront this siege is to lie there between the sheets and bear it out, in the clammy pool of his own incontinence.

In silence and in solitary confinement: to travel through the great seas of time in the tipsy craft of the chair in which you have been deposited, it is a terrible journey. Jack is beginning to know his condition as a few halting words come limping to memory, inapplicable to anything much, and seemingly scrambled, or in some foreign tongue; but words just the same. Words are put to him by the workings of an indefatigable mouth which presents itself to his eyes for this purpose on what seems a regular basis. *Book – book – a book* explains the mouth. *Jack – Jack – Jack*, it maintains. *This – is – Jack's – book*, it concludes with a smile; and repeats; and repeats. Jack fixedly and steadily stares at the mouth. He stoically refuses to be terrified by these osculations, which remind his picture-teeming brain of the soft, deliquescent sucking pads of a mollusc prised from a rock. That the mollusc should address its message to himself in so dictatorial and designing a manner is in itself a mystery too terrible to encounter. The words which are pressing on Jack's resistant awareness invite him to despair. Through them he will come to know the misery of his segregation. *Jack's book* is a history of bright revelations of all that has been forfeit. As things stand, his mind just crawls with shadows, veilings, obscure auras and ripples left by that which once has been. But words are worming in, one by one, sidling across at odd angles, declaring themselves in casual clusters or manacled in grammatical rows, against his better, Elysian, judgment.

Sleep, sleep. He likes to sleep. He likes to suck. His left hand by strange and guileful artifice manages to reach his mouth, and inserts its little finger; he sucks; it is good; his breathing lulls; he sleeps. He has found by trial and error that if he wishes to achieve some purpose, he must attempt the opposite. It is a sinister, left-handed world, in which he has forgotten to be right-handed; a mirror-view. So to get the hand into the position in which he can obtain comfort from it, he must push it strenuously downwards, and think of his toes. He sees them now in his mind's eye, the high-instepped, rather small foot with its rows of – of – *piggies. This little piggy* . . . said the shade of – of *Who?* and he felt his small toe nipped and tweaked between thumb and finger: Oh mocking voice, laughing *Eee eeh eeh, all the way, all the way home. Don't Mother laugh at me Mother.* These terrible digressions, the trap-door of Jack's mind unhinging and he drops right down through a fall of air, the pit of his stomach rises to the floor of his heart, and he pitches down the hole of memory, to touch his toes. They are a long way down, Jack in his vertigo hasn't a hope of reaching, but he tries anyway – just once more – think, think, Jack – strain, unbend that paralysed arm – yes – he's there, the pioneer, the entrepreneur, his finger is in the side of his mouth and he can suck it all he likes. Had intended his thumb of course and is mildly surprised to find himself nursing his little finger, but still has a sense of victory, and the reward of the restful doze the comfort brings. Pavlov's Jack will try this again, over and over; and maybe, being more than dog and never less than man even in his ruin, devise other more spirit-nourishing means of deliverance from his own despair.

A flock of migratory children wings its way round the island of Jack and executes bird-calls in the sanctuary. Jack forbids them not. Jack's dark-grey trousered legs are the steep cliffs on which such life has formerly with impunity clambered, perched, gee-upped, bucked or nestled. Now they take no notice of Jack, and Jack bestows no explicit attention on them. He neither recognises nor fails to recognise them. They disclose themselves more as aberrations in the composition of the light and in the tonal texture of the room than as individual human presences. For instance they flit across the fire upon which Jack is given to meditating; sometimes they dart to and fro across this warmly radiant field of vision, their silhouettes like the pinions of birds traversing a window to visit their nest beneath the eaves. These interferences in no way irritate Jack, and neither do their outbursts of noise. When they halloo wildly 'Wah-owah-o-wah', palms beating a tattoo over open mouths, or yell 'Snap!' or 'Rummy!' under the lamp, Jack does not feel testy as in his earlier incarnation. A good thing too, for now he could not disengage by locking himself in the den with pursed mouth, clamp a book down over his eyes, and leave the children to the women. The beating clock upon the mantelpiece, whose chime he used to like, is to the present occupant of Father's chair a more punishing bedlam than the whirligig of moving shadows, which ebb and flow but the clock remains: *pic pic pic*.

There is a baby in the room and it keeps crying. That distresses Jack. He cannot concentrate on nursing his own condition while the baby is around. And it wears a label: round its neck, like a noose, designation of mortality, the word *baby*. *Baby*, Jack thinks, whenever the child is dandled in his sight; then 'rock-a-bye-baby', they sing, more terribly; then 'is Baby hungry?' they enquire. Jack understands all this, with perfect clarity. It is too terrible an outrage to his excoriated feelings, it is simply too much to be borne without articulate protest. He stares at the baby, with rivalry that feasts upon its own black bile, he condemns its existence with the absence of ruth belonging to the hopelessly dispossessed. Yet he pities what he curses, and wishes it would not cry.

One, two, three, the mother undoes the buttons of her pink lambswool cardigan, her face averted as she chats with someone out of the picture; her hand cups under the heavy tense breast and scoops it out. The breast is white and distended, with a tracery of blue veins, mottled around the dark nipple. Milk squirts before the baby can batten, its superfluity overflows, in a bluish-white dribble, the side of the mouth that tongues but hardly has to suck the source that yields its life. *Baby, baby*. Jack's finger slides from the corner of his mouth, his hand, that inanimate package of sterile matter, drops to his lap. He has to wait for them to realise that he might be hungry, his lips might be dry, and sometimes they forget. He sees the coffee-cups lifted to sipping mouths that cannot crave the warming fluid in the raw way that he knows need; and he can neither say 'Please' nor reach out and grab. He will go mad. He *will* go mad. There is nothing and there is nobody. Out here, beyond the circle. No. No; no; Jack will hang on, he can do that.

A small figure arises, most surprisingly, in the gap between his legs. For once he gets a glimpse of the whole figure: normally when they come in close he concentrates on a single feature, mouth, hand, ear, even a button, a check on their garments. But the gallant little emanation which springs up takes him by surprise, and he sees a boy. The boy has crinkly brown hair and a freckled face. He wears a purple T-shirt bearing the picture of a steam-engine, and he holds a dinner-plate on which are painted honeysuckle and clematis. Two cakes are on the plate.

'Granpop have a cookie?'

Yes yes, Jack's eagerness rises to receive the benediction that has been offered. This boy is his grandson, he knows that, he himself is Granpop, the cake is for him and it looks so delicious. There is a simple harmony and grace about this giving and receiving gesture, and the recognition which it has brought about. He wants to accept the gift from his grandson. But it will take time. He summons his left hand and imaginatively projects it in the opposite direction to his desire; but the plate in those small hands wobbles crazily and distracts him, it tilts and the cake coasts across its circumference. It rights itself, then sways, finally makes a landing on his knees.

'Excuse fingers,' says Granpop's grandchild, and places the cake in his hand.

I have it.

He holds his token which the world out there has somehow passed in across the forbidding threshold between self and self.

I have it.

The words of this sentence heal like connective tissue across the dead patches riddling his mind. He sits with his eyes closed, his hand softly resting round the circle of the cookie, testing his bliss, enjoying the sensation of wholeness, hearing himself repeat that bounteous sentence again and again.

I have it, I have it, I have it.

Are there more such precious compensations in his brain's trove of buried eloquence? There must be. Let them surface. All things are the more pregnant for having descended into the grave. Jack pays no attention to the removal of the boy and the plate, having his testimony in his hand. He is uninterested in the swishings of persons around him, the fluttered voices raised in consternation. Hence is unprepared for the raid. They try to pluck the cake from his hand, they bend over him, talking to one another, not to him.

'Granpop isn't hungry right now,' explains the thief to the giver. 'Okay, Chickabiddy?'

Swiftly Jack sends the message to himself to open his hands, *that* hand, *now*, wide, wide, *do it do it*. His fingers clamp tight, much too hard, they crush the brittle cake into a mass of crumbs. Rage. Rage. Utter loss and fury and the wish to strike at them, curse and hurt them somehow, at least to roar and beat the arm of the chair with a massive fist, scatter them from where they bear in upon him,

in the old days I'd have –

now what can he but, weakly, weep, and the tears course down, which he cannot wipe away for himself, he the foolish old man, he the great weight of leaden baby who hates them all, their intrusive faces, their impertinent hands.

'Quieten down there, quieten down. There there. Don't cry. Molly shall give you another cookie, much nicer. Hush, dear.'

Jack won't eat the substitute. He closes his teeth. Jack was hungry but not in that way. He has stopped snivelling, he looks her in the eye. *In the old days you were all afraid of me, I had the mastery, do you think I'm beat?* They fear him still, he scents it, gagged and bound as he is, though somehow they have been licensed to rifle his modesty, dress and undress him, clean his bottom, wash his face, blow his nose, and a thousand other acts of horror and humiliation. But if he were to stand up now to his full height, every inch the man he was, Jack Middleton still, as it is latent in him to do and they know it, and judge them, saying *I pardon you*, wouldn't they quail and flinch? They would; he knows it.

'He doesn't seem to want it now.'

'No, dear, never mind. Just as cussed as you ever were, Jack.' And it's as if she taunts him, *Come on out: I know you're there.*

The fall has come, he greets it in the bright scarlet stars which are conveyed in on twigs and set in vases around the room: and *maple*, thinks Jack, *maple*, delighting his eye upon that rubeous red. It meets his spirit in the pendulous cones of spruce and pine, prickly beechmast, nutlets and the winged seeds of maple which those scavenging scoundrels his grand-children bring in in polythene bags and assort in a parliament on the mat by the fire. As early morning light spreads over the forest outside his window, Jack's eye alights on the fall in a consummate golden age of birch and beech graciously, royally dying amongst the constant gloom of evergreen. The conflagration of the fickle, deciduous aspect of nature astonishes his senses like a wanton manifesto of a life flamboyantly vital in its decay. With this location of himself at a point in time, some of the nightmarish horror which shrouds Jack is lifted – the crawling of his scalp, the floating void of the undesignated inner world. His spongy eye drinks liquor of colour, so that the life of interiority achieves a passionate, filmic quality, sensually compensating for his abject deprivation. Life within Jack intensifies; engrosses and fulfils itself as, infant Narcissus, he gazes dreamily into that lascivious and fantastic mirror within.

Power gathers in Jack as never before in his old incarnation. The power to utter that which is dormant coils tighter and tighter in his chest, in his gut, in the helix of the brain, tensely convoluted: energy such as splits the mouth of the seed and articulates the shoot. The spring awaits release. He has learnt so much in this short while, 'a remarkable adaptation', the doctor said in his hearing. The evenings draw in, Jack broods at the chimney-corner as the pine-logs steam out hot balsam and smoke puffs up like the vagrant wisps of memory which now uncurl in smoky wraiths trailing smoky nouns. *Proper nouns*, announces memory, *the name of a person or place*: the most important, numinous secret of all makes itself accessible to Jack. He has laid hold on the world of objects with a net of common nouns – sheathed the dangerous crimson star with its several slicing edges in the familiarising *maple leaf;* swaddled the poking, insinuating horror of those five-angled instruments in the felt of *human hand*. The world is tamed by his art. Now Jack's senses stir with the ache of names remembered; fugitive, fluid persons break cover from the hinterland of his mind and beckon. Merlin will conjure with a greater magic to call up the souls from these burials by that occult, endangering act of naming whose exercise will paradoxically enroll the artist amongst the mortal. Jack will die of pain when he admits the names of – *her* – and – *her*, and – the anaesthetic, amnesiac blanks filled in.

They are all gathered, curtains closed, around the logfire, he hears their conversation as a background murmur, pleasant, comfortable, like something nourishing simmmering in a pot. He generally tries not to attend to specific words which have to go through a complex and rather tedious process of translation in his mind. For out there they speak (he early worked it out, not in so many words but as a musical or mathematical concept) backwards. They are inside-outers, back-to-fronters, left-to-righters: they fail to oppose him for they mirror him. 'One side of his brain's quite gone,' said the doctor. 'But what an adaptation – I've honestly never seen anything quite like this.' In Jack's dissident opinion, it is their perception which is at fault, not his which is normative and standard for the world he lives in. Jack Gulliver will tolerate the customs of the crazy people, but he cannot possibly be expected to endorse them. Often, as now, he just blanks off. He fares on long sea-voyages where the siren-echoes beckon.

But now he is recalled by the escape of one of his interior wraiths into the outside world.

'Oh Angie, you know who that is darling. That's your grandmother – Dad's mother, Florence . . . She was God to him.'

Florence.

Mother.

God.

Three-in-one, the better trinity, of which the threefold Father is a carrion shadow. Now a photograph is passed from hand to hand across his mother's child's line of vision, and Jack sees her likeness at the eye of the whirlwind, that calm, proud face which spells all tenderness to him, and all that is threatened with loss: the primal bond and scissors both.

Took it abroad to show Jenny last year

'Nejjy,' says Jack.

It is his first word. It would have taken a century to translate into their language, which is Arabic to him, and he would certainly have forgotten the beginning by the time he came to the end, so laboured and incongruous a work it is to speak out your inwardness. That stirs them up. They seize his hands, wet them with their tears, clamour, stutter and dispute. 'I can make waves,' he once told – someone – with childish malevolence; and is satirically pleased to note that he has not lost the knack. Again he issues his creating Word.

Nejjy, he instructs – that one.

'You want Jenny,' that one replies. 'Of course, my lamb, of course.'

There is a wave but he has not made it. It arches now at

the back of his mind and seems to hang there in balance, a tidal wave high up like Florence's roll of precipitous hair; and under it the drag of the undertow is a terrible hollow in which Jack cowers, hunkering down. He remembers lying with Jenny *oh Jenny, blessed Jenny, sweetheart, beauty* between navy-blue sheets in some rented room whose door is closed on him forever *my darling may I? Please please receive me* both her arms crooked round his neck, little and pale upon the sea of dark sheets, both his embracing her loosely, fondling the small of her back *lovely my loveliest gentle generous girl* cherishing her and being cherished, the marvel of how soft her skin and how much silkier it grew under his touch *am I nice for you sweetheart, am I, do I please you? Say I do* her face quite foolishly blissful and open, giving him small kisses with swollen inside-lip *if I pull the quilt down, will you be cold?* smiling, teasing, murmurous and tender, the feeling of closeness unutterable *I worship you Jenny, you are God to me, God help me;* and how totally at her mercy he was overwhelmed him, and how total was her mercy. Now he is a terrible death's head from whom all human creatures rightly turn.

The dog at his master's feet noses in and nestles; Jack's hand reaches down between his parted legs and gestures with small, faltering motions of his outstretched fingers to come and be loved. One need not command in language *Thoby* or *Bot-y* or *Good dog* or *Bad dog*, or *Come:* the dog was always there. It had no autonomous life separable from its allegiance, but put forth its own needy state of moment-by-moment dependence as a source of warmth and solidarity. The dog humorously walloped its great soft tail against Jack's calves, *here I am*, or butted its face into his lap and groin, scrambling up with eager paws, snagging his sweater, *it's me as usual*. The dog had no need of tether, bearing such attachment. Even across the length of the room the tie stretched so taut between them, others might have been sent sprawling over the trip-rope of eye-contact.

Jack looks up, Thoby comes padding; is a moist cold nose and wet rough tongue in Jack's palm, sniffing up the safe, familial, exciting smell, licking in the salty taste of Jack; is a breathing weight of subsiding creatureliness as his haunches relax against his master's half-paralysed but still sentient legs. Is there; is *there*, so solid and foursquare an argument for the integrity of the human with the animal. Is a darkly glistening forcefield of amiable energy, with his black curly coat in the firelight sleek with a gloss like that on coal. Is a power-house to which Jack may always turn: witness the resistance of Thoby's barrel-like body to being dragged out by Maureen and Tom at night, sets firm with every muscle in his broad chest, and a leonine snarl upon his lips. Is a swarm of disobedient desires such as Jack would give his eye-teeth to emulate, sitting here chairbound and tame, while his animal snatches profiteroles from a neglected plate, trots off fast with the baby's best red musical rattle, at which its fastidiously hygienic mother, Emma, complains that the slobber has communicated germs of an ineradicable nature to the toy, which will have to be thrown away. Is a black spirit Jack sends roaming from his magic circle, to the ends of the earth to do his bidding; and retires to his mute master at day's end.

'That wretched wretched creature. Look what he's done now,' that one fumes.

'I don't think he's right in the head. I'm sure he's dangerous. I worry for the baby.'

'Can dogs have paranoid schizophrenia? If so he's a prime candidate.'

'He barks at Mother, you know. Show Tom where he nipped you.'

'Goodness, did he do that? You really ought to have him put down.'

'He's Jack's dog really: not mine,' says that one doubtfully.

'Yes, well, Dad isn't in much of a state to look after him, is he? In any case I'm sure Dad would be the first person to agree that a dangerous animal is just not a safe pet to keep around the house.'

'Well, he's not that bad, dear. I shouldn't like – '

'You have enough on your plate as things stand. How long do you think you can go on like this? Good God, look at him now, he's taken against the damn goldfish for Heaven's sake – hey, get down you witless hound. Down, I said, down.'

'Thinks he's a cat, not a dog.'

'Never been the same since – '

'Don't say I didn't warn you, Mother, that's all – '

'I promise I won't. Oh Thoby, come on over here: what are we going to do with you?'

'Sometimes these pedigree dogs suffer from inbreeding, you

know. We had that poodle, Minta – she was quite berserk, used to eat herself – '

Jack's dog skirts the group suspiciously, anxiety widening his eyes. He slips behind the settee and is there heard to pant. Is cajoled and commanded to emerge; will not; finally, exasperated shoots out and bounds at the enemy, barking furiously. Makes for the male with the heavy scents of hostility at hands and groin and armpit and mouth. That male staggers back under a hundred pounds of launched ferocity. Bedlam; a woman calling; shrill children stampeding. Jack's dog still maddened, seeking atonement for the tempest of terror still loose in his skull, sights Jack, stony Jack the hieratic king, aloof on his throne. Thoby shrinks back snarling on his haunches, frothing at the mouth, his eyes bloodshot. He barks savagely at his master.

No no no no no no no

Thoby pounces on the adversary and snatches the cuff of his sweater in his jaws, saliva flecked with Jack's blood where teeth and claws have scored the parchment skin, he yanks Jack's arm madly to and fro, his eyes lifted and rolling as if in direst puzzlement, blindly seeking the chastening control of *master, master. No no no no no no no*. Jack in the maelstrom unravelling feels the cord slacken and snap between himself and his creature, falls backward under the tempest of violence into that abortive pit of wordless rejection he came from whose exit has been so hard and rare.

Thoby, called off, suddenly loses all impetus. From slavering he passes to abject cringing. A thousand enemies surround him, he sees their gimlet eyes, from which it is useless to try to hide. He backs into the far corner and hunkers down there, his chin flat on the floor, his long black ears fanning out like the curly wig of a Restoration courtier.

'Is Dad all right?' They bathe his hand. They place their palms over his thunderous heart. 'Are you all right, Dad?'

'I'll take him to the vet. There's no option now.'

'Yes. Take him now. You must. This would have broken his heart.' She strokes his hair, her face is crumpled with rue. 'Poor old lad.' They speak of Jack as if his body were Jack's effigy, or he himself were out of his wits, or elsewhere.

'Should we get the doctor? I'm sure he shouldn't have shocks like that.'

'I doubt, quite honestly, if it registered. Probably just like a bad dream. But maybe call the doctor, Angie – it's as well to check.'

Jack's dog is manhandled out of the room by his son and his son-in-law. Jack knows; he sees. Thoby resists every single inch of the way. Jack keeps his eyes fixed on the door through which his mortal shadow quit the theatre of his vision. Later the doctor arrives and listens to the huge throb of Jack's betrayed heart and takes his fast pulse. Just to be on the safe side he administers an injection of sedative; and Jack goes out like a light.

4
Grace

It is like a childhood illness, these long doldrums, disincentived. As sixty years ago he lay inert and let the featureless adults pass to and fro across his indifferent field of vision, so now Jack opens his eyes upon a lacklustre world drained of colour and purpose. His bored eye travels the sallow rectangle of daylight at the window; his mind recedes to the half-world where the shades spawn twilit verbal confusions upon which he plays in apathy.

I had a stroke.

Oh Jenny may I stroke you there?

On the stroke of midnight he died.

His hand steals down to hold the dwindled root of his sex, that flaccid unstirring has-been, which gives him a limited infantile comfort to coddle in his palm, as if he there protected a defencelessly vulnerable aspect of himself. But when they pull off the sheets to cleanse or change him, they discover his hand there and, embarrassed, remove it. They straighten his body out and lie it flat as if we should all march to Heaven with regimental precision in starched pyjamas. Nothing embarrasses Jack now, he submits tamely to whatever rules are laid down in a house no longer his.

Stroke-stroke, stroke-stroke, chimes his heart.

There-there, there-there.

Home-time, home-time, rings the school bell.

Little by little Jack's body creeps and spasms its way back into the attitude of self-solacing, foetally curled, his hand between his thighs. As patiently, the powers-that-be uncurl him from his hibernation and expose the reluctant ball of his eye to the lackadaisical light of day.

'Jack, darling, you have a visitor.'

He does not stir. He is well used to this kind of interference. If you take no notice, often they will go away and leave you in peace.

'Jack, dear, open your eyes.'

They have pulled the curtains wide open, to allow the troublesome glare to drill into his shut lid.

'I don't know if it's any good. Don't be too disappointed, sweetheart. He has good days and bad days, more often bad. Do you want to sit with him for a while?'

Scraping chair, be still. Breathing stranger, go away. The jittery birds outside the window make some querulous fuss at inordinate length in their incomprehensible code. Jack is falling asleep – good, good – his breathing deepening. The sac of self huddles down into the stale, airless pocket of the womb-lining.

'You always did have a quite spectacular snore, you know, Jack,' says Jenny's voice conversationally.

He smiles involuntarily before he is really awake. How long has the dear old girl, leaning up on one elbow, been viewing his stertorous self upon the pillow? *Poor Jenny. What bad nights I've given you Cherubino with my decibels. How do you stand it?* Wry face; mop of dark, tangled hair; tired kind eyes, most beautiful. So she will be, he predicts; this time he has not dreamed her. He smiles broadly, the inner complicit smile of one who never has to be alone for she breathes by him. Oh sleeping with her in naked sharing tumultuous joy, who was it told him – poor fool – that in the end we are on our own? That in the last analysis we slink out single-file through the narrowest of exits? Never never never never never. Not in a million years while Jenny shares his sleep. *I satisfied you last night Cherub didn't I? And I will pleasure you today until you beg for mercy; and will that pay you for my snores and your insomnia?* Sometimes in the night he awakens; pads out to the bathroom; pads back in, and through the gloom, last thing and first thing, sees her dark hair spread upon the pillow with such an agony of tenderness, his hand hovers above her head in the likeness of benediction for he dare not touch her if she's asleep, she sleeps so thin; and Jenny's cross if you wake her. *You're not cross now, you're asking me to waken.* The smile is yielding and involuntary, but opening his eyes an act of will: portcullis of lashes, secured against all intrusion, crusted together somewhat, hard to unlock.

There is a face he used to know and ought to recognise, close by his pillow but not sharing his estate. It has the look of a listener, an attentive inwardness. All its hair is shorn: strange alteration. He knows the face but it is vastly changed: older, certainly. One sees the laughter-lines about the eyes, revealed by the cropped hair, creases in the skin pictured as so wholly smooth, recollected on the very whorls of his fingerprints as an identity of his own. She is leaning with her elbows on her knees, her head bent to a level with his own, peering into his eyes, with a reader's frowning concentration. She is a lot older, there in the shadow. At the same time, more fully herself. An image of risen power, the eagle ascended, looking down on his own shameful ruin and decay. She is a soul in bliss, but he – closes himself against her desperately, brings down the blinds. No Jenny no earth no eyes no God.

'You're terribly patient with him, Jenny.'

'He was patient with me when I needed him.'

'But you know darling he really doesn't know you're there. The doctor told us. He's almost brain-dead. At least in the parts that matter.'

'I don't believe that, Maureen. Do you?'

There is a pause. The quiet voice again: 'I've come to a point of acceptance. I like to care for him. Whether or not.'

'I haven't – come to any point of acceptance.'

'That's not your way.'

'I think he hears me.'

'Do you, sweetheart? Honestly? Perhaps he does then. I'd trust your instincts.'

'Why don't you hate me, Maureen?' the voice bursts out. 'Why do you let me come here and love him out loud in front of your very eyes?'

The other voice tenders neither answer nor absolution, and dimly Jack wonders, sunk down in the comfortable dip of the bed dozily tuned in to this radio-world of transmitted whispers, how the actors can accord such life-and-death significance to the old bag of bones trussed up here so snugly incommunicado.

'Do you still have that old tape-recorder, Maureen?'

enquires the burster-out in more level tones. 'I'd like to play him some music I've brought.'

'Of course, honey. In fact we have a new one, the latest thing in technology. A lot of Jack's old junk has had to be got rid of.'

And here is Olly at her heels, trotting along behind her finding more security in a week of Maureen than in eight and a half years of the volatile Jenny. The blond cuckoo would gladly settle here amongst the tall pines of the magical country and nest within the solid walls eighteen inches thick, and keep his borrowed sweaters and mittens, go tobogganning with the grandchildren in the winter, and camp and swim in the summer. There is nothing here to which he takes exception, save perhaps that quilted hump in the four-poster bed which he sees from the landing and is said to be a sick old man, whom he fears and will not approach. He would not like to see the sick old man's face, though his mother says there is nothing whatever to be frightened of. He looks through the gap in the door and observes her madly conversing with that silence, apparently perfectly content with no answer. Now Maureen delivers the tape-recorder to Jenny, and 'Hi!' sings Olly, on the wing, migrating past the sinister doorway.

The warm smell of self deep in the foetal bed: a shame to abandon it for the desolations of the upper world, eye-stabbing light, rape of the spirit by those remote, vexed voices they have up there. Jack does his level best to abdicate life, digging down into his chrysalis, wallowing in the low estate of Jack. But she is like a mocking-bird at the window of his privacy, calling his curiosity to see what throat could generate such bantering calls.

Jack likes the folds of his sheets, pillows and eiderdown to be just so and not otherwise. If they are not to his liking, he feels put out. After all this is his world, shrunk to a cocoon, and he ought to be able to dispose it according to his convenience. The flannel sheets swaddle his face, hands and feet like bandagings for an ancient wound. They should be loose to his skin so that a chamber of warm air can surround him; and so that his fingers may clasp and gradually work into his grip a significant handful of the flannel material, which he may rub between finger and thumb. It comforts Jack and helps him drowse. Once upon a time when he burst into the emergency of living for the first time, caterwauling (being Jack) at the top of his already considerable voice, they wrapped him up tight, by happy chance, in just such a piece of flannel, which his fingers caught and his mouth sucked; and it became his dearest friend. Until he was ten, Jack kept the dingy, fraying fabric under his pillow, and sucked it to get to sleep at night. Brays of male derision – father and step-brother – could not deter. The friendly cloth slept at his cheek folded to a special shape in a nightly procedure of infinite soothing – until it vanished all of a sudden, and he didn't really miss it, he felt at the time, though now with its return there is an atavistic pleasure, as of a pot rescued from boiling over, a half-forgotten danger obviated.

But when they raise the bedclothes the roof of the world lifts away, and it is sheer terror then. They rip off his pyjamas and take a layer of skin with them. Flayed Jack hangs raw and red in space as when he first sailed into view, and has his chin razored and his exposed surfaces scalded and scoured with soap and washrags; and when they have done rolling him over, twisting him back, the taut sheets are arctic wastes around his sterile isolation.

And he can bear no more. He will open his eyes and see if anyone here can put him out of his misery.

Dawn of day and gracious light. The profiled figure at his bedside is quiet and still, leaning forward, chin in hand. Early morning sunlight burnishes the back of her head to copper. She wears a daffodil-yellow blouse of some silky texture, and behind her stands a vase of russet and tawny-coloured chrysanthemums. Jack watches from the underworld without being noticed, and drinks upon his eye the riot of autumnal colour in the land of the living. Her forefinger taps gently on her upper lip to the rhythm of the music.

He knows the music, Strauss' *Four Last Songs*, written in the composer's eighties. He knew it always, as far back as he could remember, the vast, lush rhetoric of orchestration that sees no reason to hold back, so late in the day. Is the music inside or outside him? Its tides sweep away the frontiers between Jack and all which is not Jack, the woman's voice sings in his own head, she is Jack and he is the woman, resolving in bittersweet solution the nerve-strung, garrulous dilemma of it all.

'I know exactly who you are,' says Jack on the light-stained pillow, slowly but with all his old doctrinaire assertiveness. 'You're Jenny in the mirror.'

5
Snow

The first snows have hit Pennsylvania, not in blizzards but with stealthy footfall night by night so that when they awaken, the land lies deeper in drifts, but the snowfall has paused. Ankle-deep, knee-deep, thigh-deep it mounts the walls of 'Red Earth' and 'Shadows' in a geometrical progression which will bury the door in a week. Nicki loves it, the glittering forcefield of violent white that annihilates the domesticated garden-world; the two-dimensional black presences of the pines and firs and those strange foreshortenings in which the far white world pushes forward between those dark living pillars. She relishes the vivid air on her cheeks, the leaden clouds gravid with more to come.

'You are a winter lady,' says Marguerite to her, seeing her childlike eagerness. 'I didn't know that before. See how much I've still to learn about you.' It is the first winter of their lives together, though it seems they have known each other for ever.

'Yes I suppose I am. A winter person. How odd, it never occurred to me.'

'*My* winter lady,' corrects Marguerite. '*Mine*. Not just anybody's. Not even your own. All mine.'

'Greedy.'

'You're damn right I am. As far as you're concerned.' Marguerite is glad of the heavy snowfalls: they will maroon the two of them at 'Shadows', cut them off, with any luck, from the incursions of the rivalrous world that interrupts their beatific exchange and steals Nicki's attention from her. Marguerite likes the idea of being muffled and shrouded in this counterpane of snow. Other voices have no resonances here. The very birds are muted, pianissimo. Perhaps even the hateful Middletons at 'Red Earth' will be cut off from

'Shadows' by the snowfall, though when Marguerite opens the curtains she sulkily observes that the strange foreshortening light-effects have thrown the great pale house forward in their direction over the tree-tops. Brittle, insecure Marguerite wears a *Trespassers will be prosecuted* notice over her breast, she knows that Maureen uncannily read and respected it, but Nicki seems oblivious. It's Nicki she fears, her outgoing, free-and-easy loving nature. The snows will hem her in.

'I'm going to dig,' says Nicki.

'What? Snowmen? Igloos?'

'No, you silly girl, dig us out. Come on, it'll give you an appetite.'

'What do you want to dig out for? Let's dig in. Just us. Together.'

'Marguerite – *Marguerite* – we've got all our lives – just us – together.' Nicki brushes her cheek with one finger, very softly. 'Don't you know that yet? Hasn't it sunk in?'

It has sunk in. *All our lives*. It is enough, even for Marguerite's huge hunger, spreading her beak like a ravenous nestling for more more more: *all our lives* is (surely?) enough. The vows she has extorted from Nicki, and yet she ought to have the power, the command in the relationship. She is only twenty-eight, darkly beautiful. Need forfeited sovereignty. It capitulated instantly. One day this craving need will lose her Nicki altogether: *I'll make her hate the sight of me with these inexorable, unappeasable demands*.

'Of course. Just teasing. Why don't I go and call Maureen and Jack for you, sweetie, make sure they're still in the land of the living?' That goodwill is the concession she owes and drags from herself, small change from an impoverished pocket.

'Do . . . But we'll go over later. Or I will – you can stay and build snowmen if you want.'

'Maureen fine. Jack fine. Josephine is out with the kids and a shovel making a path for us to come down,' Marguerite reports, with honey voice. She stands in her red sweater, mittens and boots, watching her breath condense against the black-and-white morning: black boughs with their impossible freight of snow, the cord of a washing line swollen to a fat cable, the expectant stillness all around.

'Thanks, sweetie. You *are* thoughtful. God, your hair. It's raven against this snow. My God you're breathtaking. You're ravishing.'

I am not, after all, without my power, thinks Marguerite, digging energetically, face and hands scalding. *And when all's said and done she's an old woman, on the wane or somewhat past it, and I'm a young one, waxing.*

'Look at them now, Pete. Did you ever see or imagine anything quite like it?'

Nicki's children, Shelley and her younger brother Pete, lounging in their dressing-gowns in an upstairs window-seat, survey their parent and her friend with disdain from a great height. Pete peers and shrugs.

'God,' he says, and turns his back.

'They seem so – embarrassingly juvenile,' says Shelley, a bright, composed girl of eighteen summers. 'It's that awful giggling of theirs I can't stand. I got over that stage ten years ago.'

'I've diagnosed dear Marguerite,' says Pete. 'I've been studying her behaviour-patterns.' Having lately decided on a medical career, he has diagnosed a number of painfully Latinate diseases, mainly rare and frequently terminal, in his friends and their families. Nobody would have taken notice of this aberration had not his friend's mother visited the doctor and got hers confirmed. Pete's practice thrives.

'What's she got then?'

'Two things just for starters. She's a manic depressive. And she's anorexic. The giggling is the manic bit – the soulful drooping is the depressive – the fact that she never eats is the anorexic. We are harbouring a nut.'

'Oh come on.'

'Do you ever see her eat?'

'Not a lot. She does look rather emaciated but she probably thinks that's fashionable,' says Shelley, who, being herself hale and well-rounded, knows that it is not.

'And Mother is menopausal. She is experiencing a mid-life crisis. This is why we have to be saddled with the manic depressive anorexic nut.'

'Oh well, at least she's happy with her nut. That's something to be grateful for.' Shelley, leaning on her hands, nose against the cold pane, looks down with a rueful proprietoriness upon her mother's vigorous shovelling activities. The spade clangs on the path with a thin echoing ring. Marguerite, a bright crimson stain on the dazzling world, is leaning gracefully on her spade; she looks up and meets the eyes of the enemy she can least afford to offend; smiles with cat's eyes; waves up. 'Hi there, nut,' murmurs Shelley, waving back. 'Peace be with you if you really are making her happy.' Do all offspring, she wonders, labour under this yoke of solicitous responsibility for their parents' perpetuated adolescence?

'She *is* thin. And Mother is really manipulated by her, you know.'

'Typical of the syndrome,' advises aged Sapience.

'Their generation seems so much less able to cope than ours. In the end, you just have to leave them to it.'

Nicki, sweating, has finished clearing the path. But it is beautiful out here, she stands looking through the steam from her cocoa, over the oceanic lawns and the black sea of trees towards 'Red Earth'. It was so good that Jack made that excellent, if partial, recovery. She has learnt to love him now, not just for Maureen's sake but as a person who can mean something to her in himself. He seems to like to talk to Nicki, and though his language is more than a little inchoate, they make up for the hiatuses in signs and good-natured silences. The music he has been composing since his recovery is extraordinary, she cannot claim to understand its quirky signals, clues, innuendoes, silences, but she marvels all the same at the reservoir of creativity revealed in the depths of this old, sick man. He's like a human radio telescope. He has traced his music from the dark side of the moon, taking at dictation the intimations of the remote stars and the spaces between.

Around Jack revolves Maureen, describing her eternal ellipse, now coming in close, now reeling out far, never less than centred. In relation to Maureen, Nicki remains burdened with the discomfort of imperfect understanding, an attraction never fully purged or outlived. She cannot put that love in the past, but it had nowhere else to go. There is still the pang, whenever she sees the serenely cryptic face, at a window, across a table, framed in the car window. There is still the little-girl rush of longings to dash towards her and urge her own case. But now there is Marguerite – no primal comfort there, but a charge like an electric voltage, dangerous and exciting. Anger and jealousy and rows and returns. Lyrical times of gentleness, lying together, searching one another's lives with feathering fingertips: sure as of a childhood playfellow, unsure, unsure.

'Aren't you coming in? The fire's roaring. Your appalling offspring are taking the sledge out to the slopes round the Scott estate. They say do you want to go with them? I told them no.'

'No, I don't want to go anywhere near the Scott estate.' Where they found Jack's dear old dog that time last spring, bloody on the barbed wire. She couldn't forget the anguish of that first view of Thoby, prone on his side, gashed all down his beautiful glossy chest, one bent paw raised in the air as if in greeting, one eye open. Extraordinarily sad. The open eye's silent asking. It is as if she has been permanently saddened by it: as if that vision of creaturely suffering had aroused her sensitivity to the whole lacerated creation. Because of Thoby's open eye, the dead squirrel on the highway cries in her hearing for redress, the vermin the owls eat are sentient mortals and their dying call is *Why*? Undoubtedly it changed her. It threatened her foundations in commonsense, and the undemanding Episcopalian Christianity which she had worn like a comfortable, baggy old suit of clothes all her life. The following day, Thoby's eye forbade her to repeat the *Our Father* with her Sunday school class; she choked on 'Thy will be done' and developed a strategic coughing fit over the question of asking pardon of the carnivorous God. It was the sort of thing she might have taken to Maureen, and found in her wisdoms an assurance, a way of seeing things whole with quiet eye which would have answered Thoby's accusations. She would have counselled how we live with all this and are not subject to it. But Nicki was beginning then to perceive Maureen too as subject, a suffering victim helpless on the chain, able to be uprooted, capable of catastrophic fall. Now when Marguerite invites her, so sprightly, *Come to the Scott estate*, Nicki sees in her mind blood on snow; the black coils of barbed wire, flecks of Thoby's blood soaking the white crystals, in a terrible epitaph which she would happen on if she ever went there again. An atonement that was no good to anyone. A sign from God to mankind of his malevolent indifference.

'What are you doing out here in the cold? Oh Nicki, don't look so lost.'

'Do I?'

'You do, you do. This isn't like you. You're naturally so joyous, we all rely on you for that. All of us who love you.'

Sometimes Marguerite surprises herself by the generosity that pours from the surplus of her love unbidden; the crossbias, against her jealous possessiveness, of her urge to cherish and share. She must really love Nicki then, if she can forget her own insecurities. That's good; that has to be good. She wraps her arms round her friend now and sways her like a child from side to side.

'I have you, Marguerite. I have you, for all time. Against all the odds. That's what counts.'

'What were you thinking?'

'Oh – I was thinking earlier about how Jack and Maureen were married on this lawn forty-five years ago.'

'Why was that sad?'

'I don't know. I don't know.'

'Because of his illness?'

'Perhaps. No, not really. Just the strangeness of the thought. Under those larches over there in that snowdrift the minister stood, and the host of guests stretched up to the house. Afterwards they had champagne and danced on the lawns and that night Josie was conceived. Isn't it *strange*, the past, Marguerite, how it loiters around in some pockets of the earth like mist (do you know what I mean?) and suddenly you're in it – the inconceivable time before we ever existed.'

Marguerite looks about. The minister arises in his white surplice from the snowdrift at the lawn's altar and asks if the icy groom takes this white transparent lady to be his lawful – and the wedding guests, drowned up to their armpits in snow raise their chalices of champagne filmed with ice, and you hear the thin chink of glass on glass – while Jack Frost and his snow-maiden take hands for the first waltz, skimming the crisp surface of the frost. Above the nuptial feast the starving crows and other carrion circle.

The northern hemisphere is shrouded in snow. Jenny and Oliver saw on the news last night pictures of Americans skating on a frozen river. *A new Ice Age*, warn the meteorologists. *Button up well and wear thermal underwear*, advised the hearty newscaster on the radio this morning. *Check on aged neighbours*, the newspaper pleads. *They might be dying of hypother-*

mia. John Street, Clayton, is remarkably rich in aged neighbours. Rosie, out of the superabundant goodness of her heart, raps on five doors, gets the coal in for one grateful senior citizen but sows the seeds of long-term rancour in another who, at the age of fifty-eight, takes mortal offence at Rosie's imputation of decay and dependency: 'When I want charity, miss, be sure I'll ask for it.'

Oliver is in his seventh heaven and, though he is supposed to be in disgrace for running out in the snow in his slippers and hurling himself full-length into an inviting drift, is in a roseate state of cherubic joy. His best friend Aziz from next door has been up and down the hill with him on an improvised sledge, they have built a teddy-bear out of snow and pelted each other with snowballs, a game which ended in Aziz's tears when Oliver – who is subject to fits of roughness – ran his hand along the wall and stuffed the resultant handful of snow down his collar. Olly has been made to apologise, which he did with a good grace, and brought in to sit by the fire and await his tea. His face is scalded bright red with fierce extremes of cold and heat. He kneels in his blue tracksuit and toasts crumpets over the flames on a fork, then lashes them with margarine and golden syrup, and eats them oozing and hot.

From the little kitchen Jenny hears him stirring his usual heaped teaspoons of sugar into his mug of bloodcurdlingly sweet tea. She stands at the window with her hands in suds, looking out at the low grey sky and registering the awful Bradford draughts at her neck and calves; the waves of cold emanating from flagged floors and the stale chill trapped in the cellars. Being a full-time mother is a monotonous business. It mainly consists of hanging around in rain and gales at the school gates in the midst of a choric discussion of ear-ache, diarrhoea and the right way to boil suet; yelling furious instructions to get ready, look both ways, don't punch, hurry up, and stop clicking those bloody castanets at once; calling the doctor in the middle of the night, and peeling potatoes at the kitchen sink. She cannot say, standing here under the drab ceiling of the Yorkshire sky, with this staggering cold piercing the soles of her slippers and numbing each individual joint of her toes, that it is a profession she would have opted for. This is not to say that Jenny regrets her choice of Olly.

'Don't take too much sugar, Olly. It's bad for your teeth,' she now admonishes her child, through the open doorway.

'I haven't,' replies his injured innocence. 'I've only taken one and it wasn't even full anyway.'

'I quite distinctly heard you put in three spoonfuls, Olly, so don't tell me fibs.'

'How can you hear sugar going into a cup?' enquires Oliver, scientifically. There is a pause. 'There, did you hear that?'

'Olly, stop it.'

'Stop what?'

'Bring the sugar-bowl out here. It shouldn't be taken into the sitting room anyway. You know what it's like when it gets spilt.'

'Horrid little crunchy bits in your socks,' agrees Olly, bringing out the bowl.

'And we do have to take care in Rosie's house, love. It isn't our house. Please do try and remember.'

'Rosie doesn't mind,' says Oliver, putting his arms round Jenny's waist from behind and counselling peace in her through his rocking motions. 'Rosie is ace. Rosie sticks up for me when you nag.'

'Do I nag?'

'Not absolutely all the time,' Oliver says judiciously. 'You are okay. Can I go out again and play with the snowbear?'

'Oh Olly it's almost dark.' Darkness comes down like a stone slab up here in the hills, there's hardly any twilight, just the sudden blackening of the gritstone walls of the terrace and the sun absconded into the lightless shoulder of the moorlands. Rosie still raves about the lightscapes on the heath, the tempestuous light raying through the brew of cloud. For Jenny, maternity's exposure to the bitter monotony of winter weathers has obscured her susceptibility to that kind of beauty. The absence of Jack has drained reality of its power of transfiguration. Colour is elsewhere, in that festal, magic country whose opalescent skies rained warmth and brightness. By and large she accepts the dourer conditions prevalent here, and does not grievously pine for what lies over the hill. 'Oh all right, Olly,' she capitulates. 'The snow doesn't last for ever. Go out and have a last play. Put on your boots.'

The snowbear keeps vigil in the yard by the coal-bunker, within the pale of the fluorescent light from the kitchen window. She helped to create him, aggregating his portly body by rolling a ball of snow around the drifted pavement until its fat mass could be shoved no further. The snowbear looks back at Jenny through borrowed eyes of inscrutable coal, and he wears a jerkin of sack to protect him against the barren climate. Behind the spotlit bear, whom now Olly pats, adding last embellishments, the background is densely black. He seems to be peering in at her as she works, an amiable but puzzled pioneer from polar regions. And now it worries her, drying her hands on the washing-up cloth, hanging up her apron: the fact that Jack is snowbound in that far continent, where the planes are all grounded, telegraph wires are down, and if you lay the bare palm of your hand on metal, the hand will come away skinned. Although over there, of course, they are quite used to such arctic conditions, they take it in their stride. Cars have snow-tyres and there are plenty of ploughs. You just stay in with your family and enjoy a more intimate privacy until the weather stabilises or clears. They have told her that many times: Jack excelled himself at boring narratives on that topic. 'Have I told you about the bad winter of 1946? . . .' She groans even now to think of it. But she can't help but wonder, as the chilblains twinge in the balls of her feet, about Jack's feet – whether they are cold, she would give the earth to chafe them for him as now she chafes Olly's as he burst in from the garden, having at last had enough, kicks off his boots and allows her to cradle his feet in both hands by the fire. The television's on. He dozes in her lap.

Oliver has a half-sister two weeks old, Zoë: he went there last weekend and gave her permission to continue existing, though he admits that he could not really see the point of her. He displays little overt disturbance at separation from his father, despite Alexander's infatuated obsession with his new daughter, which he took little trouble to hide from that devalued currency, his son. Olly threw off his royal blue school uniform, his blazer, cap and tie, without regret, and seemed to have left his racial prejudice behind in Harrogate: out of his three best friends at the primary school, two are Indian, one a white girl. Jenny notices that he chooses shy or weak-seeming children to befriend, as if carrying some consciousness of impairment, a difficulty in locating a world the exactly right size to receive him. He vacillates oddly between bouts of rowdy bossiness and lulls of extraordinary tranquillity. The peaceful boy at the kitchen table who turns from his work to disclose 'I've taken up the study of art' is drawing a painstaking picture of an apple set in an egg-cup. That Oliver is the same as the one she takes to the swimming pool on Saturday afternoons who, in the welter of churning, splashing, bellowing children, lies floating on his back barely moving his arms and legs beyond what is needed to keep him buoyed, rests back upon the mother-element with his eyes wide open, an expression of utter beatitude upon his yielded, quietened face.

Water lapped in an oval around the corners of his eyes, the line of his chin and forehead. His hair, darkened in the turquoise water, rayed out loose as a sea-anemone. Jenny sitting on the side amongst the tumbling, antic forms of the storm of Saturday swimmers, fed her eyes upon his comely limbs, his well-made hands, his beautiful wistful eyes. A line of boys leapt in, their indistinct shouts racketing to the roof; in the turbulence of their watery landings, Olly just lay there trustfully, rocking in the many wakes. Jenny's twanging nerves were calmed. She slid into the pool, approached him, and lay on her back beside him, sustained by his confidence and peace in the water; and how she swam in Jack's pool came back to her, and how he took her for a boy. *All is one*, said Oliver's rocking peace to Jenny's lifelong distress. *All's one, don't worry. Not too much anyway.*

That stabilisation of Jenny upon the restless medium, going with the turbulence rather than resisting, marks an access of faith for which she can't account but for which she's grateful. Not faith in God precisely, although she has started to attend communion occasionally, and sits in the back pew behind the congregation of ten elderly ladies and one lame old gentleman which represents the entire flock of that moribund institution. It is more a faith that something that was out of her is at last in her. She has seen one most precious to her ruined beyond any hope of retrieval. The burning creativity of Jack has been subjected to disintegration, the magician reduced to a cabbage, his rod broken, humiliated utterly. She has sat at his bedside for long oppressive tracts of time, nauseated by the sickroom atmosphere, experiencing his dereliction. There she meditated helping him to die; to make a decent end. She was ready to do it for him when he spoke. *Fiat lux*, said Jack, from the alchemist's crucible of his intolerable and desecrating pain; his spirit flamed out like a candle amidst the corruption of the flesh, and there was light. She seemed to rise from her own ashes. She can't now put out the composing light in herself, she will have to live with its modest illumination.

Jenny hopes to visit him again in the spring: Maureen will pay her passage. Time is short for him, long for her. She dare not look forward even as far as the spring, but reflects instead on how beautiful it was to see him back in his chair by the fire at home, speaking, smiling, sharing. Communion: it was worth living to have known that. If now she could bathe his feet, wash them with her tears, cup them in the palms of her hands as she can Oliver's – if now there were some small practical office tenderness might discharge – her heart swells, tears salt her eyes, but not corrosively. There are still the letters. She is learning music to try to understand the letters. Jack, who cannot write much in the way of coherent English, sends daily messages in the language of musical notation. He writes as it were from outer space, in the only language that is known there. Yesterday, taking Olly to school, Jenny saw the fleet of postmen on their red bikes flowing out of the depot. She followed Bradley her postman home, zigzagging through the treacherous overnight snow, and he handed her Jack's latest Airmail composition, addressed in Maureen's handwriting. As she received it from his gloved hand into her own, it came to her with a shock that these communications would one day cease. The postman would not call with the thin wafer of the blue envelope. She trembled with cold as she let herself in, slit the envelope and hummed an approximation to Jack's latest riddle from the end of the world.

Marguerite and Nicki ski home from 'Red Earth' in good time before dark falls. Snowflakes are eddying down as they descend the slope into the lap of the valley, their calls and laughter belling against the tight-packed legions of trees, those black, dispassionate sentinels. They fly their scarves behind them like pennants, red and green. The cutting blades of their skis fizz through the untouched snow. Nicki, who loves physical exertion, executes a dextrous turn at the base of the valley, with a swish of her skis and a tilt of her hips and shoulders. Marguerite, unused to the sporty life, buckles at the knees, ploughs and somersaults her way to the bottom, her laughter clapping against the army of trees with a report like gunfire.

Now they march on splayed feet up the steeper part of the home-slope, and ski the rest, not sparing any oxygen for speech. As they rise, the effects of an apricot-coloured sunset register in a strange tinge of pinkness to the snow as if it were a crystallisation of some unknown chemical. The higher they mount towards 'Shadows' the more that light-effect intensifies, and Marguerite has the urge to blink it off her eye, as if a drop of dye had flowed across the lens. Rounding the final bend, half of 'Shadows' can be glimpsed, its white paint glowing with a pinkish sheen, the glass of its windows reflecting a fiery liquid gold from the sun boiling upon the horizon. The effect is curiously freakish and disturbing, as if one met a man with golden eye-ointment daubed upon one eye and a patch over the other. Nicki's children's voices can be heard hellraising out there in the grounds. More like the entire contents of a football field than just the two of them: Marguerite scowlingly wishes for the thousandth time that those two inconvenient pairs of watchful eyes and no doubt satiric tongues could be despatched from her living-space. She feels the hostility spun out from their polite neutrality like spiders' webs, and picks her way with care among their glances. Never mind: they'll be packed off to their father at the weekend.

Nicki slows down; stops altogether, stabbing the spikes of her ski-poles into the snow.

'Jack was rather queer today, I thought. Didn't you think so?'

'I can't honestly say I noticed any difference. He's always pretty – weird. I can't claim to understand much of what he says at the best of times. He sort of gargles the words in his throat as if he were trying to swallow what he's saying: and when I do get the message it's oblique to anything – outlandish. What was wrong with him?'

'I couldn't put my finger on it. Something.'

'Maureen said he was up in the night – fretful – seemed to feel he'd lost something and had to hunt round for it. It must be so hard for her.'

'Yes, in a way. But she feels good when she's caring for someone, Marguerite, so maybe it's not such a trial for her as it would be for you and me.'

'You mean I'm a selfish bitch compared to her?'

'*No*! I *don't*! I didn't mean it and I didn't say it.' Nicki grabs the red ends of Marguerite's scarf and yanks. 'You make me wild. You make me want to strangle you when you talk like that. *Why* do you?' She gives another throttling tug. 'Why?'

'Because you compare me with her. I know you do. I see it in your eyes. And find me wanting. Which is unfair.' She glares at Nicki with lynx-eyes from under the curling mass of black hair.

'I never do. I never have compared you.'

'Because *she*'s incomparable, I suppose.'

'I give up. I really do.'

'Good. So do I.' Nicki has dropped the scarf, allowing Marguerite to stalk off up the incline to 'Shadows', her dignity somewhat impaired by the necessity to frog-march on the skis, and her own ineptitude. Nicki easily catches up.

'How could I compare you with an old grey-haired woman? – old enough for God's sake to be my mother.'

'Exactly,' replies Marguerite evilly. 'How could I possibly hope to reach up to that high standard? After all I'm a child-in-arms – an impediment you have to lug around – compared to that old woman.'

'Don't call her that.'

'Why not, it's accurate. What else is she?'

'Just – not that. Stop being so sickeningly childish.'

'See – I told you so. You just want a mother-figure – you're the baby, not me. Leave me out of it. I just wanted an equal relationship. I wish I'd stayed with Polly.'

The pinkish field of snow up which their sweating figures labour, the great pines which have receded into black silhouettes without distinguishable interior, the metallic shriekings of her now visible children, are all emblems, to Nicki's eye which suddenly gushes smarting tears, of some intolerable anguish which she can't name, but is always in there. Primitive losses, separations and fears, the fear of shadows, of falling, of being left out alone in the snow when it darkens. Of not being perfectly grown-up, even at the age of forty, and needing some exorcist who is grown-up to turn to, and finding that no one else had ripened fully either. You had to carry yourself along in your own arms, labouring all the way and pretending there was nothing to it. But no, *But no: I loved her with a genuine love, an equal love. It was more subtle and luminous than anything Marguerite can conceive.* 'It was before your time, Marguerite,' she says in coldly level tones. 'You simply don't have the emotional equipment to understand it.'

Marguerite shrinks into herself, as that fragment of scalding ice touches her; blushes deeply. 'Anyway,' she concludes. 'I hate you.'

There are Shelley and Pete, with their friends Victor and Sandra from Scott's, in the company of a giant snow-king eight foot high. The snow-king, his head crowned with spears of golden wheat that ray out in a six-inch radius from his head, reigns over the lawn of 'Shadows' from which his person has been rifled by the builders, and now resembles a tousled white quilt tossed about by some delirious sleeper underground. His shoulders are invested with a red robe, his eyes are walnuts, his nose an aquiline carrot, and a long pendulous pine-cone represents a disdainful mouth, turning down at either end. He looks down on his subjects with ineffable scorn from his majestic height, his demeanour exhibiting a backward list, mildly provoking to the laws of gravity.

'Do you want to help us to stone him to death?'

'But he's beautiful,' protests Nicki. 'Let him stay. I like him.' She registers her daughter's flushed face and hectic eyes mournfully. Sometimes one's children are hair-raising. Like savages: you can't believe they came from you.

'No, no, he's got to go,' yells the tribe. 'His time has come.'

'But you must have taken all afternoon to build him.'

'It won't take us five minutes to smash him. Filthy tyrant! Fascist pig! Down with him! *Vive la liberté*!'

'Vive la what?'

'The Ancien Régime and all that stuff,' says Victor, the sun reflecting on his round spectacles to create a manic effect of eyelessness. 'Down with it.'

'Quite right. Kill the king, kill the king,' mutter the circling populace. The *Sans Culottes* revolve around their sacrificial victim shaking fists, doubling up with laughter and uttering what tags of Revolutionary French jargon spring to mind, in execrable accents; all save Victor who majors in languages and waxes oratorical.

'Have you lot been drinking?'

'Us, Mother. Perish the thought. It's our natural exuberant high spirits.'

'Pete. You haven't been at that bottle of Benedictine have

you?' Pete, Nicki knows, takes a swig before school some mornings; claims it as his medical opinion that this stimulates the brain-cells. He is a nervy boy, she worries for him; breaks out in eruptions of excitement like a fiery rash and then can't steady himself. For an answer, Pete's gloved hands send the first snowball flying at the snow-king. 'Death to tyranny!' The snowball glances harmlessly off the king's right shoulder and falls in a shower of powder.

'*Don't*.'

'Why not, he's only snow. You shouldn't waste your pity on a heap of old snow. We'll show you.' Shelley takes meticulous aim; hurls; and misses.

'Pathetic.'

The regicides jeer at one another's ineptitude. They will fight each other maybe and forget the king; the imminent fall of dusk will save his snowy glories for another day. Shelley is stuffing snow down Pete's neck or vice versa. Wearily, Nicki takes off her skis and leans them up against the wall; prepares to go indoors. The sun seems to have slid down behind the hillside in a sudden rush, the pinkish glow is off the world and a blue gloom descends like a bruise on all vision, darkening moment by moment. Nicki has the sinister feeling which these days comes upon her at all sorts of odd times, of something inexpressibly unkind and unwholesome lying around a corner, through a door. She wishes she had not said the bitter things to Marguerite, nor heard them. She is tired and stiff, she feels her age suddenly. Turning in the doorway to call out a conciliatory phrase to her friend, she is struck by the sheer enmity of the expression on Marguerite's face.

Marguerite's red cap is pushed to the back of her head, straining back her hair so that her malignity is oddly barefaced. She pulls off the skis and throws them like javelins at the snow-king. They skid at his feet; are followed by a ski-pole which misses its target. Marguerite's cheeks are livid, her dark eyes violently disturbed. She stares round at Nicki, the traitor; at her fellow orgiasts.

'I'll help you smash him,' yells Marguerite. 'Come on, I'll help.' She makes common cause with the rising young against the decadent old monarch; with the new warm year against the old and cold; with Nicki's children against Nicki and the claptrap of her played-out sentimental allegiances.

'Kill the king.'

'Smash him.'

'Decapitate him.'

'Pulverise him.'

There is a cheer. His eyes are out. Another cheer. Half the king's face and half his wheaten crown are smashed to pieces. His left arm with the orb is shorn off at the shoulder. With a salvo of shouts, the pariah's ear and his urbanely sneering pine-cone mouth are despatched into eternity. His whole face is now wiped out and only the rear portions of his skull remain. Now the black windows of 'Shadows' appear through the patch of air which was his head. Still his aloof body stands, it holds against the battery. Its monumental bulk is well-compacted ice, and shows no inclination to topple despite the Pisan principles of its architecture. The wintry king by a quirk of divine right can survive his own decay, brother to the hen whose headless body goes on scampering in apparently everlasting circles of posthumous panic.

Nicki feels sick, there is something obscene about the violence invested in the game.

'Stop it! *Stop it!*' she yells at the top of her voice, hands over her ears, but no one hears.

'Let's ram the bastard.'

'Get that log. We'll do it in the good old Roman fashion.'

The four young people are manhandling the log but Marguerite beats them to it. She runs full-tilt at the king with the remaining ski-pole, and plunges it in his breast. The body quite suddenly gives; had only been standing by a thin root of ice, a whisper would have demolished it. A slow and creaking capsize lays him with a thump on his back, which smashes. Marguerite finds herself in the middle of a total silence, pierced by eyes. As if she had been caught out in the performance of some most shameful rite. Nobody speaks to her as she takes the vacated place of the sacrificed king.

'The king is dead,' announces Marguerite, thin-voiced, clambering upon the ruin. 'Long live the king.'

'Dwarf.'

They turn from her, shrugging, with raised eyebrows, conspiratorial heads leagued together. They file past Nicki into 'Shadows' and are heard smothering hoots of laughter up the stairs. All the lights go on. The two women linger outside, in one another's arms, not speaking, just holding on as evening intensifies. They stand so still that late-flying crows come down and peck up the grains of the king's crown, and a renegade squirrel, the clock of her hibernation maladjusted, filches the walnuts that were his eyes.

Also of interest:

Stevie Davies
Arms and the Girl

'*Arms and the Girl* talks about the unspeakable, giving voice to raw need and intolerable deprivation of love.'

Stevie Davies

Scotland. 1959. Prue and January Cahill – British army children – are subject to outrageous family betrayal and violence. Prue survives by clinging to her schoolbooks, but most of all by developing an unlikely friendship with the rector's daughter in her loving, middle-class world. But January is the outcast in her family, its scapegoat and its reject . . .

Arms and the Girl is a shattering, breakthrough work by a major contemporary writer.

'Stevie Davies' first novel won the Fawcett Society Book Prize . . . it was not just a flash in the pan.' *The Scotsman*

Fiction £6.99/£11.99
ISBN 0 7043 4309 6 pbk
0 7043 5063 7 hbk

Stevie Davies

Boy Blue

Winner of the Fawcett Society Book Prize 1989.

It is December 1944 and Hitler's silent V2 rockets fall over England. Chrissie is working in a munitions factory. Just eighteen and painfully shy, she is desperate to quit. Then she meets Jim, an airman, and can escape into marriage and pregnancy. But as her confinement approaches, Chrissie beings to dread the birth of her baby boy, whom she cannot help associating with the war . . .

An exceptional, haunting novel, *Boy Blue* marked the acclaimed début of a remarkable novelist.

'Davies' writing is uniquely beautiful.' *City Limits*

Fiction £3.95
ISBN 0 7043 4031 3